The Legend Of

BY
H. L. GRIFFEN

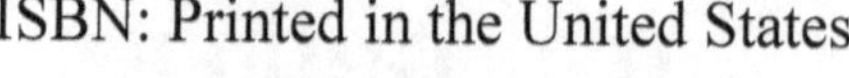

HEMINGWAY
PUBLISHERS

To my wife Tami

TABLE OF CONTENTS

FOREWORD

"The Legend of Fast Eddie" books are inspired by and dedicated to the memory of Eddie Gantt, AKA "The Southern Shaker" and others like him. Men and women who became legends by virtue of just being themselves. For the most part, they were ordinary people who were willing to take on the arduous, sometimes dangerous but mostly mundane task of driving an 18-wheeler back and forth across the country, hauling whatever to wherever, all the while enduring the rigors of the road. Traffic, weather conditions, mechanical problems, and a host of other unpredictable things that, seemingly, no mere mortal could or would want to deal with.

These individuals exemplified the American spirit of adventure and the freedom of chasing their dreams, one mile at a time. They did things and went places that most people only daydream about. They made it sound like fun to be a truck driver. Many, including myself, were inspired by the stories of their skills, determination, charismatic personalities, and sometimes crazy stunts. Aside from being a race car driver, sports star, musician or movie star, I can't think of many other professions where you can become a legend and have songs written about you just by doing your job. Least of all, driving a truck! The rest of us should be so lucky. Many thanks to those men and women who desired to color outside the lines at times. We could use some new legends today. Good stories instead of all the bad that is going on out there. In the meantime, let's try to keep the old legends alive by telling their stories. In this way, they never really die.

There are still some ghost stories floating around about some truckers that still haunt the highways to this day. Stories of a lone trucker showing up out of nowhere to help someone in distress. Of a good Samaritan driver giving a stranded person a ride to a truck stop to safety only for that person to find out later that individual died years ago. Are any of these stories real? No one knows for sure. So, don't be surprised if some night you're on a long run, late at night on a long desolate stretch of road. Maybe a little weary and bored from the drive, when all of a sudden, a set of headlights appears in your mirror's way behind you in the distance. You glance occasionally, wondering if it's another truck or maybe even a cop. Out of curiosity, you reach for the CB to call out but, no one answers. You keep checking the mirrors as the lights get closer. You key up your mic again and call out. Still, no answer. Finally, you see the chicken lights, so you know it's a rig and you breathe a sigh of relief.

Now, you're rocking along doing ninety-plus, maybe even a hundred-hundred and ten or so, but he is reeling you in fast. You call again but still, no answer from the radio. The rig is steadily getting closer, and you think, "*Man, this cat is strollin'.*" And then, all of a sudden, he passes you like you were painted on a fence. Startled, as your unit rocks from the turbulence of the passing rig, all you can manage to make out is that it is a black-striped, short-nose Kenworth with chromed stacks and a polished aluminum trailer, making a sound like nothing you've ever heard before. You stare in disbelief, trying to make out some kind of identifiable markings on the back of the trailer, but before you know it, his tail lights fade quickly into the night and just as quickly as he appeared, he's gone.

You say to yourself:

"Who the hell was that, and what did he have under the hood?"

And was it even real? No matter. You couldn't see the driver's face, but trust me, he was smiling the whole time he was going by you. Why? Because he knew you would ask that very question and then tell your story at the next truck stop. And that, my friends, is what it's all about. The story.

To quote Benjamin Franklin:

"Write something worth reading or do something worth writing about."

Alright, let's get to it.

I want to give a special thanks to Janice Gantt, AKA *"Mrs. Southern Shaker"* for her blessing and contribution to this series. She is a friend and a great lady of trucking in her own right. Now, let's go for a ride.

CREDITS

These are just a few of my family, friends and acquaintances who gave me their support, input, and reviews to help make this first book possible.

Patty Delany-Butler

Jonathan Blake

Cindy Pastore-Kemetz

Kim Lincoln

Kane Segura

Fred Young

Kathy Wager

Lori and Ronnie Roof

John Dunn

Stewart Ginsburg

Holly and Cindy McDermott

Bubba Broman

THANKS

To my wife Tami who, after hearing another of my crazy stories, said, "You should write a book." To my best friend Mark Ricci who said, "Sure, I'll help." Six years later, here we are. To Janice Gantt, for her blessing and support. To Eddie Gantt, "Southern Shaker," just for being who you were. To all the drivers back then that I rode with, drove with and listened to all your great stories. My buddy Pete Wagner, miss you every day bro. To Charlie Roberts Car #77. Boss, Friend, Mentor.

PROLOGUE
"AS THE STORY GOES"

At an old truck stop in Lincoln, Alabama, sits one of the last true Mom & Pop diners, a relic of a fading era where the smell of home-cooked meals and fresh coffee welcomes weary travelers. Here, you can still order a plate of crispy fried catfish, country steak smothered in gravy, golden fries, and a slice of warm apple pie—all served with bottomless coffee that keeps the road warriors going.

The waitresses and staff are always friendly, and the atmosphere is reminiscent of the old days when truckers were the revered 'Kings' and 'Tamers' of the highway and were treated as such.

It still holds onto the echoes of that era, its décor, worn but proud, its ambiance thick with the ghosts of old highway legends.

It's one of those places where, if you sit there for a while and listen, you can almost hear the echoes of old trucker tales, stories of men who hauled impossible loads and crossed entire states on little more than coffee and stubborn willpower. They talk of passing a cop so fast that the wind from your truck sucked his hat clean off his head. Of waitresses with unforgettable smiles, and of gallows humor shared over midnight meals.

Then there are tales of horrific crashes, legendary storms, and impossible deadlines that were met by sheer luck and skill. But most of all, they talk about the friendships, and the brotherhood forged on the open road. The stories may fade with time, but in places like this, they never truly disappear.

And if you stay late enough, just as the neon sign flickers against the dark, you might swear you hear the faint crackle of a CB radio. One last call from a trucker who never quite left the highway behind.

Yes, it was a time when legends were born. The original tellers of these tales have long since passed, but the stories live on through those who have heard them from friends, relatives, and sometimes, even a few of the remaining old timers who were maybe, once legends themselves, when they show up and talk about the 'Good Ole' days.

Of course, the road is different now. There's less room for legends and fewer places for tall tales to grow. But every once in a while, a story drifts in from the highway, something so wild, so impossible, that it refuses to fade away.

A "Hell no! There ain't no way that happened!" kind of story. A story about a trucker who defied physics, logic, and pure common sense. A story so unbelievable, it can't possibly be true—and yet, no one can quite prove it didn't happen. Well, this is one of those stories.

On this particular evening, the truck stop hummed with its usual rhythm. New-age rigs rolling in and out, drivers hunched over their phones, filling out their log books, calling home, checking in with brokers, or just grabbing a quick meal before the next long haul.

At one of the designated 'Round Tables,' there was a discussion taking place between some of seasoned truckers and a young driver named Mickey Davenport. He had only been driving over the road for about a year or so, and because he was still a newbie, he made it a practice to get advice from these and other older drivers whenever he had a chance. Mickey was smart enough to know that they had years of experience and could save him some headaches down the road and maybe teach him a few things. A rare thing these days as most graduates fresh out of school believe that once they finished getting their CDL, they were ready to be a trucker.

The men at that table saw a young driver who wanted to do things right, and in a world where experience matters more than any license, that meant something to these truckers.

Mickey had been coming here for a while now, drawn not just to the knowledge, but to the good-natured ribbing and dry humor that came with it. The old-timers teased him about his rookie status, but underneath it all was a quiet respect. They saw a kid who wanted to learn, and in their world where most find out the hard way and some never make it, that still counted for something.

Since joining in on the conversations with these local drivers, Mickey had been advised on a variety of topics because although they enjoyed ribbing him, they were happy to share their knowledge and respected his eagerness to learn. The best tires, oil, shortcuts, best way to tie down a load of pipe, how to have the loaders stack the freight properly in your trailer, sliding the tandems to balance your weight across the scales, and the always popular, *"Stay outta the Pickle Parks and away from the 'Lot Lizards'"* lecture.

Tonight, however, was different. The thick fog settled in like a heavy blanket, making even the neon lights look ghostly. Few drivers dared to brave the elements and the truck stop filled up fast. Everyone knew better that out in this soup, one wrong move could mean disaster.

Tales of horrific wrecks and deadly pile-ups filled the air, stories of truckers who never saw the danger ahead until it was too late. Many were the stories of horrific accidents involving trucks colliding with other trucks or cars, causing huge pile-ups and death tolls, because as they say *"When it's this bad, you can come upon a situation before you have time to respond,"* said one trucker. Another told of a driver losing sight of the road completely and going off the side of a mountain, careening to the depths below in a fiery heap! Along with a host of other grisly tales.

Also tonight, the regulars were up for a story that had been debated several times before. A story that seemed to raise the ire of George Willingham.

Ralph Moore was the one who started it and George gave his usual response.

"I still say that's bullshit, Ralph. I mean, it makes for a great story and all, but that's it. A great story. There's no way a truck can go that fast in those circumstances, even if he was comin' down a mountain at a decent speed. He'd have to have been doing at least 150 mph just to get to the guy in time!" He jabbed a finger on the table for emphasis and continued.

"And in a mile, no less. Besides that, how was he able to see through that fog when nobody else could? Impossible, I tell ya. Just impossible!"

The other two regulars, Hank Amick and Red Horton, had heard it all before but were still up for debating and listening to these two go back and forth.

Ralph Moore countered, "I'm tellin' ya, George, my cousin knows the guy he saved and the guy swears by his story."

The doubting trucker shook his head unconvinced, "Not possible.

"If he was outta control, there was no way he could have been paying attention to time and distance. He'd a been crappin' in his britches tryin' ta hold on to that rig. No, I tell ya, not possible," George concluded.

While staying neutral, Hank and Red weren't dismissing it outright. They'd heard the same story from different folks, drivers who swore up and down they'd caught parts of it over the CB that night. And if enough truckers were repeating it…well, maybe there was something to it.

Mickey sat forward, his curiosity burning now. "So what exactly happened?"

"Well, kid," Ralph started, "as the story goes, a driver named Bobby Ray Tucker was comin' down I-77 out of Wytheville, Virginia, one night, going to Charlotte with a load of electronics. Said it was foggy as hell. Said you couldn't see five foot in front of your truck. Well, as he started down the steeper parts of the pass after going through Fancy Gap, his brakes started giving out, and before he realized it, he had picked up too much speed to try for an exit ramp. Knew for certain if he tried, he would roll it and maybe hurt innocent people and himself in the process.

"He got on the CB and started hollerin' for anybody that might have a marker number for a runaway ramp. No one knew right off but tried to help him with other advice. No going, though. He knew he was well on his way to a certain death if he didn't figure something out fast!

"As he tells it, he was up around 80 mph and climbing with nothing for brakes. He started looking for something he could throw the side of his rig up against and maybe slow it down. Suddenly, he hears this driver come over the radio asking him what mile marker he was at. He looked out the side window just in time to see the 199.5-

mile marker fly past him. He shouted it back over the CB and waited. The driver came back on the radio and told him he was coming past the 198-mile marker and to stay in the slow lane if he could and that he would be right there. Told him to do exactly what he said when he got there and he would help get him to the next runaway ramp.

"Bobby said okay, but wasn't sure how he was going to do that and wasn't sure how much longer he could hold onto his rig! He said within seconds, this black streak went by him so fast it scared the bejesus outta him.

"The roar it unleashed was unlike anything he had ever heard before. A thunderous, earth-shaking sound that sent chills down his spine!

"The driver came back on the radio and told him to aim for the back of his trailer when it came into view and keep it steady when they connected. Out of options, Bobby did as instructed. When he saw the trailer and aimed right at the back of it. The other driver matched his speed and as Bobby eased up and gently bumped into the trailer, he felt the other driver instantly hitting his brakes.

"Bobby said at that moment, his speedometer was showing 125 mph! He was scared out of his wits but held it as steady as he could. Shortly, he felt his truck slowing. He could hear the other driver's Jake Brake and said it made a weird sound, too, like a whooshing or a whistling type sound.

"They started slowing down, and as they rounded a few more turns, the driver came back on the radio and told him to get ready and, when he gave him the signal, to hook a slight right and he would be pointed towards the runoff.

"All Bobby said all he could see at that moment was the back of the driver's trailer and nothing but fog swirlin' around them. He kept watching the speedometer and listening to the CB.

"When they got down to 60 mph, the driver told him, 'Now!' Bobby veered to the right and there was the runaway ramp as promised. He aimed right for it and held on for dear life. Said he almost went through the windshield when he hit the stones, but when he finally stopped, he said couldn't get outta that truck fast enough. It took him a minute to catch his breath and for his heart to stop pounding, but he was safe and, on his knees, thanking God. Said he promised to go to church early and stay late!"

"Wow! That is awesome!" said Mickey.

"Yeah, then Bobby said he heard the driver come back on the radio, asking him if he was okay. He said he jumped up in the cab, grabbed the CB mic, shouted that he was more than okay, and wanted to buy him the biggest steak dinner he ever had, anywhere he liked and asked him for his handle!

"'That's okay, driver, no need,' he replied. 'Just lucky I was passin' through and happened to be in a bit of a hurry. You just be more careful next time and get home to the wife and kiddos. Gotta go! Catch you on the flip side! We're outta here!'

"And he heard it again, that deep, earth-shaking roar echoing from the distance, sending a shiver down his spine. Bobby gripped the radio tighter and tried calling out a few more times, his voice laced with urgency. Still, just silence. No reply.

"Said that he told him that he thanked God for him and wished him a safe trip and that he would never forget the man who saved his life, whoever he was. Said he would never forget the sound of those pipes either. Said it literally sounded like a roar, like a lion or something."

"Fascinating," said Mickey.

George let out a sharp laugh, shaking his head in disbelief. "Bullshit! Ralph, c'mon! A lion roar? Great story, but bullshit!"

Mickey was all big-eyed and smiled, exclaiming, "Aw, George. That's the best story I've ever heard. Damn! There has to be some truth to it or people wouldn't be talking about it. I mean, the guy is alive to tell the tale."

George shook his head, mumbled something under his breath, then stood up and walked away from the table, clearly not buying a word of it.

"C'mon George, don't go," the other drivers said.

"Sorry, got no time for fairy tales. I got real truckin' to do." Then, with a dismissive wave of his hand, George stormed out through the entrance door, still muttering to himself, his frustration trailing behind him.

Mickey and the others continued the debate in his absence. After a while, the other drivers parted company and went about their prospective ways. He, however, was done with his day and decided to write down what he had heard. The fact is, Mickey had been researching these stories for months, and this was the best evidence he had gathered so far. Now was the time to add to his notes.

The story he had just heard was of particular interest to him tonight as it had some similarities in the details of one that he heard at a truck stop in Pennsylvania one day. That story did not take place in Fancy Gap, Virginia, but it was a trucker barreling down a mountain at breakneck speed with another truck supposedly hitting 150 miles an hour and letting out a roar that shook the night. And it was like that report from a State Trooper in Texas of chasing a truck also going 150+. They couldn't all be coincidences.

Mickey pulled out his notebook and proceeded to jot down every detail he had just heard. His mind raced as he compared the two stories, scanning for connections, patterns, anything that could explain the impossible.

Very interesting, he thought. There has to be some validity to this because he had also heard about a truck that someone heard after it left a truck stop one time out west making an unusual sound.

He didn't write that one down at the time because the driver wrote it off to a particular exhaust system that some drivers were playing around with to get a "Cooler, throaty-er' sound."

Maybe not so much now. As he sat there musing over his notes, Mickey periodically glanced out the window and watched as trucks slowly made their way in and out of the foggy lot to the fuel islands and parking area. The next time he looked out, he noticed a black rig easing up to the pumps. From where he sat, he could see it was a new Peterbilt 579. He had looked at one before he bought his KW. The trailer was a black reefer unit, as were the aero shields underneath. Actually, most everything on the truck was blacked out. A lot of guys liked that blacked-out rat rod look nowadays. He preferred chrome accessories himself.

As Mickey went back to his notes, he began mumbling as he scribbled,

"Now, what did the driver say? He was at the 199.5-mile marker. The other guy said he was coming from the 198. The out-of-control driver said the guy went past him within seconds."

Mickey calculated 1.5 miles @ 150 mph = 36 seconds! He sat back in his seat.

"Damn! That can't be right!" he exclaimed out loud.

He thought about other factors also involved like winding turns downhill, dense fog, load shifting, braking ability, was it loaded or empty, and a host of other impossibilities at that speed.

"That's just not possible!" He finally assessed. "That rig would have flipped over at the first curve!" Mickey mulled over his notes and calculations some more.

"Even if he were empty, just the G-forces alone would make it impossible for him to go through the turns at that speed because the trailer would want to go in the direction of the inertia. There isn't a trailer out there that stable. The hero truck had to be closer than he said. He had to be at a high rate of speed and right on his ass! But what about the fog?"

Mickey himself had already driven through the mountains in heavy fog and knew it was a crawl fest at best. You literally can't see five feet in front of you. He could see why George was saying, "Not possible!"

By now, Mickey was stumped and, quite frankly, somewhat discouraged. The more he thought about it, the more he began to think that maybe it was just a tall trucker tale. Folding up his notebook in disgust he tossed it in his bag and decided to call it done with. Glancing out the window again, he noticed a driver approaching the restaurant entrance, a large, shaggy dog keeping perfect pace at his right side.

Normally, Mickey wouldn't have given them a second thought. The man looked like any number of truckers he'd seen at truck stops across the country. A jean jacket, plaid shirt, faded jeans, scuffed cowboy boots, and a well-worn Cat hat pulled low over his eyes. Just another face in the endless stream of travelers.

But something about this one, or maybe the way the dog moved in sync with him, steady and alert, made Mickey pause. He guessed the man was in his 60s.

For some reason, Mickey found the pair curious. As he watched, the dog assumed a sitting position without instruction at the front of the walkway as the driver continued into the entrance.

Very regimented behavior, he thought.

The driver came in and headed towards the restrooms. Mickey decided he would wait out the fog in his sleeper, so after finishing his last sip of coffee, he got up and went to pay his bill. As he did, the driver rounded the corner and headed to the register ahead of him with a couple of bottles of water and dog treats.

After he paid his bill, Mickey followed the driver outside and about halfway down the walkway asked, "Cool dog. What kind is he?"

The driver stopped and, turning around, replied. "He's a Briard. A French herding dog. They were real popular in England and France with kings and dukes and the like. The French used them a lot in WWII for all kinds of stuff."

"Really? Never saw or even heard of one before."

"Yeah, he's a rare one for sure. Got lots of personality, I know that."

Mickey looked toward the driver's truck. "I noticed your Pete. Nice looking rig. It's a 579, right?"

"Yeah, I like it. Has all the bells and whistles. I just use the bells right now. Still learning the whistles."

Mickey laughed at that one. He liked his humor. It reminded him of his friends back in South Carolina. They chatted for a few minutes about the particulars between their trucks and what each liked about them. They slowly strolled toward the curb and when he got to the dog, Mickey reached over and petted the dog on the head and stroked him a little on the side.

"Say, kid, what's your name?" The man turned and offered his hand.

"Mickey. Mickey Davenport."

They shook hands.

"Eddie McVane. This here is Radar."

"Hiya, Radar."

Eddie took a few more minutes and asked him for his CB handle.

"Keystone Cowboy," Mickey replied.

"Rolling Stone."

Then Mickey asked who he was hauling for, out of where, and also how long he had been driving. Eddie told him how long he had been driving and what he was hauling.

Mickey raised an eyebrow, clearly impressed. "Wow, I could learn a lot from you. Do you get down this way much? I'd love to talk more."

"Occasionally. Tell ya what. Gimme yer number. I know a company that is always looking for good talent. They pay good, too."

"Sure!"

Mickey quickly rattled off his number and address, and his voice filled with gratitude as he thanked him again.

They lingered in conversation for a few more minutes, exchanging some last words before Eddie finally checked the time and let out a small sigh. He said he had to go. "Gotta operate to own, you know."

Mickey looked over at the exit area and could barely see it. "For real? You going back out in this?"

"Unfortunately, I have to. Hot load. Not much further, though. Birmingham."

"Okay, man. Be careful. Glad to meet you."

"You too, kid."

After shaking hands, Mickey patted the dog on the head.

"See ya later, Radar."

He watched as the two of them headed back to their truck and turned and headed toward his own truck in the back of the parking lot. As Mickey climbed into his rig, he heard Eddie's truck fire up and glanced over through the fogginess as they headed out of the lot and down the road.

Better you than me, buddy, he thought. *Nice guy, though. I hope he hooks me up. I'd love to talk with him more. I bet he's got some stories to tell.*

Mickey could still hear Eddie changing gears as he entered onto I-20. Easing up into his sleeper, he got comfortable and settled in for the night. Despite the fog, it was nice out tonight so Mickey had the windows cracked and the side vents open to let the evening breeze come through. Shutting all the lights off, he leaned back, closed his eyes, and started thinking about the day.

Very cool, he thought. *I've met some very cool people in this job.* Mickey put his hands behind his head and settled into his bunk. He had just closed his eyes and started to drift off when suddenly, a sound off in the distance made him sit straight up in his bunk. He wasn't sure if he was dreaming.

Sitting there wide-eyed with the dim light of the truck stop yard lights peeking through the curtains, Mickey wondered aloud, "Did I just hear what I think I heard? Was that...a lion roar?!"

And so, it begins.

"Sir, this is Texas. When the legend becomes fact, print the legend."

(Quote from The Man Who Shot Liberty Valance)

CHAPTER ONE
GOING HOME

Dave Dudley's song "Six Days on The Road" was just finishing up on the radio as Eddie checked his gauges and mirrors, easing in and out of early morning traffic. He was more than ready for a break, craving a hot meal, a moment of peace, and the comfort of a bed beneath him. He saw the sign for Walcott, Iowa, flash by followed by a billboard for the IOWA 80 TRUCK STOP at EXIT 284, 12 MILES. That's where he would stop for fuel and breakfast.

As Dudley's song faded to the next tune, Eddie started mentally preparing himself for going home or the lack thereof. *Home* was something he hadn't really known in the three years since shutting himself off from everything. As far as he was concerned, his world ended when his beloved wife of thirty-two years passed away. The only things left are memories of her and the short time he had with his grandchildren, the enduring lifelong friendship with his eccentric best friend and business partner, Jimmy Wagner, and a strained relationship with his son.

His long hood Peterbilt Truck, "Fat Betty," so named for his late wife's mother, was Eddie's home now. Every so often though, he would check into a motel as a brief escape from the endless road, and a chance to recharge, rest, and maybe reclaim a small sense of normalcy. Otherwise, he drove in his truck on the road during the day and slept in it off the road at night.

It hadn't always been this way, though. Once, he had a normal, happy life. A time when laughter filled his days, when the world felt right, and everything seemed to fall into place. Eddie had always been a hardworking, happy-go-lucky, wisecracking kind of guy with a passion for cars and a knack for driving the wheels off them. His dad, Eddie Sr., owned a small trucking business in Morganton, North Carolina, and raced cars on the weekends. Eddie was always right at his side, underfoot, getting greasy and messing with everything in the shop. Every chance he got, he would climb into his dad's race car, dreaming of the day he'd take the wheel for real. Eventually, his dad built him a go-kart to keep him occupied, fueling Eddie's passion for speed.

As his dad watched him ride around the homemade track at the back of the garage, he began to notice the boy's skill and fearlessness, commenting one day, "The boy has two speeds—dead stop and wide open. I don't think he even knows what a brake pedal is." This eventually grew into bigger and faster karts and then cars. Eddie became totally immersed in the racing scene and absorbed everything he could learn from his father and other local drivers. They could see he was a natural and were often amazed at his skill level for his age. Of course, there was the occasional temptation for mischievous behavior like the time Eddie was in high school and his dad got a call from the chief of police. It seems they had picked up Eddie and had him in a holding cell. According to the chief, he tried to outrun two squad cars in his alcohol-powered go-kart after driving through the middle of downtown on the double yellow line at 75 mph! Apparently, there was a dare involved. The officers only managed to catch him when he ran out of fuel.

Eddie Sr. went down to the courthouse, paid the fine, and took Eddie home from the jail. Sitting in the silence and looking at his dad's stern face during the drive, Eddie thought for sure he was dead. Then his dad looked at him and asked, "And what did we learn from this little adventure, son?"

Eddie thought for a moment, then replied, "It's really dumb to do something like that on a dare, but if you do, make sure you got enough fuel to get away."

His dad's stern face erupted into laughter so hard, he almost ran off the road. Eddie Sr., who was also Eddie's biggest fan and supporter, told that story at least a million times over the years.

Eddie's best friend, Jimmy Wagner, AKA The Hammer—so named for his temper when things didn't work as they should Jimmy would take a ball peen hammer and beat the offending item into a million pieces—joined with Eddie and his dad to make a formidable racing team. The Hammer, in between administering ball-peen justice, was quite a mechanic and extremely tech-savvy. His close friendship with Eddie enabled them to work together almost with a single mind.

It was during these early days that Eddie discovered he had a gift when it came to machines. As was often his routine, he would go to the garage and just run his hand over the fenders and across the hood of a car, getting a feel for it. Nothing special about that. Any number of drivers have and will do similar things to get in tune with their cars and the race at hand.

However, one day, something strange/weird/scary/exciting (Eddie didn't know quite which word to use) started to happen. As he moved about a car that was running, he went into what felt like a trance and all sounds around him faded away. It was just Eddie, the car, and silence. Slowly he began to hear sounds, but different from the ones he was used to.

First, it was a light, pulsing sound. Then came a series of mechanical noises. As they continued, Eddie found his vision dropped into a blur. The blur then tunneled as if he were in a tube moving at full speed. His peripheral sight remained a blur, but the lane in front of him was now clear, and Eddie felt like he was traveling at speed just standing there. It was as if he had become part of the machine, hearing and feeling every piece of it. At first, it startled him, and he snapped out of the trance. Not knowing who to ask about such a thing, he kept it to himself for quite a while. As time went on, though, Eddie grew more at ease with it and it became part of his pre-race routine.

After that, when he drove, he could identify every sound and vibration to the point where he could relay information to Jimmy when he felt something was wrong or needed adjustment. Eddie could even tell whether a new car was a contender or not. Eventually, he confided in Jimmy about his newfound gift, and although Jimmy didn't fully understand Eddie's experience, he finally concluded that, "The boy is definitely connected, and that's good enough for me." He also suggested Eddie keep that to himself thinking it would weird people out too much.

From that point on, they were rarely beaten at any track, and if they were, it was by Frank Palmer. Frank was Eddie's arch rival and a former high school bully who had a habit of putting him into the wall or over the bank if he had a chance.

Still, Eddie and the team thrived, and the wins piled up to the point where they were recognized everywhere they went. A local track announcer gave Eddie his nickname one night by telling everyone in the stands, "Fast Eddie McVane takes the checkered once again." From there, the handle stuck. Soon, he was getting all kinds of offers. Once, he was asked to pilot a car at tryouts for a local NASCAR team at Daytona. He did well and impressed a lot of people, but couldn't get the ride. They said he was too young and needed more experience. Things were different back then in NASCAR. Yes, he had made a good impression, but the old-timers said he had to pay his dues and work his way up the ladder.

So that's what he did. Eddie resented the snub, but went back and started working his way up that ladder. At the same time, he also began driving trucks with his dad, helping with the business part-time during the week and racing on the weekends. It was all about the speed, even with the trucks. This was evident by the speeding tickets he got a little too often.

He had his life planned out and was well on his way to paying those dues. Sure enough, new driving opportunities were offered again a few years later. It looked like Eddie's chance to get a shot at the big time had finally come.

But then tragedy struck and everything changed. He got a call that his dad had died suddenly from a heart attack while working at the shop. Eddie was devastated. His biggest fan, his tower of strength and inspiration, was gone. Nothing was the same after that. His mother, always the anchor of the family, seemed to lose her fire and zest for life. She showed little interest in the business then, so it fell to Eddie to carry on.

He put racing on the back burner with the idea of picking it back up when things settled down. But that day never came. Life changed and the responsibility of running the business took over.

With the team dissolved, Jimmy went off to study at MIT, but returned home after only four years claiming it was "too confining." He started his own performance shop and did well, even got married and had a few kids. Jimmy couldn't seem to hang on to his women, though, because he was always at the shop, doing research and development on this thing or that, and building killer engines for everybody around the area. After the fourth wife, he told Eddie he felt like he was more of a "catch and release" kind of guy and never married again.

Eddie, meanwhile, eventually got married to his high school sweetheart, Kate Morgan. They had a son and named him Eddie, Jr. The two worked well together: Kate managing the business and Eddie managing the repair shop and driving trucks. Like most marriages and businesses, there were some obstacles and they almost lost everything a couple of times, but always managed to pull through. As the years passed, Eddie accepted his fate, and although he regretted not being able to pursue his dream of racing, he was content.

He was about to settle in for what was to be a respectable retirement, spending time with his son and grandkids, and traveling the country with his wife and seeing the sights. Eddie could not know that everything was about to change, but he soon would.

He received a set of texts one day with pictures of his wife kissing another man. The texts alleged that she'd been having an affair with a man named Russell Cortland, Eddie's banker and good business friend, while Eddie was on the road. Eddie was furious and blew up at her the moment he got home and saw her.

They argued and she tried to tell him otherwise "It's not what you think. Russell is not a good guy like everybody thinks," but Eddie's Irish was up, and he was too angry to listen. Frustrated, Kate left the house to let Eddie cool down and then she would come back to explain the misunderstanding.

Sadly, she never got the chance. Kate was killed in a car accident shortly after leaving the house. In an instant, 30+ years of marriage, memories, and all they had built were gone. No chance to make amends, no way to take back the ugly things that were said, and no opportunity to ask for or offer forgiveness. If it had not been for Jimmy physically restraining Eddie later that day, Russell Cortland would surely have been dead.

Eddie would later discover the truth of the matter after finding his wife's diary and reading how Russell had been after her for years. It was Russell Cortland who had set her up, planted the rumor, and doctored the pictures. He was trying to split them up so he could have her for himself. Kate had kept that from Eddie, partly because Russell held the loan for the business but more to protect Russell from what she knew Eddie would do.

A despicable, selfish act for personal gain by this man had cost Eddie his wife and ruined his life. Even if Eddie wanted to tell people—he didn't and he especially was not telling his son—who would believe him? There was no real proof. And Russell certainly wasn't going to confess. How do you tell people that such a respected businessman and member of their community, as well as a church deacon, would do such a thing?

No, as far as anyone was concerned, Eddie's temper over something stupid had caused Kate to leave the house that day. Eddie kept the truth to himself, letting people believe whatever they wanted. He felt he had no other choice. But every day since, he had damned Russell Cortland to hell.

Eddie shut the world out almost completely. During this time, he rarely spoke to his son or his grandkids or any of his family. When he did, it was always awkward, and he was sure it was uncomfortable for them as well. Eddie would send cards and texts during the holidays, but that was the extent of him reaching out. Everybody had judged him and felt they knew the truth of the matter, and therefore, it was settled. The only one he saw regularly, and the only other person who knew the truth besides himself and Russell Cortland, was Jimmy Wagner. Eddie made Jimmy swear an oath that he would carry it to his grave. Jimmy agreed but begged him many times to tell Eddie, Jr., but Eddie would not hear of it.

"I won't have him think badly of his mother in any respect. Trying to convince him of what Russell did sounds like I'm making excuses for myself. If I had listened to Kate instead of believing some bogus made-up photo and rumors, she would still be alive. I should have given her the benefit of the doubt. I didn't do that. That's on me. People can think what they want of me, I don't care. I'm on the downhill side of life anyway. Kate was the best of the best and that's how I want her remembered."

Eddie said it with a finality that Jimmy knew all too well. His mind was made up, and there was no changing it.

Over time, everything felt different to him. Family gatherings lost their warmth, and even familiar stops at local restaurants and stores no longer felt the same. All he felt was emptiness and the cold stares of judgment. After several months of this, Eddie couldn't take it anymore and felt he no longer belonged there. He became more and more depressed. Everything he knew was gone. Without Kate, he felt lost and out of place.

Finally, Eddie sold the business, invested in Jimmy's research and development business, bought a new rig, and disappeared behind the wheel of his truck.

He headed West where the roads are long and the people are few. Out there, it was easier for Eddie to lose himself and his past. You also don't have to explain yourself to anyone and no one really cares anyway. Just show up on time and drop your load. The "sign this paper" and "see ya next time" conversations were just fine with him. Whether it was driving the wide-open expanse of the plains and deserts of the Southwest, climbing over the Rockies, or navigating the barrenness of the Badlands, he hauled whatever to wherever.

For the most part, Eddie had moved on, met and made a few new friends and acquaintances on the road, and even got back some of his sense of humor. Still, there was a vacancy in his soul that could not be filled and it took almost three years of hard driving, long hauls, and endless hours of being alone before he began to feel somewhat normal again. That was a dark time for him. It seemed the fire of life and love had been vanquished by disappointment, heartbreak, and deceit. Kate was his soulmate, and no one since seemed to measure up.

One thing that the three years didn't change was the hatred for Russell Cortland that still burned in Eddie's gut. How could a trusted friend do something so despicable? No matter how many miles he put behind him, Eddie could not forget that day. He blamed himself as well for not listening to Kate. His temper was in full force and he was not in a mood to listen to reason. It was something he would always regret.

Today, however, Eddie was going back home so Jimmy could upgrade his truck's engine. While he was there, he would bring his grandkids gifts from the road and surely get a cool reception from his son. For the most part, though, he would try to keep low and out of sight of anybody he knew from his and Kate's past. He had pretty much accepted this as his life now. It was what it was, he felt. People are going be what they're going to be and there was no changing that. Eddie told himself that he didn't really care one way or the other anymore. He was content to die behind the wheel, one mile at a time. And so, he drove.

The closer he got to North Carolina, though, the heavier the weight of memories felt, and the darker it seemed, even in the sunshine. The only thing that compensated for the torment in his mind was getting to see grandchildren and his son, and spending time with his best friend.

Then he began to wonder again why he was still here at all. What was the point? He had lost everything and cared about little these days. It seemed a cruel fate to be stuck in a world he no longer cared to be in.

But fate wasn't quite through with Eddie McVane just yet. He didn't know it, but his life was about to get a whole lot crazier and a lot more interesting.

Before he is done, Fast Eddie McVane is going to be dragged kicking and screaming back into life's merry-go-round. He will once more have to deal with things and people that he tried so hard to run away from. In the process, he will have the adventure of a lifetime and discover that life is far from done with him and his self-imposed "End of Life" scenario, but not in the way he imagined. For one thing, he's getting out of it alive now.

CHAPTER TWO
WELCOME TO GEEK UTOPIA

It was seemingly innocent: a trucker asking his good friend and mechanic for more power to get up and over mountains to make better time. A simple request, really, but one that gradually took on a life of its own and opened up a whole new world of possibilities and innovation for Jimmy. For one thing, it led him to develop what would ultimately become the fastest truck on the planet. And there would be more.

It began when Eddie complained to Jimmy that he was getting passed by much faster trucks going up the mountains and on the long straightaways. They would just leave him in the dust. For Eddie, this was more than inconvenient; it was humiliating, and that was unacceptable. After all, no self-respecting race car driver worth his salt likes being passed by anything. Even in a big rig.

So Jimmy went to work diligently learning about diesel engines and how he could strategically apply his racing technology and skills. During his research, he discovered the world of government grants and how surprisingly interested they were in green technology. Jimmy kept in touch with Eddie and would periodically update him on his progress.

After a year and a half or so, he called Eddie and told him he had an engine ready for him and to come home. Meantime, Jimmy had moved into a spacious, larger facility and was adding new staff and equipment.

"Good for you," Eddie replied "Glad to hear business is good."

"Better than good, man!" Jimmy exclaimed, his voice practically buzzing with excitement. "Rachel hooked me up with these government grant programs for doing research and development on diesel engine technology. I told them I had an idea for a green diesel engine, and man, these people just threw money at me! It was awesome!"

"Okay, sounds like fun. You said, Rachel? Your ex?"

"Yeah," Jimmy confirmed.

"Number?

"Um…three, I think...yeah, pretty sure number three."

Shaking his head, Eddie just chuckled and replied, "Okay, cool. See you soon."

"Done! Beer, steaks, and cigars will be ready when ya get here."

"Copy that. 10-4. ETA two and a half days."

****

Two and a half days later, Eddie rolled up to a bustling complex at the address Jimmy had given him. It was a massive three-story building under construction.

"Damn," Eddie exclaimed while looking at all the chaotic activity. "What the hell have you got going on, Jimmy?"

Eddie shut the truck down and sat there watching all the construction workers, concrete pumpers, and scaffolding being erected, and a team of planners looking over the blueprints of whatever this was. At first, he wasn't even sure if he had the right address, so he called Jimmy.

"Yes, sir!" answered the exuberant voice of his friend.

"Hey, are you building a new building?"

"Yeah, man! You outside?"

"I think so. Either that or I drove into the building scene of an *A-Team* episode."

"Yup, you're here. Be right out."

Eddie climbed out of his truck as Jimmy came bouncing out the front entryway, weaving and dodging construction workers. Jimmy was a tall, gangling-looking man in jeans and a lab coat, his signature look. He was always smiling with a large toothy grin, and had seemingly endless energy. His once blonde hair was white now and always seemed to be going in every direction, making him look like a mad scientist. Waving, he came over and, after hugging Eddie, turned and threw his hands toward the new structure.

"Whaddaya think, man! Awesome, right?"

Eddie, smiling, replied, "Dude! You have been a busy little geek, haven't you? Quite the new setup."

"Old friend, it is on. We are into R&D in a big way! Dude, we got some of the coolest stuff going on now. I mean, we got tools, technology, and equipment I never even knew existed! We have some of the latest diesel technology that hasn't even hit the market yet. C'mon, lemme show you around."

Without waiting for a response, Jimmy grabbed Eddie by the arm and led him through the building entrance past the construction, through the lobby, and into the back of the complex. The lobby itself was sleek with modern polished floors, large glass windows, and walls lined with framed diagrams and blueprints that looked far too complicated for Eddie to understand.

Along the way, Eddie saw people in cubicles, sitting at drawing tables and desks, busy working on computers—doing *what*, he didn't know. But it all looked important and very high-tech.

As they continued through the different departments, Jimmy was stopped by different people who asked about what they were working on or about carpet color or the placement of a cabinet. Eddie just followed behind, taking it all in, listening and marveling at what he was seeing. His best friend certainly had come a long way from those years of building racing engines and doing his own R&D work in a rusty warehouse complex.

Jimmy continued on, showing Eddie the fabrication department and then the machining department. "And here," as he spread his arms wide and smiled broadly, "is where we can make any kind of part from a drawing produced by the designers up in the front office."

Eddie was doing his best to keep track of it all, trying to understand and memorize as best he could.

"Welcome to 'Geek Utopia,' he said under his breath.

That's when it hit him: Everybody was so...so...*clean*! Lab coats, sweater vests, and khakis. Short-sleeve, button-down shirts tucked in with precision, and he even spotted a few pocket protectors full of pens. Plus, lots of bespectacled folks who seemed to be deep in thought about complex calculations on several very big computer screens.

Eddie was suddenly feeling wildly out of place in his Canadian tuxedo and cowboy boots.

After a few more departments, they went out to a large open area where it was a bit noisier. There was a massive high-tech gantry crane overhead carrying a pallet of diesel engines across to a destination at the far end of the building. Looking up and watching all this activity almost made him dizzy, but he kept moving and following along.

Shortly they came to a support pillar along the way that had an intercom. Jimmy pressed the button and shouted into it, "Ange!"

Nothing.

"Ange!"

Silence.

"*Ange!*"

"YO Boss!" came the reply finally.

Frustrated, Jimmy asked him, "Why do I have to call you three times?"

"Because I never answered my mutha' on the first two. I gotta keep my streak alive!" Jimmy shook his head in surrender.

"You at the Dyno?"

"Yassir!"

"Good, we'll be right there."

"Roger that!" Jimmy looked at Eddie and shook his head.

"Crazy little Italian. Cat knows his stuff, though."

They continued until they were outside a room with a sign over the door reading: CAUTION! DYNOMETER ROOM.

Jimmy led Eddie into the brightly lit white room filled with flashing controls, high-tech screens, and controls with gauges, and introduced him to the voice on the other end of the intercom.

"Eddie McVane, meet my chief engineer, Angelo Giuseppe Marco De Franscella!"

Good grief, Eddie thought. *Couldn't they make up their mind naming this guy? It must have taken days!* Shaking his hand, Eddie took in Angelo Giuseppe Whatever's features. He was a short, dark, stocky, Italian fella with salt-and-pepper hair and thick black-rimmed glasses.

"Hi ya, Eddie. Pleased ta meet ya," Ange said with a very heavy Long Island accent. Even speaking in a normal manner, he was louder than most folks he knew when they were yelling.

"Got a stout one here for youse," Angelo exclaimed. "Got er' bangin' out about 1,500 ponies without da turbo."

The big Caterpillar engine was visible through the glass enclosure where it was hooked up to an assortment of hoses, wires, and gauges. Angelo and Jimmy showed Eddie how to read the graphs and what each line meant.

"Dat's youse peak horsepower at 1,550 RPM," Ange declared.

Angelo directed Eddie's attention to another screen to show him what the engine was doing internally, and how they modified certain parts to get more performance and longevity out of the motor.

Eddie nodded as if he fully understood, but this wasn't his strong suit. He did the driving and Jimmy did his thing with the motors. That had always been the combination that worked. He was good with that.

"So, whaddaya think?" Jimmy asked, his grin wide and expectant.

"Awesome," replied Eddie. "Can't wait to take her for a ticket chase. What's her name?"

Jimmy had always named his engines because he said it made it more personal for him. To build an engine, Jimmy put so much heart, sweat, and passion into every piece and then into the assembly of the complete motor that he felt like he gave birth to it when it fired up for the first time.

Eddie told Jimmy one time that had he put the same kind of love and attention into his women, he would stay married longer.

"Yeah, maybe," Jimmy had replied with a chuckle. "But at least when my engines blow up, I know how to fix 'em. When my women blow up, they stay blowed up."

"Meet Rosie," he said to Eddie, pointing to the engine.

"Rosie, huh?"

"Yup. when the turbo starts churnin', her pipes get Rosie Red."

"Gotcha. When can we introduce the two?"

"If we can get Fat Betty in here tomorrow, we should be able to have her ready to rock and roll by Friday. I also wanna do some new tests while I got her here."

"Cool. Now, about that steak, beer, and cigar."

"Done! Seven work?"

"If yer waitin' on me, yer backin' up." Eddie replied.

They both grinned at the same time. It was their way of letting each other know there was no debate about the matter in question. When they were back outside, Eddie turned to Jimmy with a look of admiration. He was truly happy for his friend.

"Man, buddy, you've come a long way from Warehouse Row. Look at you, all 'Mr. Big Time.' I'm proud of ya, man. I really am."

"Thanks. You're in this, too, don't forget. I wouldn't be here if it wasn't for you. Wait till you see your stock report. If this green diesel thing works out, you'll be set for life."

"I'm good, buddy. I was glad to help. If it goes, great. Looks good so far."

"That ain't the half of it, Eddie. I can't tell ya everything right now, but we got have some seriously cool stuff going on down in the basement. I mean, *super* high-tech. We're talkin' Elon Musk kinda stuff."

"Who?"

"Tesla cars, high-speed trains, spaceships...?"

"Nada."

"Boy, you have been out of the loop for a while. Never mind. Anyway, I hired some of my old MIT buddies and I even found some people that used to work for NASA, Boeing, and the military."

"Damn, man. That's big time, sure enough. Wait. A basement?"

"More like a bunker," Jimmy corrected. "It's like a whole other world down there." Eddie wasn't quite sure where Jimmy was going with all this, but then again, he didn't understand "geek speak" very well, either. He would let it ride for now.

"Okay, well, tell me more at dinner."

"You got it!" They shook hands and hugged each other as they always had. Ever since high school, they considered themselves brothers. Eddie headed for the motel. He did have some questions, though. A lot of questions.

What kind of crazy stuff did his eccentric friend have going on now? Geeks at computers? MIT grads? NASA and military techs? Sounded like a lot more besides green diesel engine research and development.

And did he say spaceships?

CHAPTER THREE
GET YOUR TICKET HERE, TEXAS

At dinner that evening, they talked about "the good ol' days" of racing, and what might have been.

Then Jimmy caught Eddie up on the local news.

"Frankie Palmer is still a jerk. He works at the textile plant. Foreman or something like that. I heard he tried to bully his way around with this one guy and the guy knocked him out cold!"

"Serves him right," Eddie replied. "The guy will never learn."

"Yeah, I still remember the look on his face that day in school when you finally stood your ground and knocked him on his ass. It was beautiful. Still has that scar on his lip, too."

Eddie grinned. "Yeah, that did feel pretty good."

"Have you talked to Jr. yet?" Jimmy inquired.

Eddie shifted in his seat. "No, not yet. Left a message. Was gonna stop by to see the grandkids before I left again."

"You ever gonna tell him?"

"We've been over this before, Jimbo. How do I do that? Nobody, not even my son, is gonna buy that story. I've played it a thousand times in my head and even I wouldn't buy it. No, best to let a sleeping dog lie. Besides, nobody is gonna believe me over Russell anyway. Mr. 'Pillar of the Community' and church deacon."

Jimmy could see the old wounds opening.

"Okay, let's change the subject then. Let me tell you what's going on at the compound. We're doing some intense R&D on a bunch of stuff. I got diesel techs building monster motors that can put out some serious horsepower combined with high-speed electric drive systems."

Eddie sat back in his seat. "Really? How's that work?"

"Well, we are mating the two technologies to produce a hybrid system that can handle a big truck in special situations."

"Why not all electric? Isn't that what everybody else is trying to do?"

"Well, yeah, but we're taking a little different approach because we have a different goal in mind. And that's not all. We're also working on a gyroscopic stability control system integrated into the suspension system."

"Sure… What's that do?"

"Well, in theory, it will counter the inertia of the weight of a load in your trailer to prevent it from tipping over in a turn or cornering on a mountain road."

Eddie was impressed by that one. "Now, that, my friend, is a great idea! Think of how many accidents that would prevent."

"I know, right? Not to mention, dropping insurance premiums and no more cargo spills. Jimmy leaned in and started painting Eddie a bigger picture.

"All right…we just bought two new Pete 579's to set this stuff up in, and a couple of trailers. There's a lot of other stuff we're doing to these things and I mean from the frame up. Stuff that's never been done before. We even have a full-size truck dyno coming so we can measure the horsepower, torque, and potential speed once everything is mated together.

"And that's where you come in, my friend."

"Me?"

"Yes, you. I need *Fast Eddie* to put it through its paces."

"How so?"

"Okay, well first, you need a little schooling on how to engage and work the computer that operates the systems."

Eddie squinted his eyes as he listened, cocking his head a little while he contemplated where Jimmy was going.

"Why do I get the feeling there's something you're not telling me?"

Jimmy smirked slightly and replied, "Whaddaya mean?"

"I mean, what have you got up your sleeve that you haven't told me yet? You forget who you're talking to. I have been in some of your crazy contraptions before!"

"True, but I haven't killed ya yet."

"Not yet, but almost! Twice!"

"C'mon, yer on your way out anyway, might as well go out in style."

"Thanks! They'll put that on my tombstone: 'Eddie McVane, he went out in style!' Crashing and burning in a science experiment, and he looked cool doing it."

Jimmy laughed. "Hey, it would be an epic finish!"

"Just what I always wanted," Eddie quipped.

"Okay, here's another thing. We're preparing for the future of high-speed transport."

"How so?"

"Well, along with the engine and electric drive system, we are using some stronger and lighter weight materials on the chassis and body panels so you can carry heavier payloads."

"Hmm. Less truck and trailer weight, more payload capacity. Makes sense. And...?"

"And faster. A lot faster."

"Okay, I'll bite. How much a lot faster?"

"Two hundred plus," Jimmy deadpanned.

Eddie's eyes almost popped out of his head as he sat back in his chair.

"Say what? Are you crazy? That's just nuts!"

"Theoretically, of course."

"Oh, theoretically. Why didn't you say that in the first place? I'll answer myself: because that's theoretically insane! A 200-mile-an-hour tractor trailer? And, is that even possible?"

Jimmy watched Eddie's expressions as he was trying to process what was being said while continuing to vent his thoughts aloud.

"Also, you do know that's a lot of weight to try and propel at that speed. And then there's the whole stopping thing, Jimmy. Let's not forget about that."

"I know. But it's totally possible and we are building the truck to do it."

Eddie thought about the idea and eyed Jimmy over for a solid minute before responding.

"Okay, let's say you do build this thing. Just where do you propose we test this idea out?"

"I'm working on that."

"Are ya now?"

"Yeah, I got some ideas of places out West that would be perfect. I mean, like, a straight line fifty miles of open road to just let 'er rip! Couple of places out in Texas, some in Oklahoma, New Mexico. There are some in South Dakota, too."

"Uh huh. I dunno, buddy. Sounds sketchy to me. Theoretically, of course."

Eddie pondered some more and then continued his query. "So, let me get this straight. You want me to take this, whatever...hybrid thingy truck, and drive out to 'Get Your Ticket Here, Texas,' so *we*, meaning *me*, can try to get a loaded, almost 100,000 pound rig up to

200 mph? You think that's not going to draw some attention? Do you have any idea how insane that sounds?"

Jimmy started to respond but Eddie wasn't finished just yet.

"And what happens if I break it? Now I'm stuck out in the middle of nowhere! I don't think the geek squad makes those kinda house calls.

"And what about cops? Am I just supposed to stop by the local sheriff's department and say, 'Hey guys, I'm just gonna be rippin' along on one of your long roads at 200 mph in this here 100,000 pound brick missile, doing a test for my crazy friend back home because 'we're building the future,' so, ya'll just be cool, nothing to see here. Okay?"

Jimmy laughed. "I know it sounds crazy, but it can be done. I'll have it all worked out when the time comes."

"Yeah…I dunno about that one, Jimbo. That's a tall order, buddy. I mean, a 200-mph rig? And what's the point again?"

"The future, man! Elon Musk and several other companies are working on stuff even crazier than what I'm doing. Musk has got spaceships that will be taking people on vacations to outer space pretty soon. Underground high-speed trains, all kinds of future stuff.

"Transporting products is the next big hurdle, moving them across the country faster, safer, and more cost effectively. It's what's ahead for trucking. That's what I'm working on, man."

"Well, sounds like an ambitious goal, all right, Jimmy, but at 200 mph? I dunno, I'm kinda old to be going that fast anymore. Hell, I'm almost 70! Reflexes and senses aren't what they used to be. I really shouldn't be going half that fast. Well, very often, anyway."

"C'mon, man, you still got the stuff. You are the only truck driver I know that's driven at 200 miles an hour before. You know what it's like! Plus, you got that…that...thing. You know, the Vulcan mind meld or whatever you want to call it."

"Vulcan mind meld? Seriously?"

"You know what I mean."

Yeah, I do. But you forget. That was in a prepared race car with a helmet, roll cage, a five-point harness, and a fire suit. Not to mention a crew of crash squirrels to come and scrape up your parts if you hit the wall so there's something to send home to Mama. Oh! And another thing, they were okay with me going 200 miles an hour on their pavement. Big difference there.

"Plus, there are a lot more variables with a rig. Handling, aerodynamics, shifting loads, suspension dynamics, tires, just to name a few. You want me to go on?"

Jimmy started to say something but was cut off again.

"Then there are the cops, road conditions, weather, critters, and again...cops."

"Okay, okay, I get it, but here's the thing. I know about all that. I've taken all that into consideration," Jimmy responded assuringly.

"Really?"

"Yes, really. You forget. I knew what it took to get you out in front back in the day and I know what it's going to take to make this rig work. I am close to some breakthroughs that nobody has even thought about yet and I intend to be the first."

Looking down at the table, Eddie shook his head. "I hear ya, buddy, but I think you need a younger guy for this gig. This sounds way beyond me."

Jimmy shook his head in disagreement exclaiming, "But we're a team, man! We were the best. Nobody is better qualified for this gig than you."

"Maybe back then, but this...I dunno. This, I gotta think about. This is waaay over what we used to do. This is outta my wheelhouse, my friend."

Jimmy sat back in his chair and waved off the response.

"Nah. You still got the goods. I got faith in you."

Eddie thought about it a little more before finishing his thought on the matter.

"It won't be ready anytime soon anyway, will it?"

"Well, depends on my man, Bobby Chu. You haven't met him yet. He's the kid that's designing and building the mechanism that will mate the two systems together. Maybe a couple months?"

"Okay, we'll look at it then. No promises, though."

"Fair enough."

For now, Jimmy felt he had given Eddie more than enough to think about. He knew it took time for him to process such things, and this was by far his biggest challenge yet. It was a lot to absorb.

They sat and chatted for another hour about the latest local news and gossip, what the local race teams were doing, who was moving up, and what sponsors were backing who. In some ways, Eddie missed going to the local events, the racing, the football games, and the county fair with his son and grandkids. Seemed like forever ago, he thought. Finally, he decided he had enough for tonight.

"Okay, I'm going to call it a night, my friend. What time you want me there in the morning?"

"Eight should do. I think Angelo is more excited than we are about this new motor. I told him you were the man to put it through its paces and see what it was made of."

"I'll do my best not to break it."

"Okay, see ya in the AM." They said their goodbyes and Eddie headed back to the motel.

Over the years, Jimmy had offered to have him stay at his home several times, but Eddie had always preferred to be in a motel room. He hadn't felt comfortable anywhere else since Kate died and he felt no need to buy a house or condo, or even get an apartment. Why? He would just sit and stare at the TV or at the walls, and think about the past. He didn't really socialize much anymore, mostly because he didn't trust people. He even kept his trucking family at a distance.

In Eddie's mind, he no longer had a home nor did he belong anywhere. His truck was his cell and the highway was his penance. He will drive until death comes for him, and when it does, he will welcome the reaper and offer him a beer.

Chapter Four
This Home is Where His Heart Was

Eddie rolled into the complex the next morning. Jimmy instructed him to go around to the back entrance and pull in the back bay. As he climbed out of his truck, two technicians in lab coats took over the rig and continued driving it into the garage area to give his beloved Fat Betty a new heartbeat. Eddie watched as it disappeared into the shop and the door closed behind them. The truck was his pride and joy as well as his home now and he didn't like strangers pawing all over her, despite knowing she was in good hands, even if those hands were wearing lab coats.

Eddie walked back outside where Jimmy picked him up. The cool, "Hey," and nod weren't fooling Jimmy.

"Relax. We'll take good care of her."

"I know, just feels funny, that's all."

"All right, well I got a surprise for ya."

"Yeah?"

"I figured you'd want to cruise around a little so I dug Lucille outta the barn and cleaned her up for ya."

Eddie's eyes lit up then.

"Cool, man. Thanks!"

'Lucille' was one of the few things Eddie held onto from his past life with Kate, aside from a few pictures and mementos he keeps in the truck with him. It was a custom built 1985 Chevy K-20 4x4 pickup, triple black, long bed, with a high performance 454 big block that had a rumble like no other. Eddie restored the truck several years ago with Kate and Eddie Jr.'s help along with one of Jimmy's engines stuffed in the engine bay. It was one of his better memories.

As Jimmy pulled up to where Lucille was parked, Eddie eyed her lovingly. She still looked good. Long, tall, black, and sexy. As they sat there, Jimmy asked him what he had planned for the next two days while they worked on Fat Betty.

"Well, I'll probably go see the kids and then maybe ride over to Hickory and see some racing. Nobody else around here I care to see."

Jimmy knew it was useless to try and convince him to stick around the area. Not everybody blamed Eddie for what happened. He still had friends, but Jimmy knew Eddie just wasn't comfortable there anymore.

"Okay, my friend, I will call you when she's ready." With that Jimmy left Eddie to get reacquainted with his pickup.

As Eddie got behind the wheel, he looked around the cab at everything he and Kate and Eddie, Jr. had done to it. All the memories flooded his mind. The bodywork, the interior, and the night they stayed up late to paint it. He remembered when he and Junior picked out the wheels and tires, and how they all took a ride together as a family the day it was finally finished. That was a good day.

As he fired Lucille up, he listened to the throaty rumble for a couple of seconds before putting her in gear. He eased out of the space and headed out of the complex toward town. Not much had changed in his old neighborhood, just a few different stores and some new construction here and there.

As expected, there were memories at each turn. As much as he knew he shouldn't, he drove by his and Kate's old house.

The new owners hadn't drastically changed it, but Eddie noted every change. There were different flowers and they had planted some new trees. They also repaved the driveway and fixed that fence Kate had been after him about forever. Gone was the basketball goal and the tire swing he put up for the grandkids, and the shutters he and Junior made for Mother's Day along with the flower boxes that always had dahlias and cascading vines. The garage looked clean and organized. There was a minivan and mountain bikes inside instead of a cool hot rod project. It was a mere ghost of what it once was, but it was still where all the memories of his married life were made.

The house in Eddie's mind is where his heart is. The one he was passing by now is just a house on a street.

As he drove on back toward the highway, Eddie thought he saw a few of his old neighbors, but he didn't look too hard. They had nothing to say that he wanted to hear. Most of them had forgotten all the times he had helped them with flat tires, locked keys in the car, good deals on parts and repairs, the cookouts, the football games, and race day parties. All their kids had been in his house and yard at one time or another when Junior was in school.

No, the only thing folks seemed to remember now was that day. Eddie had never been a judgmental person toward people who had made mistakes in their lives and he had forgiven many over the years. But it didn't seem to work in reverse.

Eddie finally admitted to himself, now, that he was probably more hurt than angry anymore. However, it didn't lessen his hatred of Russell Cortland. Many was the time he plotted revenge in his mind but stopped himself, if for no other reason, that it would bring shame on Junior.

Russell was indeed lucky in that respect. Eddie buried it deep within himself and took it all out on the road and his equipment.

Now, being back with all the memories and feelings, testing these engines for Jimmy and pushing them to their limits would have to do. Eddie was going to push them like he pushed his race cars back in the day. Right to the very edge! If an engine didn't break in those days, it was a good one. Well, the Fast Eddie engine rules haven't changed. The new motor Jimmy and his team were putting in Fat Betty would get a workout after tomorrow, for sure!

****

The drive over to his son's house was always hard. Eddie had to mentally prepare himself for when he spoke to him. Junior was cordial enough, but Eddie always got that underlying feeling of resentment that he was there when his mother wasn't. Although he didn't blame Junior for his feelings, Eddie wished many times over that there was a way to fix it.

When he got to the house and turned in the driveway, the garage door was open and he saw the 68' SS 396 Chevelle that he and Junior had started to restore all those years ago was still there, covered up with all kinds of boxes and miscellaneous items piled on top of it. Eddie remembered how excited Junior was when they got that car. It was in real good shape and they had big plans for it.

Bonnie answered the door and gave him a hug. "How you doing, Pop?" his daughter-in-law asked.

"Not bad for a worn-out old dude."

"Well, you look good in spite of that. Junior's at the store, he'll be right back. Kids are in the den."

His grandkids were all excited to see him as he passed out their gifts. Cody McVane, the oldest, was a die-hard fisherman. He had been since he was old enough to hold a fishing pole and fished nearly every day since. He was almost taller than Eddie and was filling out into a solid-looking young man.

"I heard you were into fly fishing now, so I did a little research and got you this." The look on his grandson's face was priceless when he opened the box.

"*Wow*! An Orvis Mirage! No way! He hugged Eddie and thanked him several times.

Jessie McVane was Eddie's princess and the apple of his eye. She looked so much like her grandmother it was unreal. Like her brother, Jessie was also tall, with long brown hair, tanned skin, and big brown eyes. Just a lovely young lady.

Eddie was always overwhelmed when he saw his grandkids. He couldn't believe how beautiful they were and how much time had passed from when they were first born. He reminisced when he and Kate held them in their arms.

He knew from talking to Bonnie that Jessie had been wanting a new computer for school so he got her the new Chromebook with all the upgrades. As always, Eddie also got her a new set of earrings with some cute critter on it because she seemed to like odd trinkets with different animals on them.

"Oh, thank you, Granpaw!" she exclaimed. After giving him a big hug, she started chattering about all the new things she could do.

"Now I can do some really cool stuff. This has more storage and a faster processor, plus you can..." And off she went about all the stuff she had in mind that she would now be able to do, and doing this while putting on her critter earrings.

While Jessie was talking about her computer, Cody had gone out to the garage and gotten one of his fly-fishing rods. He had already mounted the new reel on it and now he was all about that.

Eddie just smiled and sat and listened. He loved his grandkids and was always happy just being in the same room with them. They could rattle on about anything. It all sounded sweet to him.

In the meantime, he heard Junior's truck pull into the driveway. When he came into the den, the kids showed their father what Eddie had gotten them. He was excited for them and said how cool the presents were. Then Junior looked at Eddie and smiled.

"How you doing, Pop?"

"Good, son. You're putting on some weight there, aren't you?"

"Yeah, it's Bonnie's fault. She cooks too good."

As they exchanged pleasantries, Junior came and sat in the adjoining chair. Cody went outside to play with his new fishing reel setup and Jessie went to her room to explore her new computer. Eddie asked Junior about his job and all he was doing there, but Junior quickly changed the subject. Eddie noticed but didn't push it.

"They have me working split shifts this month. Makes it tough to schedule things here at home, but we manage. Jimmy working on your truck again?"

"Yeah, he's putting in a new motor. Says he's got some other things he wants to do to the truck that he wants me to try out. I have no idea what they are."

"I see he's got that new building going up. Some kind of research and development facility?"

"Yeah, you ought to see this place. It's like some kind of futuristic science lab or something. Wall-to-wall geeks, computers, and high-tech equipment everywhere. Says it's all about green diesel engine technology."

"What's that?"

"I have no idea, son. You know Jimmy. He could be trying to make them run on maple syrup for all I know."

Junior chuckled. "He is out there, for sure."

Bonnie called them both for lunch.

"Junior, you and Pop go wash up for lunch."

"Yes, ma'am," came the reply from both of them.

As they ate lunch, Bonnie asked Eddie about his trips, where he had been lately, and how he was doing overall.

"All things considered, pretty good, I guess."

After they finished eating, the kids asked to be excused and went back to their activities while Eddie, Junior, and Bonnie chatted about different things.

Eddie felt awkward, like he was just a visitor or a neighbor stopping by. Even though this was his son's home, it wasn't like it used to be. He wished more than anything he could go out in the garage with his son and tinker with that old Chevelle.

After a bit of quiet, Junior came out of left field with his next question.

"So, Pop, given any thought to retirement?"

"Um, well, no. I haven't thought much about it at all, actually. Why do you ask?"

"Well, you are going to be 69 this year, I was just wondering what you had planned."

Eddie paused for a moment realizing that he really hadn't thought about the subject at all. As a matter of fact, he was so wrapped up in driving and burying his sorrow in his work, he had barely come up for air in the past three years.

While he was still thinking about the question, Bonnie chimed in.

"We were just thinking it might be something for you to consider, that's all. How's your health? Are you still smoking those cigars?"

"Yeah, it's my only vice. Maybe a couple fingers of Jack when Jimmy and I go to dinner, but other than that, I just drive. I feel pretty good, though. Don't do junk food, pretty careful what I eat, lots of water and I did cut back on the coffee."

"You ever think about buying another place?" Junior asked.

Eddie knew that Junior was fishing for something. As he looked his son in the eyes, he wanted so bad to say how much he hated this town and being this close to Russell Cortland and the people that judged him, but he held back.

"No. At least, not right now. And if I did, I'd want to be up in the mountains. But I'm not ready to hang it up just yet, though. I have my hands full with Jimmy and his craziness. That keeps me young right there. As for everything else, I do have my will and everything in order with the Bessett law firm. You and the kids get everything I have plus the life insurance."

Bonnie reached over and patted his arm.

"We weren't worried about that, Pop. We just wanted to make sure you're okay."

"I'm think I'm pretty good. I've still got a little gas left in the tank yet. I'll let you know when I'm ready to hang up my keys."

"Fair enough."

Bonnie and Eddie talked some more while Junior took out the trash.

"Believe it or not, he worries about you," she said. "I know things have been difficult for both of you, but maybe it's time to try and mend some fences. He thinks you should come home, settle down and spend more time with the kids. Some folks at church were asking about you, even the pastor asked how you were and that he hoped to see you one day when you were in town. People do miss you, Pop."

Eddie thought about that all the time. Was he being selfish? Couldn't he find a way to cope? Was there a way to be close to his family and not have to see or deal with anybody from the past? As much as he wanted to believe that, he couldn't see it happening. But he promised her that he would work on it.

Bonnie knew that Eddie was just making conversation and saying what she wanted to hear. She knew he didn't want to see anybody from the church or anybody else for that matter. He resented their judging ways and she really understood that. She had been trying for the past three years to make his son understand as well how hard it must be for his father and how he had to be hurting more than anyone could imagine. For now, Bonnie dropped the subject and gave Eddie a hug, telling him to be safe and that she loved him and he is always welcome there.

"Thanks, kiddo. I appreciate that. I'll keep you posted."

After all the goodbyes were done and Eddie hugged the kids "just one more time," Junior walked him out to his truck where they shared an awkward moment of silence.

Eddie hated the feeling and spoke up to break it.

"For what it's worth, kid, I'm really proud of you and Bonnie. You both have done a fine job with Cody and Jessie. They are turning out to be great kids. You two should be proud."

"Thanks, Pop, that means a lot."

Another moment of silence, then Junior comes back again.

"I really wish you would think about retirement. The kids would like you being around more."

Eddie looked over at the garage where the Chevelle was.

"Maybe finish up that project one day, eh?"

Junior looked over at it as well.

"Yeah, maybe."

Eddie figured he got all he was going to get out of his son for today. It was more than he had gotten in the past three years. He would take it.

"Okay, I'll give it some thought. Love you, and I will keep you, Bonnie, and the kids posted on my whereabouts. Thank Bonnie again for lunch."

"Okay, Pop. Stay safe out there."

They shook hands and Eddie got in his truck and headed back to the motel. He watched Junior in his rearview mirror still standing there watching after him as he was leaving. Although he could tell that his son wanted to talk more, Eddie didn't want to make it harder than it was already so he made his exit to relieve the pressure for both of them. It was progress, though. He would see how it went next time and maybe hang around a little longer.

Now, there was one more stop to make before his day was done.

****

Eddie was on hallowed ground: the gravestone of Katherine Lilian McVane. A flood of emotions came over him as he stood in front of it. The first time they met, the day they got married, and the birth of their son. The good times, the bad times, it was all there. Thirty-plus years of memories playing in his head like a DVD movie on fast forward. Her smile, her laugh, her comforting and encouraging words during the hard times. The fire in her eyes when she was mad at him for doing something stupid. The warmth of her sitting next to him when they were on the porch at night or just piled on the couch watching a movie together. All gone. Eddie was in tears as he softly spoke to the place where his wife lay.

"I'm so sorry, Kate. I'm sorry I didn't listen to you that day. I should have known it was a lie. I was so jealous at the thought of some other man touching you, I couldn't think straight. You were my world. I loved you more than words can say. Please forgive me."

He talked on and told her how big the grandkids were and how Junior was doing at his job. He talked about his life on the road now and how she would have liked some of the places he had been and seen the past three years. He told her about Jimmy's new place and the technology they were working on.

"He's still a nut job, but doing well with the new facility. You know Jimmy, always dreaming up newer and crazier things. Junior and Bonnie are worried about me now. They want me to think about retiring. What do you think about that? How do I retire? What would I do? I could spend some time with the grandkids, but they'll be ready for college soon and then they'll go away. Everybody here has judged me without knowing the truth. A lot of them are our so-called church friends. And Russell Cortland? How am I supposed to live here with that guy still walking the earth? You always knew what to say in times like this. I know you would probably tell me to forgive everybody and move on."

Eddie could hear her saying one of her favorites to him: *"Don't let that crap live in your head. If they're living in your head, they're living rent free."*

But he sighed in defeat of that request.

"Believe me, honey, I'm trying, but it sure is hard. I'm just not there yet. All I know is that I miss you more than words can say."

He stayed for a while longer, just talking about whatever came to mind. As he talked, he plucked the weeds from around her stone and set new flowers in the vase.

"There. I know how you liked things neat and trimmed. I got you some purple flowers. Don't remember the name right off, but I remembered they were your favorite color. Hope that's okay."

He checked the arrangement of flowers one more time before leaving. Silently, he reached down and rubbed the top of her headstone and sighed.

"Well, hon...time to go. Say hi to Nana and Poppy for me. Love and miss you. And yes, I know. I'll try not to do anything stupid and get myself killed."

****

Two days later Eddie was at the new complex bright and early, waiting as Jimmy drove up.

"Damn, son! Are you anxious or what?"

Eddie had already stopped to pick up coffee and biscuits, and smiling, he handed one to Jimmy.

"Always ready, my friend." They headed inside.

"Come on in the office," Jimmy said, "and let me go over some stuff with you on this new unit."

They were followed by Jimmy's Maine coon cat, Nikola, so named after the famed inventor. The cat took his place on a specially prepared platform just behind the desk. He was dark gray with a lighter gray mane and was the biggest cat Eddie had ever seen outside a zoo. Nikola was Jimmy's pride and joy, and he treated him like royalty. Eddie always joked about the cat's loyalty.

"You know that if you passed out or fell down and couldn't get up to feed him, that cat would eat you, right?"

"Stop! He would not. Nikola loves me." Jimmy reached around and petted him.

"Don't ya, buddy?"

"Yeah, just don't forget to feed him. What does he eat anyway, like half a deer or something?"

Jimmy laughed. "No, he has a special diet. Actually, he eats better than we do."

"No doubt."

Looking around at Jimmy's new office, Eddie was amazed at his collection of movie, TV, car, and science fiction vehicles. Plus every kind of memorabilia imaginable. The walls were covered with movie and TV posters of virtually any genre you could imagine. As Eddie took it all in, there was *Knight Rider,* the Bond cars, and even *Airwolf!* All the Batmobiles plus *Ghostbusters,* the Eleanor mustang, the Bullitt Mustang and Charger, *Starsky and Hutch's* Gran Torino, the *Back To The Future* DeLorean, and all the *Fast and Furious* cars. It was amazing. Like a museum, no, a shrine to the vehicles. Eddie looked behind him and there was even more. *Transformers, Mad Max, The A-Team, Christine,* and Eddie's personal favorites, *Vanishing Point* Challenger, The General Lee *and Smokey and The Bandit* Trans Am. They were all there.

Then there was an entire bookcase with all the VHS tapes, DVDs, books, die-casts, and bobble heads. You name it, it was all there. Eddie turned his head and saw actual detailed drawings and diagrams of the Starship Enterprise, beginning with the original series, and other sci-fi craft in frames mounted in another area of the room. Truly a complete collection if ever there was one and as if to say he hadn't forgotten about the people, Jimmy even had autographed signatures in framed snapshots of Barris, Roth, Dean Jefferies, Gene Winfield, Alexander Brothers, Chip Foose, Boyd Coddington, and others.

"Damn, Jimmy, is there anybody you haven't got in here?"

"Not many. I always wanted Von Dutch's signature but never got out that way. I went to all the shows I could get to when these guys were there. They were the pioneer builders of the day. They were my main inspiration for designing and building. Tesla, Edison, Marconi, Gates, Jobs, and Musk in the technology and science department. These guys were visionaries, way ahead of their time."

"Well, I am sure they would be honored if they ever came here. Man! This is something."

Jimmy reached for a tablet on his desk.

"Okay, here is your assignment, Mr. Phelps." He showed Eddie a series of icons and what to do in sequence when he starts his tests on the new engine.

"Here, this monitors all that the engine is doing. This one shows the horsepower it's putting out at what RPM range. This graph shows the turbo performance, and this one shows all that's going on internally, each glow plug, timing, fuel consumption, and so on. All you have to do is make sure when these lines hit these marks that they turn green. If not, then adjust each slide button here until they do."

"Okay, sounds easy enough. How about these icons over here?"

"No, those you don't need to worry about right now. They're for something else later on."

"Later on? What else is there?"

"It's something I've been working on for a while. Basically a different performance setup."

Jimmy didn't want to overwhelm Eddie with too much information at the moment. Those icons on the side were what he was working on downstairs, and it was probably the most ambitious endeavor he had ever tackled in his life. Trying to explain it right now was hard, even for him. Jimmy needed time and a way to ease Eddie into a proper introduction to the truck of the future.

"Okay, sounds good. That it?" Eddie asked.

"Yeah, that will do for now. C'mon, let's go see if Angelo has got you ready."

Eddie stroked Nikola one more time before he left, whispering to the cat, "Remember, Jimmy's our friend. Don't eat him while he's sleeping."

They went out of the office and through the maze of cubicles that were already buzzing with activity as Egghead City was fully awake and doing egghead stuff. Intermittently, one would poke their head up and say, "Morning, Boss."

As they were nearing the entry door to the back, a young Asian man wearing black-rimmed glasses and a lab coat burst through the door and almost ran into them.

"Ooohh! So sorry, Boss man!"

Jimmy calmed him down.

"It's okay, Bobby, relax." He turned to Eddie.

"This here is Bobby Chu, my main assistant. Bobby, meet Eddie McVane." Bobby's eyes lit up and he seemed to get all excited. He grabbed Eddie's hand and began shaking it vigorously.

"*Oooh*! So glad to meet you! I hear much 'bout you. You famous driver! You Fast Eddie!" Eddie was taken aback by the young man's enthusiasm and was wanting his hand back.

"You big deal! We all follow you career. We build you good motor and make neat stuff for you."

Jimmy cut him off at that point. "Okay, Bobby, Eddie has to go. Thanks."

"Oh, yes! You busy guy. It pleasure, Mr. Eddie." With that he hurried off to where he was headed with Eddie looking after him as he went.

"Okay? What was that all about? And what kind of 'neat stuff' did he mean?" Eddie gave Jimmy a quizzical look while Jimmy deflected the question.

"He saw our scrapbook in the office one day and went nuts over it. I told him some stories and he's been a fan ever since. He came from South Korea on a student visa back in 2015 to go to MIT. He liked it so much here that he applied for citizenship and eventually got it. Even worked at NASA for a while, designing stuff for the space shuttle. When I called some of my old professors looking for recruits, they all gave Bobby high marks and said he would be perfect for what we were doing here.

"Aside from being a genius, he's also into the tuner scene and a big gear head. Not to mention he's good at solving complex engineering problems. We are trying to mate two technologies together, something we've been working on for a while now. Bobby has a pretty good handle on it. He's also really good with AI." Jimmy continued walking toward the back of the shop trying to distract Eddie and move him to the back where his truck was.

"What's AI?" Eddie asked

"Artificial Intelligence. It's like that new technology they put in cars and trucks now that warn you if you're weaving into the other lane or if you don't stop quick enough, it will do it for you."

"Oh, yeah. I've seen the commercials. I think it makes people lazy. What if it quits working one day? Who stops the car then?"

"It's more foolproof than that."

"I dunno about that. I've seen some pretty sufficient fools out there lately."

They finally came to the back shop where Fat Betty sat, all cleaned up and ready to go.

"There's my girl," Eddie said smiling and happy to be back at his truck. Climbing inside, he hung his clean clothes up and put his briefcase in its usual spot.

Jimmy climbed in the passenger's side and installed the tablet in its place on the dash. As he turned it on, it indicated everything he had shown Eddie in his office.

"There ya go. Just do like I said and it will record and store everything that goes on with the engine."

"Perfect. Well, time to see what she can do. Mike Jenkins has got me a load going to Albuquerque, New Mexico. You said you had some stretches for me to run out there?"

"Yeah, I have some satellite feed coming that we can check out. I will be able to give you the mile markers by the time you get out there because I'll know where the safe zones are. By the way, how did it go with Junior and the kids?"

"Good, actually. Although they are worried about me getting old and want me to retire soon."

"Really? How do you feel about that?"

"And do what? Sit on the front porch and yell at people to stay off my lawn?"

"What about the grandkids?"

"Thought about that. They will be going to college soon. Besides, you know I don't fit here anymore."

"You still have friends. They ask about you all the time. It could work."

Eddie looked down at the floorboard.

"Can't do it, Jimmy. Too many memories and too much pain. I would die of misery here." He looked back at him.

"No, my life will end on the road somewhere, as it should. To be honest, if it weren't for Junior, the kids, and you, I would never set foot here again."

Jimmy put hand on his friend's shoulder. "I understand, buddy, I truly do. I won't ask again, I promise."

"Thank you."

Just then another tech in a lab coat came to Jimmy's door. "Sir, we're ready for testing downstairs."

"Okay, be right there. Eddie, you take care, my friend. Stay safe, man. See ya when you get back."

"Till then."

They shook hands and Jimmy hopped out. Eddie fired Fat Betty up with the new motor named Rosie. She had a deep throaty sound that commanded attention.

"Wow, Rosie, you sound good! Now that's a growl if ever I heard one. Come on, new girl, let's see what you got."

Eddie backed out of the bay and into the sunlight of a new day. He headed out to the Interstate and down to Charlotte to pick up his load going to Albuquerque, New Mexico.

As he headed out of town, he looked in his mirrors and was happy to see the town getting smaller. The further away he got, the better he felt. That place was no longer home to him. It was just a place where his son and grandchildren lived and where his best friend and partner worked. As far as he was concerned, his home was waiting for him in Heaven with Kate. He would drive the wheels off his truck until then.

Chapter Five
Just in Time to Say Goodbye

After Eddie took a left turn out of Albuquerque, he jumped onto I-40 heading east. When he got up to speed, he gave Jimmy a call to give him an update on how Rosie was doing. So far, she was performing well with no issues. "As a matter of fact," he told Jimmy, "it's the smoothest-running engine yet."

"Cool. How about performance wise? Did you save the info on the computer like I showed you?"

"Yep. She jumped up to speed pretty quick. Lots of torque. She pulls like a bear. It showed all green buttons, so that's good, right?"

"Yes, sir, that's a good thing. Now we have to see what she can do when you take her for a gallop. I have a couple of mile markers checked out, and according to our satellite images, this would be the perfect stretch to try her out and see what she can do."

"Okay, text me the mile-marker numbers. What am I looking for?"

"When you get within a mile of the stretch, call me and I will show you what to set the monitor at. It will tell you what RPM range you are shooting for per gear, and it will also show you the peak horsepower range per gear and whether it starts to drop any before you shift. If it does, that's when you adjust the setting I showed you."

"Got it. Just curious, did you do anything else to this thing? Feels different somehow."

Damn! Jimmy thought. *How does he do that?*

"Um, I did have the guys in Engineering make some new gears for better takeoff and top-end."

"Thought so. Told ya. I can feel everything that goes on with my truck. I can even feel the air in the tires." Eddie was grinning when he said it.

"Come on! That's not possible!"

"I'm tellin' ya. I can feel everything. So just tell me next time."

"Okay, okay! Jeeze! You are a genuine freak of nature."

Eddie chuckled to himself.

"Okay, Jimmy, I'll call you when I get within a mile or so of the test area."

"Copy that. Later."

Eddie hung up and settled in for the drive. He was right, though. A good driver knows his truck, inside out. He can feel every vital part that pertains to the handling and performance of his rig. So much so that he can tell when the engine doesn't sound or feel right, doesn't shift right, the brakes feel spongy or pulling, whether it's handling properly under a load, or in this case, the shorter rev time to shift through the first five gears. It didn't match the usual engine sound Eddie was used to. He could also tell it had a taller gear on the uppers because he was at 75–80 mph and was only in 16th gear (out of 18) and hovering right around 1,300 rpm. Definitely different from before.

****

He was about an hour out of Albuquerque, when he saw a bus on the side of the road up ahead with smoke coming out of the back. There was no other traffic on the road, so Eddie slowed down and decided to stop and see if he could help. He pulled over on the shoulder about fifty feet behind the bus, grabbed his extinguisher and hustled to the back of the bus. As he got up to where the driver was, the smoke was starting to dissipate.

"You need this one, driver?"

"I think I've got it. Thanks anyway."

Eddie sat his down.

"I'll just hang for a bit to make sure." He walked around to the side of the bus and looked over the group of people milling around. The bus driver came up beside him.

"I knew something was wrong when it started losing power. I started seeing smoke coming out the back and got off the road right away.

"Good thing, too. Much longer and it would have gone up completely."

Both Eddie and the driver had seen bus fires before. They knew they could get out of hand quick.

"You got somebody coming?" Eddie asked.

"Yeah, I already called it in. Supposed to be a Roadside Assistance vehicle and a replacement bus on its way. Roadside Assistance guy said he would be here in about twenty minutes. He is bringing extra water for the passengers. The terminal said it would be about an hour to an hour and a half before a bus replacement gets here. Eddie looked around and it seemed like it was mostly younger to middle-aged folks. They looked like a hearty crowd and could make out okay in the heat for an hour or so.

"Tell ya what, I'll hang until the Roadside guy gets here just in case you need my extinguisher or something."

"Thanks, mister. I appreciate it."

"Eddie McVane."

"Josh Burnside." They shook hands and chatted for a while.

As they were talking, Eddie noticed a young blonde-haired kid in an Air Force uniform on his cell phone pacing back and forth, and he seemed to be distressed about something. Eddie surmised from his appearance that he had the look of a kid from the Midwest. Tall, muscular, and tanned. Probably from working outside a lot, farm boy maybe, he thought. He didn't think much about it as it seemed everybody nowadays was distressed about something.

The kid hung up his phone and came over to where Eddie and Josh were talking. He was visibly upset and asked Josh in a polite Midwestern accent, "Excuse me, sir, but did they say how long it would take another bus to get here?"

"They said about an hour or so, son. I'm sorry."

"I understand, sir, but do you know how far we are from the nearest town? Maybe they have something."

Eddie spoke up, "Sorry, son, but we're about halfway between Albuquerque and Santa Rosa, with nothing in between, so either way it's about the same."

"Okay, thank you anyway, sir." He turned around and slowly walked away. Eddie could see he was wiping away tears from his face.

"Wonder what's up with him?" Josh asked.

"I don't know, but it must be something serious. You can tell the kid has been crying."

Eddie thought about his own son and what would it be like if he were stuck out in the middle of nowhere with some kind of need like whatever this young man was dealing with. Pondering that for a moment, he decided to inquire.

"I'm gonna go check on him and see what's up."

Josh nodded in approval. Eddie walked along the side of the bus and found the young man sitting at the front of the bus on the ground. He was obviously in a sad state.

"Hey, kiddo, don't mean to pry, but what's going on?"

The kid looked up with tears in his eyes.

"It's my mom, sir. I got the call yesterday that they put her in the hospital and she's in a bad way. They don't know how long she has and I was trying to get home to see her before she went. I just graduated from the Academy in Denver and all I could afford was a bus ticket. She worked all kinds of jobs after Dad died to send me to that school. I owe her so much and I just wanted to at least let her see me in uniform before she died."

Eddie's heart sank when he heard that. He thought about not being able to say goodbye to his dad when he died. He decided that he had to try and help the kid out.

"What's yer name, son?"

"Zachary, sir. Zachary Dennison."

"And where is it you're trying to get to, Zachary Dennison?"

"Russellville, Arkansas, sir."

Eddie reached his hand down to the kid. "Just so happens I'm going right by there. Come on, I'll give you a lift."

The young man's eyes grew big and he grabbed Eddie's hand to come up off the ground and bear-hugged him so hard Eddie thought he was going to pass out.

"Okay! Okay! Gotta breathe to drive, kiddo."

"Thank you. Thank you, sir. I don't know how I could ever repay you."

"Don't worry about that, just call whoever you need to, and tell them you're on your way."

"Yes, sir!" Zach got on the phone as they were headed back toward Eddie's truck and grabbed his duffel bag on the way.

Eddie stopped and briefed Josh on the story and made sure he didn't need anything before they left.

"No. I see the Roadside guy coming now. We're good. Thanks again and take care. Good luck."

Eddie helped Zach put his duffel bag in the sleeper and they headed out. Once they got on the road, he called Jimmy to let him know he was making a quick stop in Russellville, Arkansas, and filled him in on the deal.

"Okay, man, no problem. You still up for a test?"

"Sure, why not. After all, this is an emergency." With that, Eddie set the cruise control while Zach told him all about his growing up in Russellville, playing football, working on the local farms during the summer, and how hard it was when his dad died and how they struggled. He teared up when talking about his mother and how she made him stay in school even though he wanted to quit and get a job to help with the bills.

"No, sir, she wouldn't hear of it."

Eddie let the boy talk. He knew Zach was worried that they wouldn't get there in time and wanted to keep him preoccupied with conversation to help the time pass. He didn't get to say goodbye to Kate, either, and Eddie knew what that felt like, so now he was on a mission to help this kid get home in time.

He listened as they cruised along and was calculating the distance and time it usually took for the drive on this stretch of road. From where they started, it was about twelve hours to Russellville. If Jimmy could find him some clear stretches, Eddie figured he could shave some time off. It was dark now and Zach was still talking. He had gotten to his time at the Air Force Academy and how he got a job offer from an office in Washington, DC, as a systems engineer.

"Wow Sounds pretty impressive. I'm not sure what that is, but it sounds important."

"Yeah, I also studied to be an analyst, which I really liked. They said I was good at it. That's where you sort through all kinds of information for the intelligence community to see what's going on in the criminal world to find bad guys."

"Well, with all that's going on today, I can see where that's needed." Just then Eddie's phone rang. It was Jimmy.

"Hey, are ya close?"

"Yeah, just about a mile and a half away."

Jimmy rattled off instructions in Eddie's Bluetooth about what to look for on the computer screen.

"Okay. Got it." He set the computer up as instructed.

"How's the kid doing?" Jimmy asked.

"Good. I've learned so much about living in Russellville, Arkansas, that I could go there now and know everybody in town by name, the best places to eat, and the best fishing holes."

Zach laughed as Jimmy wished Eddie good luck and hung up.

"Sorry, I didn't realize how much I had been talking."

"It's okay, I don't mind. Besides, it's good to have someone to talk to sometimes."

Zach's curiosity got the best of him. "Mind if I ask what you're monitoring there?"

"Not at all. That was my business partner back in North Carolina. He and I used to race back in the day and he has always built my motors and done the tuning on them. Not my thing, I'm just the pilot. Now he builds diesel engines and this here is a new one. He set up this computer to regulate the performance and keep tabs on what it's doing. That call was to show me how to dial it in for peak performance.

Zach's eyes got big as he talked. "Cool! I mess with tuner computers on cars myself. I do all the tuning for my buddies back home. Hondas mostly."

Eddie glanced at Zach with a grin.

"Nice lawnmowers, I hear." Zach chuckled at that.

"I know, you're old school, but they are cheap to work on and they actually go pretty fast. I've never seen a setup like this one, though. It looks much more advanced than what I'm used to working with."

"Well, Jimmy is an MIT grad and has been doing his own R&D work for years. I think he designed this very program."

"Wow! He must be pretty smart?"

"Crazy as a bat, actually, but yeah, he's pretty smart."

"Always wanted an old muscle car myself to fix up, but my mom made me save for college. One day I'd like to restore a Chevelle or Camaro from the 70s.

Eddie began sharing some of his stories of the cars he and Jimmy had back in the day.

"Wow. I would have loved to have been there back then."

"Yeah, they were some cool cars. Wish I had them back now. Be worth a fortune."

Eddie saw the mile marker he was looking for so he eased the throttle down and gradually picked up speed. There was no traffic in either direction. It was 2:00 a.m. and Jimmy assured him the coast was clear for the next twenty or so miles.

"We're just going to step up the pace a little and shave some time off the clock, if you don't mind, Zach."

"Not at all!"

The power transition was smooth with just the right amount of exhaust rumble. The truck rode so nice that it was hardly noticeable. Eddie set his pace at 135 mph and held it there.

"Man! I can hardly feel anything, this truck is so smooth. I didn't know that was possible."

"Yeah, my man Jimmy knows his stuff. He doesn't think I know it, but I know they modified the suspension, too."

When they got to the assigned mile marker, Eddie backed it down to 75 mph and set the cruise control. He checked the time and read it off.

"Eight minutes fifty-three seconds to go twenty miles. Not bad. A couple more sprints like that and we'll have you home in no time."

"Wow!" said Zach. "I can't believe this thing can go that fast. That was awesome."

"Yeah. Appreciate it if you kept that to yourself."

"No problem, I understand. My friends wouldn't believe a big rig could go this fast anyway."

They continued through the night talking cars, performance, the good old days, and country living. They even had some country music in common. Zach called periodically to check on his mom. So far there was no change. Eddie liked the kid and believed he would do well in life. Apparently, he was raised proper.

Jimmy found Eddie some more stretches where he could turn Rosie loose and they made good time, stopping only for coffee and snacks.

****

It was 8:30 in the morning when they rolled into the city of Russellville. Eddie pulled up to the front of St. Mary's Regional Medical Center. He helped Zach get his duffel bag out and they said their goodbyes. Zach couldn't help but bear hug him again and with tears in his eyes, he thanked Eddie profusely.

"Glad I could do it, kid. My heart goes out to you and a prayer for your mom. Now go on and let your mom see that uniform on ya."

"Yes, sir!" He started to salute Eddie, but caught himself, then turned and hurried toward the hospital. Eddie looked after Zach and wished him all the strength he could muster in his spirit.

"Kid's gonna have a tough couple weeks ahead of him." he lamented

With that, Eddie headed out of town and back toward I-40 and continued on to Shreveport, Louisiana, his actual destination.

Zachary Dennison got to see his mother and although she was barely able to speak, it was evident in her weak smile that she was proud of her son and how handsome he looked in his uniform. She had completed her mission in life and kept her promise to her husband that their son would go to college and make something of himself. They had produced a fine young man.

An hour after Zachary Dennison walked into his mother's hospital room, Marjorie Dennison passed away peacefully with a smile on her face and pride in her heart. She had run her race and had gone home to be with her Lord.

Zachary wept while holding his mother's hand. He was heartbroken and grateful at the same time. He got there just in time to say goodbye. That night he said a prayer thanking God for sending the trucker into his life for that final gift. He would never forget the kindness of Eddie McVane.

Chapter Six
My New Best Friend

The sun was just coming up as Eddie exited I-20 onto Hwy 157 in Haughton, Louisiana, heading toward the Pilot Travel Center there. After going out of his way to help Zach, he was only an hour behind his planned schedule. The speed sprints he did in Oklahoma paid off. Eddie calculated that he shaved about two hours, give or take, and figured without the detour, he would have been an hour and a half or better ahead of schedule.

Not too shabby, he thought. The truck performed well and had no issues. Now, he was ready to get some breakfast and fuel. Fat Betty could use a bath, too, so to the truck wash she would go. Once he got fueled, Eddie headed over and told the attendant he wanted him to vacuum the inside and clean the windows after the wash. It was a sharp looking rig and he liked keeping it that way. Eddie always tried to keep his equipment looking as new as possible.

"Always take care of what takes care of you, son, and you'll rarely be disappointed." His father drilled that into him early on. Eddie then grabbed his phone and the tablet from the dashboard, and headed toward the restaurant.

As he turned the corner coming to the entrance of the restaurant, he noticed off to the side area a good-sized dog at the end of a grassy spot a little past the walkway. The dog was just sitting there watching the traffic. *Strange*, Eddie thought. The big shaggy critter looked like a brownish overgrown Shih Tzu with some black streaks here and there, and a black masked nose and mouth. *Must belong to somebody*, he thought.

Eddie continued on to the restaurant where the waitress seated him at a booth that just happened to look out where the shaggy dog was perched. Dismissing it, he got out the tablet and checked the performance readings. He saw that the engine, Rosie, he smiled to himself, had done very well and needed only minor adjustments. Happy with that, Eddie ordered steak and eggs with grits, toast, and coffee for breakfast. As he ate and scrolled on his phone, he kept glancing out at the dog. Now, curiosity set in.

Wonder where his owners are? Looks like an expensive breed. Somebody wouldn't just dump him out on the side of the road, would they? Eddie's mind was churning. They had owned dogs and cats plus a variety of smaller pets when Eddie Jr. was small, like fish and a couple of hamsters, and there was that snake Eddie wasn't particularly fond of. Mostly, though, they had retrievers. *Great dogs*, he remembered. The thought made him send Junior an e-mail to see how he, Bonnie, and the kids were. Eddie hit send and asked the waitress for more coffee.

When she came back with the pot, his curiosity had gotten the better of him so he asked, "What's up with that dog?"

She paused for a second as she looked out at him before answering Eddie.

"Well, there used to be this old man that came in every couple days to get lunch. I heard Sharon, the other waitress, say that he was a WWII veteran and that the dog was always with him. I noticed whenever the old guy came in, the dog would sit outside the front door and wait. Sort of like now. When the man would leave, the dog would go with him and they would walk across the way to where he lived. He had been coming here for quite some time from what I understand. Then one day, the old man quit coming. I saw on the news a few days later that a local WWII veteran had died and when they showed his picture, it was that old man. He was 98. Since then, every couple of days, the dog shows up and just sits there. Like he's waiting or looking for the old man."

"Really? That is something." Eddie looked back out at the dog.

"Yeah, several people have tried to catch him to take him to the shelter, but he wasn't having any of that. Sometimes people give him food and treats and water, but then he goes wherever and comes back and just sits. Always right there."

Curious, Eddie thought as the waitress went away. He studied the dog for a while and then finished his last sip of coffee, tossed a tip down, and grabbed his stuff as he slid out of the booth. After paying for his meal, he wandered over to the store to look for some dog treats. He found some and went outside, slowly walking towards the dog. Eddie always seemed to have a way with animals ever since he was kid so he figured he would give this one a try. Maybe help get the animal to a shelter where they could care for him and help find him a good home. He felt it was the least he could do.

As Eddie approached the dog, the animal turned and gave him a curious look tilting his head. Eddie stopped and started talking to him.

"Hey buddy, not gonna hurt you. Just wanna give you something to eat." He opened the bag of treats and held out his hand and inched closer so the dog could sniff his scent. The dog did so and started eating the treats.

Okay, Eddie thought, *this is a good sign.*

"Good boy", he said. After a short time, he slowly inched closer and sat down beside the dog. Eddie opened the bag and poured the rest of the contents out in front of him. The dog ate like he was starving. Eddie watched him as he ate and began to think how much he and the dog had in common. He, like Eddie, had lost a loved one and had a void in his soul. Losing that kind of relationship doesn't heal overnight and for some, never does.

As he sat there, Eddie began to reminisce about Kate and the good times they had. Her laughing at his corny jokes, the fire in her eyes when she got mad, the joy in those same eyes when their son was born, the pain whenever he or Eddie Jr. got hurt, and the concern and dogged determination when they were going through hard times. It got him back talking to the dog.

"I lost someone close to me, too, ya know. It hurts bad and it seems as though your whole world has ended. And in some ways, it has. But you have to find a way to keep going, otherwise, you just as well lay down and die. The hurt never really goes away completely but you find ways to work through it. I'm still working on it myself and it's been over three years. I still have days, like when an old song comes on the radio, or I see something that reminds me of a good day with my wife or a funny moment with her and Junior. Those are the memories you keep and the others you put on a shelf in a closet. I know you probably miss your owner, but it's time to move on. You still gotta live. There's still a lot of life left in you, I believe."

The dog seemed to be listening to him as he was now looking directly at Eddie.

"You know, there are people out there that would love to have a handsome dog such as yourself. I mean, look at you. You're a fine specimen, nice fur, and you seem like you're pretty smart...although you also look like you could eat your weight in groceries. Still…I'm betting we can find you some nice people to care for you."

Slowly Eddie reached over and petted him on the side and then on his head. The animal didn't seem to mind so Eddie continued his conversation with him.

"So. What do you think? Want to give it a shot?"

The dog tilted his head as if he understood what Eddie was saying. After sitting there for a few more minutes, Eddie stood up and walked a few paces away then looked back. The dog was still looking at him. They exchanged looks briefly and then the dog started after him. Eddie turned and headed toward his truck. The dog caught up and heeled at his right side. Eddie just kept walking and talking to him as they went.

"Good boy. I will look up some places on the internet and see what we can find for you, okay?"

The dog kept pace as they headed to the truck. Now Eddie was wondering what kind of dog he might be. He would look that up as well. When they got to the passenger's side of the truck, Eddie opened the door. The dog sat and just looked at him.

"Okay, lemme tell ya how this is gonna work. Number one, I've got a feeling this isn't your first time getting into a vehicle. Second, I ain't picking you up and third, there isn't a crane around to hoist your big butt up here, so…" Eddie took his left hand and the gestured towards the truck.

The dog hesitated for a moment longer, then effortlessly jumped up onto the passenger's seat. Eddie smiled and closed the door behind him.

"Thought so.".

As he climbed in and fastened his seat belt, the dog was watching every move he made. Eddie's tone seemed to reassure him.

"It'll be okay, buddy. We'll find you a good home."

He took out his phone and started looking for shelters. After some searching, he found one about an hour from their location. Eddie called them and after some questions, they said that they would take him.

"Okay, my friend. Got you a room for the night and some nice folks who are going to hook you up. See there? Told you it would work out."

Eddie started the truck, eased out of the parking lot and back onto I-20. As they cruised along, he put on some old country music and looked over at the dog.

He seemed to be enjoying the ride, as much as a dog could, Eddie supposed. He felt good about helping the critter out as no one else seemed to be able to do so. When a Merle Haggard song came on, he looked over at the dog and said,

"Now that's good music right there." The dog looked at him as if he were listening, too.

"That's when country music was good. Not this stuff they have nowadays. Got no soul. Same thing with racing. Ain't been the same since Ol' Dale left us."

The dog went back to watching the traffic like he was doing at the restaurant. Eddie chatted at him as they rumbled down the interstate where the conversation covered a variety of topics. He was enjoying having someone to talk to besides Jimmy for a change. The good part was, the dog couldn't argue his points.

"That's another reason I quit going to honky tonks. Everything is either karaoke or DJs. If I wanted hear somebody sing offkey, I'd record myself in the shower. No sir, ya gotta have a live band for any kind of a good time. Nope, things just ain't like they used to be and we are a sadder country for it, I say."

Eddie looked over and the dog was still watching the traffic.

"I know you agree, too, you just can't find the words right now," he said jokingly.

Eddie checked his mileage and saw they only had another couple miles to go.

"Well, won't be long now and we'll have you some new digs if you'll pardon the pun." The dog just looked at him.

"You know, digs. Get it? A dog di...never mind. It was a bad joke anyway."

When they were about a half mile from the exit, the dog started acting strange and making funny noises. Eddie looked over at him and it seemed as if he was focused on the oncoming lane.

"What's up, buddy?" he asked.

The dog started with low grunts, then started barking and staring hard at the oncoming traffic. Eddie looked, but didn't see anything. He looked back at the barking animal and was getting a little freaked out by his actions now.

"WHAT!" Eddie yelled. But the dog paid him no mind and got louder and more excited.

Eddie tried again to follow the dog's gaze and this time he saw a pickup truck had veered out of the line of oncoming traffic, gone down into the median, got airborne, and was now headed right towards them.

He barely had time to react. Instinct took over and Eddie yanked the wheel to the right while laying on the brakes as hard as he could. He knew from his racing days that there wasn't anything left he could do and what was coming was not going to be pretty. They were just along for the ride now.

Eddie turned the wheel and leaned over to his right as far as he could against the G-forces. The impact from the pickup was so hard he thought he would pass out. He could feel the rig as it started to veer to the right while he held the wheel but the impact whipped it hard back to the left. The only thing to do was hang on and wait for whatever came next

He felt the rig sliding and heard tires squealing and metal crunching. Eddie's heart was pounding thinking that surely this was his last ride. As the sliding and the noise continued, he could feel the rig going down into a ditch, and then it started listing hard to the right. Eddie knew then they were going over.

Only his seat belt and the death grip he had on the wheel kept him from being flung across the cab. Suddenly he caught a glimpse of trees out of the corner of his eye and heard the impact of the branches hitting the windshield as the truck was rolling onto its side, sliding into them, snapping off everything in its path as it went. It seemed as though it was never going to end. The noise was deafening! Scraping! Squealing! Crunching! And finally the truck came to a rest and then...Silence.

Eddie wasn't sure if he was dead or alive at first. If it was his time, he was ready and let go for whatever was next.

A few seconds later he opened his eyes. *Well. I'm still alive.* He thought.

He tried to focus and get his bearings as he hung from the seat. Broken tree branches filled his vision while the smell of pine mixed with diesel fuel and fluids dripping down on the hot exhaust filled his nostrils. Even as groggy as he was from the impact, Eddie's mind was racing now. Fire! A racer's worst nightmare after a hard crash.

Eddie struggled to pull himself up and disconnect the seat belt. As it released, he fell against the passenger's door with a fumbling thud. He was covered with bits of shattered glass and debris from the interior, and he was bleeding.

Shakily, he managed to pull himself to a standing position. He checked himself as best he could and didn't feel anything broken.

"*A miracle!*" he thought. Suddenly, he remembered the dog.

Looking around, Eddie saw the animal sticking his head out of the sleeper bunk covered with papers, clothes, and debris that had been tossed around.

Good, he thought. *At least he's okay.*

Eddie got his footing as best he could on the passenger's side door. Shaking, he stood up, bracing himself with one hand on the dash and the other against the cab corner. When he looked up towards the driver's door, he couldn't believe what he was looking at. It was crushed right against his seat. *Just a few more inches*, he thought, *and I'd be dead.*

"Thank you, Jesus!" Eddie said under his breath. "I know I haven't been to church in a while, but I promise I will check back in soon."

Damn, what a mess, he thought as he looked around at the cab. Then it hit him. His beloved Peterbilt, Fat Betty, was most likely destroyed. *Well*, he thought, *she gave her life to save mine.*

Sentiment runs deep between truckers and their trucks. Eddie was no different with Fat Betty. When something is so much a part of your life, it seems to take on a personality, and even a soul of its own after a while. It's a bonding thing that drivers and their vehicles make, a connection, if you will. He felt almost as if a family member had just died.

Right now, though, he had to get himself and the dog out of there. Eddie looked around for something to hit the windshield with and found his small fire extinguisher had broken free. The windshield was already cracked and pushed in from the impact of the tree branches. He took the fire extinguisher and began hitting at it, pushing it out and away from them to make an exit. Once the way was clear, Eddie coached the dog to come to him. He helped the animal out through the opening and the dog slid down the hood and onto the pile of grass, dirt, and debris the truck had dug up while sliding.

Eddie was pulling himself through when he heard voices and felt hands grabbing at him, pulling him out and down the hood to the ground where he fell in a heap. He felt like he was in a dream. The men helped him to his feet and asked if he was okay.

"I think so. Feel like I've been run over by a truck, though."

Eddie joked whenever he was scared or hurt. Today, it was both. That was his way to deal with such things in his life.

"Guy must be in shock," one of the men said.

"We gotcha, buddy," said another to Eddie. Two of the men helped him up the embankment and on to the road side. Once he got on flat ground and could feel stable, Eddie assured them he was okay.

"Thanks, guys. I'm okay now."

"You sure?"

"Yeah, I'm good."

After pausing to make sure he was okay, they rushed off to see if they could help others involved in the crash.

When he was able to focus through squinting eyes, Eddie surveyed the devastation before him. The pickup truck that hit him was destroyed and sitting in a mangled pile in the middle of the highway just down from his rig. There was at least a half dozen other vehicles involved. Some were crossways in the road and others were in the median. People were running from vehicle to vehicle checking on everyone as quickly as they could. The eastbound lane was stopped and drivers were either getting out to help or rubbernecking the scene. It was a mess, to say the least, with debris and skid marks everywhere.

Eddie felt blood dripping down his forehead and reached up to pick some glass chunks out of his head. He looked down at the dog as the dog was looking up at him.

"Sorry buddy, but I'm afraid yer gonna be late for your appointment. Hell of a ride though, eh?"

Eddie looked over at his rig and saw how wrecked the cab was on the driver's side. The pickup had taken out just about the whole left side of the truck, but most of the damage was up front. The wheel, air filter, and mirror were gone completely. The driver's door and the sleeper side were crushed in as was the front lower corner of the reefer trailer. Even the trailer tandems were knocked out of place.

"Damn, he sure made a mess of my truck," Eddie muttered as he walked slowly towards the mangled pickup. Seeing what was left of the driver hanging out of the truck, there was no question he died instantly on impact.

Sirens were blaring now with cop cars, rescue, and fire trucks roaring in from all directions. Paramedics were seemingly everywhere checking everyone they encountered. He watched them work as he slowly walked and surveyed the scene all around him still dazed. It reminded Eddie of some of the wrecks during his racing career and accidents on other highways. At a few of those, he remembered how he helped out.

What he never thought was that he would be the main participant in one.

A paramedic came from behind and gently grabbed his arm, then guided him over to a rescue unit. Eddie sat patiently while they checked him out, but his mind was whirling as he tried to regain his composure and get his head around what had just happened.

Through it all, as a tech cleaned him up and applied some quick bandages to his cuts, there was the dog sitting at his right side looking up at him. They continued like this, just looking at each other.

The tech working on Eddie noticed the exchange of looks and asked, "Is that your dog?"

Eddie was thinking about what happened in the truck prior to the accident for a moment and then looked at the tech before he replied.

"This here is my new best friend."

He looked back down at the dog.

"His name… isRadar."

The paramedic returned, but despite his insistence, Eddie refused a trip to the hospital stating that he had been in worse wrecks at Hickory Speedway back during his racing days. Shortly after finishing with the paramedic, a highway patrolman came over to take his information for the accident report and asked him for his version of what happened. After he finished his statement and the officer went on to the next person, Eddie called Jimmy and filled him in as best he could remember. Not surprisingly, Jimmy was very upset at the news and offered to fly down to get him.

"No, buddy. I'm okay. Really! Just rattled my cage a little, that's all. No worse than a night at Cherokee or Hickory Speedway. I'm just going to get a room for tonight, and if I feel up to it, I'll head out for home tomorrow." Jimmy protested, but Eddie won the argument

"You know I hate flying anyway."

"Man!" Jimmy exclaimed "The Good Lord must have been lookin' out for ya today!"

Eddie glanced down at his new co-pilot.

"Actually, I think He was busy so He sent His dog instead."

Puzzled by Eddie's response, Jimmy came back.

"Huh? Say that again? What about a dog?"

"It's a long story. I'll call you after I get a room and shake some of this day off me."

"Please do. A dog?"

"Yeah, a dog."

"Well…cool! Can't wait to hear about it. You sure you're okay?"

"Yeah. Yeah. I'm good. Relax. Call ya later."

Eddie hung up and called the nearest cab company. They said it would be a half hour or so because of the area being blocked off due to the accident, but their driver would call when he got there.

Seeing the tow trucks coming now reminded Eddie that he needed to call Mike Jenkins and have him alert the customer about the accident.

"No frozen fish today," he said to the dog. As Eddie was waiting for the cab to arrive, he watched one of the cops directing the two big rotator wreckers over towards what was left of Fat Betty. He headed there before the one operator hooked up and told him that he was the owner and that when they got his truck back right side up, he wanted to get a few of his belongings out before they took it away.

"No problem," said the tow truck operator. He handed him a business card and then Eddie, with Radar beside him, went off to the side to watch.

They made it look like a ballet of sorts as they worked the scene. Righting a full tractor trailer unit was not an easy feat, even under the best of circumstances. They ran cables out, hooking straps to certain key places and then they began winching his rig a little at time. They winched it upright and then began bringing it up out of the ditch and onto the pavement until finally, Boom! She was right side up again.

As Eddie looked at what was left of his beloved truck, it looked like half her face had been ripped half off. Jimmy's brand-new motor, Rosie, had been torn almost completely out of the frame on impact and all her fluids were now out on the ground. Eddie was sure it was done as well. He walked around to the other side and found that the passenger's door still worked so he climbed up and fished around to find his briefcase, grabbed a few clothes and his photos of Kate, Eddie Jr., and the grandkids. He left the rest for later.

His phone rang showing that it was the driver from the cab company.

After he loaded himself and the dog into the cab, Eddie watched as the accident scene faded behind them. Still somewhat shaken, he looked forward to a shower, food, and some rest. He was glad to be alive, but felt bad for the other people, especially the dead guy's family.

As they rode along, Eddie noticed that the dog could probably use a bath, too, so he would look up a groomer nearby. He still wasn't sure what all had just happened, he just knew that the dog had probably saved his life. Eddie was aware that animals were known to have the ability to warn people of earthquakes, seizures, and apparently, danger. But this thing with Radar was before anything had happened yet.

"How's that possible?" Eddie wondered.

Right now, he didn't care, one way or the other. He was just glad the dog did what he did and in the nick of time. Eddie was certain he would not have seen what was coming before he could take the needed action at that moment. While he always did have good reflexes, he knew he wasn't *that* good. Especially at this age.

He also knew he was exhausted from the events of the day and his head hurt from thinking about it all.

They rolled up to the motel and emptied out. The dog took his position at the entrance while Eddie went inside and paid for the room. Now it was time for that shower and food. He would call Jimmy in a bit and fill in him in on the details.

When Eddie got to his room, he took his stuff inside, leaving the door open for the dog but Radar had already parked himself at the edge of the walkway. He began watching and looking up and down the parking lot just like he had been doing at the restaurant when Eddie first saw him. Standing in the doorway now watching him, Eddie wasn't sure what to do next. Finally, he called out to him.

"You can come inside, you know. No need to stay out here."

Still, the dog just sat there, watching the parking lot. After a moment, Eddie walked up and stood in front of him.

"You know, I kinda owe you my life. I don't know what your life was like in the past, but I'd feel better if you came inside."

The dog just glanced at him and then back at the parking lot. Eddie studied him for a moment. The animal appeared to have a regimen of sorts.

"Military maybe?" Eddie wondered. *"His owner was a WWII veteran."*

The dog continued to sit and look as if he were a sentry at a post and appeared to have his mind made up.

Eddie finally gave in and said to himself, *If that is his routine, who am I to argue?*

Now he spoke directly to the dog. "Okay then, Radar. Well, you do you. Me, I've had enough for one day. I'll get you some food and water, *and* an appointment with a groomer. You look almost as bad as me. Plus, you smell like dirt, diesel fuel and, well, dog. So, um, carry on."

Eddie went back to the room entrance and looked again at the dog one more time before he closed the door.

Curious critter, he thought. *Curious indeed. Whatever. I'm just glad he did what he did. I'll take weird and alive all day long. Right now, I'd buy him a steak dinner and a new suit of clothes, if he wanted.*

After taking a shower, Eddie stood looking in the mirror at the damage. He was bruised pretty good on his left side and he had some light scratches on his forehead. He changed the bandage that the tech had put on for the glass cuts. Overall, he looked none the worse for the wear, all things considered.

He caught up on the local news and put on fresh clothes. Then Eddie called to get a rental car and also checked out groomers for the dog. There was a 24 hour store next to the motel so he would walk over to get his new companion some food and water after he called Jimmy.

Eddie made a quick look through the curtain to check on Radar as he dialed Jimmy's number. *Still there,* he thought in amazement. When Jimmy answered the phone, Eddie filled him in on the whole story.

"Wow, dude! That's crazy! So basically, what you're telling me is that dog saved your life?"

"Appears so. No way I saw that one coming. I mean, he started carrying on way before anything happened. It was surreal."

"That's crazy! Really crazy. I gotta meet this guy" They talked a little more and Jimmy asked again.

"You sure you're okay?"

"Yeah, man. I'm good. Just banged up a little. I have a rental car coming so when I get done at the tow yard tomorrow, I'll head back home. I gotta go for now. I need to call Junior and let him know."

"Okay, call me tomorrow and let me know when you leave out. And keep me posted."

"Copy that."

Eddie called his son and filled him in on the accident. Junior seemed genuinely concerned and offered to come and get him. "I'm okay son, really. I'll be home in a couple of days. I'll stop by."

"Okay, Pop. Keep me posted."

Eddie hung up and was pleased that his son offered to come and get him. He longed for the days of their father-son chats.

Putting his boots on, he headed out to go to the store. As Eddie approached Radar, the dog jumped to attention and immediately heeled at his right side. Standing there looking down at him, Eddie was somewhat surprised, but figured that action was also part of the dog's routine. Eddie just shrugged his shoulders and accepted it.

"Alright then. Let's go to the store, buddy." After getting some dog food, water, and some snacks, they headed back to the motel. He put down food and water for the dog and stood there for a moment just watching him eat and drink.

Not sure what to do next, Eddie started talking to the dog. This was all new on top of everything else that had happened.

"So, I guess…this means you're with me now, huh?" The dog didn't respond but kept eating.

"Well, I'm calling it a night. I've had enough excitement and mystery for one day. If you're still here in the morning, we'll go from there. Your groomer appointment is at 2:00. Okay?"

Still no response. "Well, goodnight, I guess. See you in the morning." Eddie walked back to his room, turning and looking at the dog one more time.

Before he turned in for the night, he looked out the window and made one last check on the dog before he crashed for the night. As he faded off to sleep, his last thoughts were of the dog barking and warning him of something that hadn't happened yet. *How did he know? How could he know?*

When Eddie woke the next morning, he went to roll over and winced in pain. He hurt in just about every part of his body. He laid there for a little while longer and then slowly eased his feet over the edge of the bed.

"Ooooh. Man, oh man. I don't bounce like I use do at all."

Slowly he got up and got dressed. Every move was an effort. He limped over to the window and looked out. The dog was still there.

"Well, he's dedicated I'll give him that," Eddie said out loud. He put his boots on and then gathered up food and water for Radar. He went out the door and the dog jumped up and seemed happy to see him. He slurped up a bunch of water and then ate while Eddie explained, "I'd sit with ya buddy but I'm not sure I could get back up again." The dog ignored him and ate like he was starving.

"Okay, here's the deal. I need some breakfast, too and then we need to go to the tow yard where I can get the rest of my stuff and then we will get you cleaned up. Sound good?" Eddie said as he reached down and petted him.

After breakfast, Eddie and Radar drove over to Broman's Towing and Recovery in Monroe, La. Pulling into the yard, he approached what used to be his truck. It looked worse today.

The owner came over as they were standing there and introduced himself.

"You the driver?"

"What's left of him." Eddie extended his hand and they shook.

"Bubba Broman. Man, you were lucky! That pickup tried to come right into the cab with you. A couple more inches and you wouldn't be here. I looked at your seat and it was almost completely crushed by the door. It's a wonder you can even walk at all."

"Yeah, I'm a hurtin' unit for sure today. If it wasn't for this guy here warning me, I don't know if I would have been able to steer away as quick as I did." Bubba looked down at the dog.

"Sounds like he was a good luck charm for you. I'd say he's a keeper."

"Oh yeah, I grew really fond of him after that." Eddie and Bubba talked a little bit more and then Eddie asked him if anything was salvageable.

"Not much. The frame is wadded up pretty good, suspension's junk. What wasn't hit on this side was pretty much wiped out on the other side when you rolled over and slid.

"What about the motor and tranny?"

"Tranny, maybe, Motor? Can't say for sure, but it pretty much puked its guts out laying in that ditch."

"Okay, here's my partner's number. He's going to want the engine for sure. He'll make all the arrangements for getting it shipped back to the shop."

"Sure thing. We can take care of that for you after the insurance company and cops get through with their investigation. According to what I hear, the driver was drunk." Eddie shook his head in disgust.

"Damn shame. Don't know what people are thinking sometimes." He had seen his share of alcohol-related incidents over the years. They rarely ended well.

"Thanks, Bubba. I appreciate all your help."

"Sure thing, Eddie. You take care."

With that, Eddie got the rest of his belongings out of Fat Betty and took some pictures of what was left. A sad day indeed for him. Aside from being his home for the past three years, the truck had been a good one and had been a good engine test mule for Jimmy.

Eddie loaded up his belongings and the dog in the rental vehicle and headed back to North Carolina and the new facility. Jimmy had told him it was complete and that he had a surprise for him. With Jimmy Wagner, there was no telling what that might be.

Chapter Seven
Thirty Million Dollar Geekmobile

It was midnight when Eddie and Radar rolled into Morganton, North Carolina and headed to the Comfort Inn. After Eddie signed everything and got the room key, Radar took his position at the front entrance and settled in for the night. Eddie had to assure the girl at the front desk that he was no trouble and wouldn't bother anybody.

"Does he always do that?" she asked.

"Yeah, pretty much. It's his thing. Don't know where he got it from but he just posts himself and watches. For what, I have no idea."

"Can I bring him some water or treats?"

"Sure. I usually do before I turn in, but I don't think he'll mind if you do. He does usually shy away from people so don't take offense. It's just a dog thing, I guess."

"Okay, I will get him some water."

"Thanks." Eddie was tired and still sore from the accident and the long drive. He limped to the elevator, thankful that she said his room would be close to it. Much as he wanted to text Jimmy, Eddie wanted to sleep more and would text him in the morning. He almost felt bad for the 30 seconds it took to fall asleep. Almost.

****

Getting out of the bed the next morning wasn't much easier than getting into it, but he was starting to feel a little more normal. Whatever that was anymore. He texted Jimmy and they agreed to meet at the Waffle House for breakfast.

"Cool, I can't wait to meet this dog."

When Eddie checked out at the front desk, the girl said that the dog did shy away from her, but then he came back and drank the water and food she put down. Eddie thanked her and left her a tip for taking care of him. He loaded Radar and his gear in the rental car, then headed for the Waffle House. They were sitting in the rental car watching to make sure Eddie didn't see anyone he might know when Jimmy drove up.

Eddie and Radar got out to greet him. Jimmy saw the small bandages and noticed Eddie's limp.

"Damn, man! You look like crap!"

"Thanks. I've felt better for sure."

Jimmy greeted Radar who seemed to like him. "Hey, Buddy, thanks for taking care of my friend here." He petted Radar and the dog responded with a tail wag.

"Well, you passed the first test. That's the first time I've seen him wag his tail. You must rate pretty high in dog-dom."

"Oh, yeah. Dogs are good people indicators. They seem to know who's got good jujube. They like, pick up on vibes and auras and stuff."

"Okay, dog whisperer, let's get some breakfast." Radar took his position outside, just out of the line of people traffic and right where he could see the entrance. As they were ordering, Jimmy began questioning Eddie on exactly what happened.

"The guy down in Louisiana sent me photos. You're damn lucky to be alive, dude. I mean, that thing was crushed right in the driver's door and the rest of the truck wasn't much better. You sure you didn't break anything?"

Eddie shook his head. "I think I would know. Leg's a little sore and stiff as hell, but no, I'm good. A few glass cuts and bruises, that's about it. Seems like it hurts more than it used to, though."

"Well, give me the details."

Eddie gave Jimmy minute-by-minute details as he remembered the accident. Jimmy sat back at the part where the dog gave Eddie a warning just before the impact.

"Whoa! That's crazy! And you didn't see it coming?"

"Nope! I looked twice and didn't see a thing until the third look. Then it was coming at me."

"Well, I'm glad he was with you. I guess Radar is the perfect name. What are you going to do with him?"

"Well, for now, he seems to be okay hangin' with me. And to tell you the truth, I've kinda gotten used to him. He's pretty low maintenance and doesn't complain much. Just makes funny noises occasionally."

"Like what?"

"Like different sounds for different responses. He seems to understand what I'm saying most of the time."

"Really? That's different."

"Yeah, he must have had some good training at some point. He's regimented in his routine and seems to be very aware of what's going on. I mean, it's like he is accessing everything going on around him and then adjusts to his surroundings. I'm still learning his nature. Doesn't take to everybody, just who he deems trustworthy or something."

"Yeah, well, lucky for you, is what I'm sayin'. I'd keep him around and take real good care of him."

"No doubt. It appears I need a keeper now. When I told Junior about the wreck, he was glad to hear I had a companion at least, although he's still on me about the retirement thing. I told him I'd think about it."

"Yeah, and did you?"

"I did. For about a minute."

Jimmy laughed. "Thought so."

"So, tell me about this truck you've got hidden in the basement. We don't have to take it apart to get it out I hope."

"Oh, no. I've got an elevator for it. Brings it right up to ground level." Eddie cocked his head at him and then shook his head.

"Really? You never cease to amaze me."

"Hey, it only costs a few more dollars to go first class. You're gonna like this truck. She's all black with a matching black trailer. The trailer has some cool stuff in it too. I know it's not like your long hood, but it's got plenty of character, I promise ya."

"Yeah, well, it will have to do for now. I got loads to run. You know I like my long hoods. I will be looking at another one for sure, but I'll take this one and work the bugs out of it for you."

Jimmy just smiled with a glint in his eye.

"Can't wait."

They finished breakfast and headed out to the new facility. As they pulled up to the new complex, Eddie still marveled at its appearance. It looked like something out of a science fiction novel. A bright, shiny three-story-high glass structure with walkways and manicured lawn with shrubs, trees, and park benches. *Even eggheads needed a place to sit and contemplate important geek stuff*, he thought. As they got out and headed toward the entrance, Radar took his place just at the edge of the walk by the grassy area near the side entrance. Jimmy was watching as he did so.

"Wow! And he does that every time?"

"Just like clockwork. He just sets there and watches everything that's going on. Probably, if he had thumbs, he would be taking notes."

Jimmy laughed. "Have you had him try that yet?"

"No, but at this point, I wouldn't be surprised if he could."

They continued into the building and headed for the elevators. They were stopped a few times by different people asking Jimmy questions about a particular project they were working on. When they got to the elevators, Bobby Chu met them there. He immediately broke into a big toothy smile and started chattering at Eddie.

"Oooh! Fast Eddie! You like what we do. We make you bad ass truck. It do lots cool stuff! We work hard. It do big things."

Eddie just smiled and tried to follow along. The doors opened and they went in. Bobby pushed the button that said "Lower Level" and was still chattering at Eddie when they got there. Eddie kept smiling and glanced at Jimmy for help, but he was smiling too, so it seemed redundant to hope for any help.

When the doors opened, they stepped out into a long hallway that went down to an entry door leading to what looked like a hangar. It was huge and to Eddie seemed to be about two stories high and at least 150 to 200 feet long. He saw a large control room with all kinds of screens and monitors, and people sitting at consoles like it was Mission Control. They were looking back and forth among the displays watching for what, he wasn't sure.

In front of him was a platform that appeared to be the elevator Jimmy referred to over breakfast, and he could see where the floor would open up to the upper floor. Eddie looked around and saw that Jimmy was already busy giving instructions to several lab-coated technicians. With all the high-tech equipment, people, and massive underground structure Eddie was seeing, it again struck him that this was something out of the future.

At one end of the platform was a roll-up door that he guessed was where the truck was stored. Bobby Chu, meantime, had made his way to the door and waited for further instructions.

Jimmy came over to Eddie with an iPad in his hand, smiling, and all excited.

"Okay! Let's get this party started!" Eddie just smiled, lit up a cigar then turned toward the roll-up door and waited for the show.

Jimmy signaled Bobby and then he tapped his iPad. As the door began rising, the theme song for *Top Gun* started blaring from speakers somewhere in the facility. Eddie just looked at Jimmy who was bobbing his head to the music. Then the lights on the rig came on as it started rolling forward. It was a beauty for sure. A brand new Peterbilt 579, tall, shiny, and all blacked out. As Eddie watched in awe, the rig rolled slowly onto the platform, trailer and all. It was truly a sight to behold.

He then realized it made no sound as it was moving. And, there was no driver! The music was getting to him, though. Finally, Eddie had had enough and motioned to Jimmy with a slashing motion to his throat.

"Too much?"

"Yeah! Just a bit."

The truck finally reached the point that was marked on the platform and stopped.

"Okay, impressive entrance. How is it moving by itself?"

"That's part of its autonomic capabilities."

"Oh, of course. Its autonomic capabilities. So obvious."

Jimmy explained, "It means we can drive the truck remotely. Like a big remote-control vehicle. We can also see what you see on a video screen. Like a video game, only for real."

"Seriously?" Eddie looked back at the truck. "Okay. I remember you saying that you were mating two technologies?"

"Yes. It has a hybrid, diesel/electric power system with a modified 24-speed transmission and an all-wheel drive system on both the tractor and the trailer."

"What? Why on the trailer?"

"I'll get to that in a minute. First, check this out."

Jimmy walked around to the front of the truck and tapped on his pad. A thin red strobe light began running back and forth in the bumper and making a familiar sound.

Eddie looked at Jimmy who was grinning that goofy grin.

"Knight Rider? Seriously?"

"Yeah, it seemed appropriate for all the technology we built into it, and it's black, like KITT. Look here."

He walked to the driver's door and opened it. Eddie recognized the sound as that of the opening of the cockpit door on *Airwolf*. Jimmy jumped up into the truck and when he sat in the seat, all the dash and interior lights came on and made the humming sound that *Airwolf* made when the pilot sat in his seat. Eddie just shook his head watching Jimmy act like he was fifteen again as one classic TV show sound followed another.

Next, Jimmy pressed the horn button on the steering wheel and the Dixie horn from *The Dukes of Hazzard* started blaring. Eddie couldn't believe what he was hearing.

He has totally lost his mind, Eddie thought. Jimmy hopped back down and began walking around the rig rattling off more technology.

"Now, this is what drives this beast." He unhooked the latches for the hood and then, taking a key fob, pressed a button and the hood began to raise electronically until it revealed a bright-green-painted engine with a lot of chrome tubing, plumbing, and wires. It was a maze of technology like nothing Eddie had ever seen.

"What the hell is all that?" Eddie asked.

"That, my friend, is CatZilla. The baddest engine I have ever built. At the moment, it is pushing out about 4,000 horsepower. It has four turbos that are computer synced with an electric integrated hyperdrive system, and according to our dyno tests so far, it has about 3,500-foot pounds of torque at the rear wheels. That's not including the electronic drive torque! We think it can do a lot more but we need to test it in the field. We have a monitoring system built in that can check it under a load. The hope is that using the electric drive system to start, it can accelerate 0–60 in about 4.5 to 5 seconds before you engage the engine. This will reduce the torque stress on the engine's drive train."

Eddie's eyes got big when he heard that.

"You gotta be kidding me! That's crazy! Is that even possible?"

"In theory, yes. Like I said, it still needs to be tested under a load and in real conditions."

"Okay, say I do get this beast up to speed. How am I supposed to stop this thing?"

"That's another cool item. It has regenerative braking."

"Meaning?"

"Meaning, when you step on the brakes, they work in conjunction with the electric motors and create a combination 'Jake Brake' style and air braking system. You can stop faster and in shorter distances from speed than any other braking system out there. It also has bigger brake discs and a larger pad contact area. When the electric motors are engaged, they automatically start slowing forward progress when you let off the throttle, and when they're disengaged, the brakes work like a regular braking system. The biggest change is that it works from the back to the front, pressure-wise. That's so it brakes harder from the trailer forward, than from the tractor back.

"The system is designed to automatically apply pressure where it's needed the most. Again, we need to test it under a load, but in theory, you should be able to stop from a hard braking scenario to a dead stop without locking the wheels, jackknifing, or losing control. It works like ABS, but in a different way. Also, we designed a gyroscopic stability control system to counter the inertia of the cargo weight in those hard braking situations and in cornering. More theory, but you should be able to go into a turn at speed and not be affected by the transfer of weight shifting from one side to the other."

Eddie's mind was reeling. He had read science fiction stories that sounded like this and tech articles about New Age trucks that sounded like this, but he had never actually *seen* anything like this. He was pretty sure that most of it was not possible, even if his friend was a genius. Jimmy had created some wacky stuff in the past, but this was off the charts. Eddie was uncomfortable and out of sorts, but willing to tolerate it a little longer. Jimmy was his friend and business partner, after all, and he owed him the time to explain.

Still trying to get his head around what he was hearing, Eddie was doing some fast calculations in his head. *0 to 60 in 4.5 to 5 seconds? That's just 2.5 seconds slower than a Dodge Demon at the drag strip. What the hell?* Now he was looking at the truck in a different way. This thing was way more than just a truck, it was a high-tech, high-speed monster!

Jimmy continued his technical rundown, pointing out the high-speed rated tires that were mounted on specially cut wheels covered with carbon fiber wheel covers. The ultralight custom frame, carbon fiber body panels, aero spoilers that deploy at speed, self-deploying ground effects, and air-braking spoilers. He also demonstrated the truck raising and lowering in sync with the trailer.

"This is how the suspension works at speed. It adjusts automatically as the down force dictates. It's completely computer controlled, so all you have to do is drive."

"That's all, huh?"

"Well, what I mean is, the system works based on the demands of the speed and wind force that are applied at the same time. What we don't know is how it reacts under different loads, temperatures, road conditions, weather anomalies, etc.

"Now, the trailer also has some cool stuff we built into it, but I'll have to show you that upstairs. We still have to set it up on the Dyno. We'll need to tie it down so we can show you the progression it goes through and how everything works together. That way, you will have an idea of what we need to adjust when it gets on the road. It's all part of the sorting things out process."

Jimmy also continued showing him some other sound effects it made when different things engaged. He then walked around to the front of the truck. Jimmy just stood there, looking at him and smiling that goofy smile, waiting for Eddie's response.

Eddie didn't move as he took it all in, steadily puffing on his cigar. Then, he turned to look at Jimmy, took his cigar out and smiled. Jimmy was all wide-eyed with excitement and smiled back at him, not realizing—yet—that Eddie was totally overwhelmed.

"Well, Jimmy, my old friend, you have done it. You have gone where no geek has gone before."

"I know, right?"

"You have created the most expensive tribute to TV and movie vehicles known to man. A thirty-million-dollar Geek Mobile. that Scotty would be proud of."

Jimmy's smile faded slowly. "Whaddaya mean?"

"I mean, I thought you had a modified truck for me to test drive. That's not a truck! That's an overpriced, overbuilt, overengineered testimony to your teenage fantasy years. A 4,000 horsepower quadruple turbocharged engine with a Hydro watszit zapic electric...*whatever*! An integrated, whatchamacallit, spritzer hickey! Seriously! That's not a truck! That's...that's...R2-D2 on steroids with the Starship Enterprise as a suppository nitrous shot!"

Eddie was waving his arms around as he walked in a circle looking and pointing at all the super technology. Jimmy stayed silent. He had seen this behavior before when Eddie got overwhelmed with his ideas. The thing to do was wait till he calmed down, although this time, it might take a while longer than usual.

"And this! All this! What *is* all this? The secret, Dr. Strange Geek's lair? This is, by far, the most insane thing I think—no, it *is*—the most insane thing you have concocted since I've known you! This is even crazier than that damn wooden-bodied race car you talked me into racing that time. And crashed! I'm still pickin' splinters outta my ass from that little escapade. And that was 1975!"

Jimmy frowned and interjected before he could catch himself, "Um...it was fiber wood, actually."

"Whatever! But this...this is more than just 'Jimmy the Hammer' eccentric stuff. This is...I don't even know where to begin." He pointed at the truck. "I mean, I know you said you were working on future technology, but man, this is Dr. Frankentruck kinda stuff here. Un-be-lievable!" Eddie paced away a few steps, then turned around and walked back to Jimmy.

"So! You got a one hundred million dollar grant to do all this?"

"Um, well...um, yeah. Of course, there were *some* stipulations."

Eddie just gave Jimmy a dumbfounded look before replying.

"What? Stipulations? Wait, let me guess: Don't accept any friend requests from Dr. Evil? Don't spend it all in one place?" He chewed on his cigar as he waited for Jimmy's answer.

Jimmy sighed. "Well, of course, we do have to produce a certain amount of green-powered diesel engines per year—at some point in the future—maybe a little sooner."

"Oh, of course."

He stared at him for a long moment while Jimmy smiled a crooked smile, nervously waiting for the next question. Eddie finally broke the silence.

"Jimmy…?"

"Yeah…?"

Eddie squinted his eyes. "What *exactly* does a green diesel engine run on?"

"Well, um, so far, not much of anything practical except for diesel fuel. I mean, there are other things like ethanol, biodiesel, propane, hydrogen, and some other stuff, but…"

"Yeah, but what?"

"Well, I may have given them the impression that I could make them run on kelp."

Eddie's head snapped toward Jimmy as he looked at him speechless for a moment.

"Kelp? Seriously? Have you completely lost your damn mind? Please tell me you have brain worms! I could understand all this much better if you did."

Jimmy shakily smiled and tried to reply, "But I have a better idea. You see…"

Eddie, still staring in disbelief, held up his right open palm toward Jimmy to make him stop talking.

"No! Just no! Seriously, my friend. Your little cuckoo clock birdbrain guy? He's sold his little clock house and moved to Switzerland where he is skiing down the slopes as we speak. Even he

couldn't take it. I can't take it. I can't do this anymore, Jimmy. I just…kelp? Seriously? No. I'm done." He turned and walked away.

"But it's got Sirius! And leather seats."

"What?" Eddie stopped and turned around.

"The truck. It's got Sirius and custom leather seating. It can get all the old country and rock stations you like. I had them put that in there, just for you."

Eddie stared for a moment, then dropped his head. All he could do now was look down and shake his head.

He said softly, "Jimmy. This isn't about music or creature comforts or any of that stuff. This is waaay out there, buddy! This is science fiction stuff, man. What the hell am I supposed to do with this thing? I mean, I'm a truck driver, for crying out loud. You need a damn college degree just to fire it up!"

Jimmy saw the opening and implored him to listen.

"Look, if you will just give me a chance to explain, I'll prove that I'm not crazy."

Eddie quickly replied.

"Brother, you ain't got that kinda time. Besides, there's no doubt you're crazy. The question is, have you finally redlined your tachometer and slung a main rod bearing or something? Man, Jimmy, buddy, I just don't know."

"Please! Just let me show you a few more things before you dismiss it all.

"There's more? There's more of this? That's supposed to make it better?"

"Please. Eddie, please. If you still think it's too much when I'm done, then you can leave. And I will never bother you with this stuff again. Ever. I promise. Okay?"

Jimmy looked at him with that "cute puppy that just peed on the new carpet but he knows he's cute and you're not going to beat him" look. Eddie sighed and rolled his eyes. He looked over at the truck for a minute and then went back to shaking his head all the while talking to no one in particular.

"God, I need new friends. The ones I have are all broken."

He paused, looking at the truck for another moment before finally giving in.

"All right. All right." Eddie put his hands up. "All right. Let's hear it. But no promises."

Jimmy got excited again.

"Okay, c'mon. Lemme show you the inside of the truck first. This part yer gonna like, I promise."

He took Eddie over to the driver's side and told him to climb behind the wheel. As Eddie reached for the door handle, he stopped. Without looking back at Jimmy, he said,

"Sound effects, off!"

Jimmy responded.

"Off!" He scrolled his iPad and tapped his fingers. "Okay, you're good"

Momentarily satisfied, Eddie opened the door, climbed up, and sat in the new leather seat. *It is comfortable,* he thought. Jimmy climbed in on the passenger's side and sat quietly while. Eddie studied the cab and its features. It did look nice and although he preferred his 389 dash, this truck wasn't half bad. It all seemed to be stock appearing with the exception of a couple of switches on the dash and a specially designed panel that was definitely not stock.

Jimmy reached over and tapped the panel. It was a touch screen that responded to his tap by displaying its screen saver—a working model of a flux capacitor. Eddie could only look skyward and give Jimmy a dismissive wave to continue.

Jimmy touched the screen again, and a complete diagram of the truck appeared. The display had rows of icons at the top and on the left side of the screen. Each icon was for a specific function.

"Okay, check this out." Jimmy tapped one of the icons on the truck diagram. Instantly the windshield displayed a topographical map of the surrounding area that started from their current location.

"It's a full screen GPS mapping system that is real-time. That means it moves and calibrates as you move. Hopefully at high speed. It works just like a regular GPS, only full scale. You can program your destination and it guides you along the same way, but the screen moves in real time as the truck moves at speed."

"Okay," said Eddie, "but wouldn't it kinda distract your driving vision?"

"No, here's the cool part." He spoke into his earpiece. "Bobby, cut the lights."

Suddenly it went completely dark in the building. Now, all Eddie could see was the map.

"Okay, what am I missing here, Jimmy? I still say it will impede my vision."

Jimmy was all smiles. "Think hazardous weather, fog, storms, or whatever. With this, you can drive in any condition, on any road, no matter what, even with no lights!"

"Yeah, but what about other vehicles or obstacles?"

Jimmy tapped again. Suddenly, the screen changed to a green/blue tint and Eddie could see everything almost as if it were daylight but tinted. Jimmy climbed down and walked around to the front of the truck where Eddie could now see him clearly.

"Night vision!" Wow! Now, that is cool! He was starting to soften a little bit. This was some kick ass technology right there.

Jimmy came back around and climbed in.

"Whadda ya think?"

"That's very cool. I can see using this on foggy mountain roads, storms, snow, whatever."

"That's not all of it either."

"Okay, keep going. You're not out of the woods yet but there is daylight now."

"Yeah, it has infrared sensors that pick up and identify heat signatures for up to a quarter mile away in a 360-degree radius."

"No way."

"Watch." Jimmy called for Bobby again. Within a couple of minutes, a figure showed up on the screen at the other end of the building with the distinct shape of a man. Eddie was now very impressed.

"Wow. Just think. If that alone was installed on cars and trucks everywhere, how many lives and how much money would be saved from deer and other animals running out in front of them?"

Jimmy's head was bobbing up and down. "I know, right!"

"All right, you're out of the woods. Now tell me more about the diagram on the screen."

"Okay, the row of icons on top is for all your communications—phone, internet, intercom, video chat. Text messages come up on it, too. The last icon represents your exterior cameras. It has a GPS link that gives you a 360-degree and aerial view, in real time. You can see everything going on around you at all times. Backing up should never be a problem, ever again. And, yes, it does have a backup sensor and camera that shows how close you are to the dock."

"That's impressive. I know that little piece of technology would benefit a lot of drivers and save on insurance claims,"

Jimmy agreed. "This icon here is for stealth mode. It—"

Eddie stopped Jimmy in mid-sentence. "Wait...what?"

"Oh, yeah, it has stealth technology. When you engage it like this, see?" The diagram changed and now had a green outline around it. Eddie was a little uncomfortable with this one.

"And why do we need stealth technology? Also, is that even legal for civilians to have?" Eddie frowned at Jimmy with squinted eyes.

"Inquiring minds need to know."

Jimmy looked like he just got caught at something.

"Kind of..."

"Kind of what?"

"Yeah...see, you can have it as long as you have a Mode-C transponder when you're above 10,000 feet and have it switched on."

Eddie gave Jimmy a look of bewilderment, but figured he already had a toe in the water, so he may as well jump all the way in at this point.

"Okay, but wouldn't that defeat the purpose?"

"Exactly!" Jimmy exclaimed. "But here's the thing. We will never *be* above 10,000 feet. See? So, yeah! I figure we're legit."

Looking at Jimmy, Eddie knew by the smile on his crazy friend's face that debating the issue would be a lost cause. But he was also happy to know that the truck couldn't fly either, so he let that one go.

"Tell me again, why do we need stealth technology?"

"Well, this is a research test vehicle, mostly, and we are trying out things that have never been done before. We want to see how it can be applied to military as well as civilian use. If we could move people and equipment fast, and at night, without being picked up on radar, think about how many lives that would save. Also, it's better than a radar detector because of the frequency it's on. We don't need to attract any attention while testing it in the field."

Eddie agreed that it made sense, but still wasn't convinced it was legal.

"Fine," he said. "Proceed."

Jimmy tapped another icon.

"This is your security system which also activates through the key fob. Once activated, it has a voice repel warning if someone gets too close. The door handles are coded to your hand print signature and it's electrified, so be sure you deactivate it before anybody else tries to reenter or the shock will scramble their eggs for about five minutes or so."

Eddie looked at him with a smirk, asking, "That's a very specific time frame. Did you..."

"No. Not me. One of our installers, Darrell. He still stutters a little, but he finally quit drooling. The doctor says it'll go away eventually. He's okay otherwise."

Definitely have to remember that one, Eddie thought.

Jimmy continued, "This here is your fire suppression system." He tapped another icon and it showed where all the major components had a sensor that would activate the extinguisher.

Also a good thing, Eddie thought.

"What's this little skull and crossbones here? That looks serious."

"That's in case the truck falls into the wrong hands."

"And, what happens then?"

Jimmy gave Eddie a serious look. "Let's just hope that never happens."

"Jimmy! What happens?"

After a short pause Jimmy tapped on his remote pad and it displayed another diagram that was covered in red lines connected to little red dots around the installed technology on the rig. Eddie studied the diagram for a minute and noticed the words, "Doomsday Scenario" at the top of the screen. Jimmy and Eddie exchanged looks.

Then Jimmy got serious, something that was rare for him. He explained,

"Let's put it like this. If that option has to be considered, that means something bad has happened to the driver and there is a terrorist-type threat from either a foreign entity or some other bad-guy scenario. This technology can be used for bad stuff as well as good, Eddie. We can't let it fall into the wrong hands."

Studying his friend for a long minute he understood that point very well, but was still uncomfortable with the idea. The idea of driving around in a rolling bomb didn't set well with him.

"Hopefully, I can't accidentally blow myself up."

"No, it has a fail-safe system. You have to activate it here at the com or via your key fob."

"I have a feeling there's more," Eddie commented.

Jimmy looked at him with concern.

"We can activate it from here if we need to. We can actually activate all the systems from here."

Eddie pondered that information for another moment.

"Okay...so, how much time do I have once this thing is activated?"

"Ten minutes. And I would suggest you be at least a hundred and fifty yards or better away just to be safe."

The concern on Eddie's face was obvious.

"That's serious business, Jimmy. What exactly is it we're doing here, buddy? I mean, why do you need me? Can't you teach one of your sweater-vested geek recruits to do this? You tell me this thing can be driven remotely, if need be. Any monkey can be programmed for that. I don't mind helping out, but this is some serious stuff you're talking about. Why me?"

Jimmy looked at him quizzically.

"Are you kidding?" he replied. "You're my best friend in the whole world! My only friend, actually. We've been together since high school, man. I know your capabilities; I've seen you do things with cars that nobody else can do. I mean, I still say you could have given Petty, Yarborough, or Allison a run for their money back in the day, if you had the chance. But you got robbed because of your age!"

"C'mon, buddy. Now yer blowin' smoke up my dress."

"No! Seriously! I really believe that with all my heart. Hell, everybody knows that. Look, we were the best combination around. Nobody could touch us."

"Well, Frankie Palmer gave us a good run."

Jimmy threw his hand up. "Bahhh! Frankie wasn't half the driver you were! He just thought he was. The only reason he raced you that hard at all was because you kicked his ass that day in school. Other than that, he had nuthin'. Nobody could catch Fast Eddie McVane!"

"Well, I couldn't have done any of that if it weren't for you," Eddie said reminiscing. "I mean, it was you who taught me how to fight and you who built the engines."

"Yeah, but it was *you* who made the magic happen, man. You're the one who had the touch, that thing you do. You know. The thing." Eddie chuckled.

"Yeah, the thing."

"Honestly, you made everybody want to be better. Hell, you're the one that pushed me to do better and go to MIT and to feed my thirst for knowledge. I mean...you're the only one who believed in me at the time. I had no father, no other real friends. My mom worked all the time to take care of us, so she was never around. When I was the new kid at school, and kind of big and dorky looking with those dumb glasses my mom made me wear, you were the only one who asked me if I liked cars and if I wanted to come and hang out at your dad's garage. I remember all the good times we had racing and traveling. You guys were my family, man! I remember how you struggled to help your mom with the business when your dad died. I know how bad you wanted a racing career, but you put your family first. And my heart broke with yours the day Kate died. Truth is, I wouldn't be here if it weren't for you, man. None of this would be possible without you. Everybody here knows this is about you."

"I don't understand."

"Okay, I'll lay it out for you. One of the most important factors that's missing with this great technology is the human factor. Actually, *your* gift. It, the technology, needs you. This is the future of transportation, my friend. AI technology infused into a programmable, full-sized tractor-trailer unit that can be used in any number of scenarios. Moving men and equipment through hostile environments at high speeds in any condition is just one. We can even add armament to this thing, if needed. Plus, some of the technology we created can be used on civilian vehicles as well, like you pointed out earlier."

Jimmy continued, "You are that human factor. You're the only one I trust that can do this technology any real justice. None of this stuff has been tested in real-world conditions. There's no way to know what works and what doesn't, what changes need to be made, what happens in this situation or that? Especially at high speeds. You're the only one I know that can read this thing better than we can. We're mating multiple technologies together to accomplish that. At some point, all this will be computer-controlled and electronically driven. The future will need high-speed transit for shipping cargo and goods all over the country. Imagine high-speed roads all over the country going to distribution centers. Okay? Now think about this: It's about 1,750 miles from New York to Texas. How long does it take you now to drive that distance, average?"

Eddie thought for a moment. "About twenty-six to twenty-eight hours or so, depending on traffic and weather."

"Right. Now imagine being able to run at two hundred plus miles an hour. You could make that trip in eight hours without detours, weather, or traffic. That would cut costs and save time and money."

"Yeah, I can see that kind of thing coming. I hear talk on the CB and the news about electric, driver-less trucks. I don't want to be here for that. I'm already approaching dinosaur status as it is."

"Well my friend, that's why you're here. It needs that Fast Eddie touch, magic, or whatever you want to call it. That's what it needs to be complete. This system will record all your driving patterns, skills, techniques, what you do in emergency situations, whatever. All these things that can only be estimated by people who may never have driven a car before, let alone a truck, let alone an 18-wheeler. But, like I said, with you driving, it will learn your every move, every response, every turn of the wheel, and everything you do will be recorded. Then, an algorithm based on those recordings will be designed and programmed into the truck's system. This will be used to train future programmers and drivers. But first, we need to test it at that speed to make the necessary adjustments. That's why we need this hybrid power plant setup so we can get it up to that speed which is also something that's never been done before. Basically, you'll live on forever in this thing, man! Cool, huh?"

Eddie was truly speechless now. Not only was he overwhelmed by his friend's confession of his feelings—something Jimmy rarely ever did—but he just finished listening to his life's story being written for the future. What's a guy supposed to do with that?

"Jeeze, Jimmy. That's a lot to take in. I mean, I'm totally blown away. I don't know what to say." As Eddie climbed down out of the truck, he began walking around, studying it with his hands clasped behind him. He quietly walked one direction, puffed on his cigar, then walked back the other with Jimmy now at his side, neither one saying anything. They stopped at the front of the truck. Eddie looked up and down at the shiny black hulk with all its techno wizardry. He stared at the grill and then slowly up at the windshield. He glanced over at Jimmy and then back at the truck.

"CatZilla, huh?"

He just looked and puffed his cigar. Finally, he walked closer to the truck, and like the old days, he gently rubbed the grill emblem. Then down the side of the grill and onto the fenders as if he were petting it.

Jimmy took this as good sign. Eddie always did this routine whenever they built him a new car. It was like a bonding thing for him. He said sometimes he could almost hear its heartbeat and could always tell if it was a winner or a runner up. Sounded weird to everybody else, but he hadn't been wrong yet. As Eddie was doing his bonding ritual, Bobby Chu eased up beside Jimmy. He seemed to always appear out of nowhere. Freaked Jimmy out sometimes.

Bobby whispered in broken English, "What he do?"

Jimmy leaned over and whispered back, "He's talking to her, getting to know her." Bobby looked back wide-eyed in surprise.

"I not pwogwam that in system. It no tawk back. You said no tawking stuff. He not like."

"Not that kind of talking, Bobby, my boy. What you're seeing here is something that can't be programmed. It's more like a spiritual connection. Something you and I don't have and can't fabricate. Only certain people have it."

"Ooooh! Him special person! Like Buddha?"

"Him very special person. Not like Buddha, but special for sure."

"Ahhh! Him twuck whisperer!"

Jimmy chuckled. "Yeah, something like that, I guess."

Eddie walked around the truck again, letting his left hand stroke the vehicle at different spots. Coming back around to the front, he glanced over at Jimmy and Bobby. Then he looked around again at the lair and up at the ceiling. Finally, he spoke, "So, you're saying I am partly responsible for all this?"

Jimmy responded emphatically. "Well, yeah! I built this place and I designed this truck with you in mind. I mean, I know you're not a tech guy, but without your skills, this is just a bunch of metal, plastic, wires, and a fancy building. I know I got a lot of smart people around me to help build this stuff, but they don't have the one thing it needs, man. It needs your soul—that Eddie thing—to bring it all to life."

Eddie studied what he was saying for a little bit without saying much. He just paced slowly, puffing more on his cigar. Then he stopped and looked at Jimmy.

"I have one last question."

"Shoot," Jimmy replied.

"Don't you think the grant people will be a little pissed off when you can't produce a kelp-powered diesel engine?"

Jimmy smiled.

"Kinda got that covered. Our chemists have been doing some amazing stuff in the lab and they have had pretty good results with cabbage, some highly modified cooking oils, and also methane gas from local landfills. Looks promising so far. Besides, I figure I can throw them a bone from one of the things we've developed and tell them we stumbled onto it while doing our research."

Eddie looked at Jimmy and Bobby blankly for a moment. They were both wearing goofy smiles back at him as if waiting for approval. Taking a breath, he responded,

"Ya know, I'm just not even going to try to follow this anymore. It's making my head hurt. Besides, I need some rest. I'm going back to my room for a while and try to let this sink in."

"Sure thing, man. I get it. It's a lot to take in and we still need to get you trained on how to operate it. There are some other things we have to go over too."

"There's more?"

"Oh, yeah. It's simple stuff, though. Plus, it's got some quirks we're still working on."

"Quirks? Good grief! How much more can there be? Should I brace myself?" asked Eddie.

"It's all good. Don't worry, it'll be okay. Listen, go get some rest and some lunch and come back later. We will get her up top and set up for a demo."

"Yeah, I need a break from you guys and some fresh air. I'll be back in a while."

"Sounds good."

They fist bumped and took the elevator up to the first floor. As Eddie was walking away, just like in the old days, Jimmy asked him,

"So, what did she say?"

Eddie turned and grinned as he was going out the door.

"I couldn't hear any of the mechanics over her purring."

Once they were back at the motel, Radar took up his post at the curb in front of the door to the room while Eddie went inside to get him food and water. While the dog ate and drank, Eddie sat on the curb next to him and puffed on his cigar. This seemed to be their ritual now. Eddie watched the dog for a bit before he started replaying the events of the morning and relaying them to Radar. He looked at the dog as if expecting a response.

"So, what do you think about all this, Radar? I mean, you're kinda in this with me now, what with you being my copilot and all. What am I supposed to do with a thirty-million-dollar super truck? I didn't have anything like this in mind. I just wanted to drive out the rest of my days in relative peace and quiet." The dog glanced at him briefly, then went back to eating.

"Sorry. I understand. Can't speak with your mouth full. We'll talk more later."

Eddie gingerly got up, still sore and favoring his left leg, and went inside. He wasted no time tossing his gear, closing the curtains, and crashing on the bed. He'd spend the next two and a half hours sleeping like a rock. It had been a long seventy-two hours since the accident totaling his beloved truck. Eddie was wondering what he was going to do next after being presented with this monster high-tech truck, the likes of which he had never heard of, let alone be the pilot of it. That was one thing, but finding out he was going to be immortalized in a computer program to help train future operators and other programmers, not to mention driving the most expensive and quite possibly fastest 18-wheeler ever built. It was a lot to take in. His simple little private world was becoming increasingly crowded and significantly more complicated. And then there's the dog. What is he all about? Where did he learn his routine and where did he come from?

He wished Kate were here to talk to. She always knew how to get him focused and organized when things got overwhelming. All this new craziness takes a lot out of an old guy. He closed his eyes and finally drifted off to sleep.

CHAPTER EIGHT
ONLY A CHOSEN FEW

Eddie had been awake for a while, just lying there with his hands behind his head, thinking about everything. It was the first time in a long time he had so much to think about. The dog, the accident, Jimmy with his new facility, all in a few short days, and none of it planned. Now, as if that weren't enough, he was about to attempt to make history.

No one could blame him for being reluctant, history notwithstanding, but Eddie felt somewhat obligated after Jimmy's emotional speech about how he felt and his vision for the future. It got Eddie to think that maybe he had been too self-absorbed in his own misery to see the bigger picture. Maybe this was a chance to set things right and leave a legacy to his son and grandchildren. Perhaps that would take away some of the pain of the past. A type of redemption maybe? He wasn't sure.

Looking over at the clock on the nightstand, it read 11:30 a.m. Eddie decided there was no time like the present to get on with it.

If I'm going out, I may as well do it in style, he thought.

Some lunch was in order first. He gathered up the dog and headed out. After lunch, they headed back to the facility. As Radar took up his post at the front entrance, Eddie headed inside to Jimmy's office where he found him with three staff members going over some paperwork. Eddie waited patiently until Jimmy finally noticed him.

"Hey, man. Come on in. We were just going over some test results." The others quickly left, and it was just the two of them. Eddie closed the door and sat down in front of Jimmy.

"Okay," Eddie started, "I've thought about it and I'm ready to do this. I'm not going to pretend I understand it all yet, but I will give it my best shot. If this is to be my legacy, I want it to be known that Eddie McVane did his best and made a difference. I want something positive for my son and my grandkids to remember me by, not my mistakes. If this truck of yours has what it takes, if it's capable of getting to 200 mph, and you need me to test this new technology, I'm in. I'll do what it takes and bring it to the front of the pack. That good enough?"

Jimmy sat back in his chair and looked at him a minute before responding.

"Wow! Now that's the Eddie McVane I remember. Good to have you back, bro. That's good enough for me. Alright, let's go introduce you to the new girl."

Jimmy grabbed his iPad and together they headed out into the shop area where the truck was set up on the Dyno. There were technicians buzzing around the truck and in the control room. As Eddie stood there watching the activity, he focused on the truck itself. It had a look all its own. Tall, black, shiny, and bad ass!

The chains that held it down to the platform didn't seem strong enough. There was something about it he had never felt in a machine before. Something…animalistic. Eddie studied it some more. As he did, he called upon something he hadn't tapped into in many years.

He focused all the mind energy he could summon. As he did, every sound around him began to fade away until there was silence, leaving just Eddie and the machine. Then, slowly, as if the volume were being turned up, he began to hear it. A sound that only certain people like himself could hear. Pulsating, almost like a heartbeat. He began to feel the truck as if he were becoming one with it. Only, this one was different. He couldn't yet put his finger on it yet, though.

Eddie closed his eyes and breathed deep. Slowly, steadily, it came. The sound increased in intensity. He felt himself going faster and faster. Now, all he could feel and hear was speed. Sheer, unadulterated speed. It was exhilarating. In that instance, he felt the adrenaline coursing through his body as never before. In his mind, Eddie was accelerating to 200 mph and except for the road in front of him, everything else around him was a blur. He was a bullet traveling down the barrel of a gun. All his senses were alert now. He felt the vibration of the engine, the steering wheel in his hands, and every part of the suspension as it worked to compensate for the speed. He felt every moving part as if he were a part of the machine. The vision, the sound, the feel, even the smells were all there. Fast Eddie McVane was in the zone again. He was at that place only a chosen few ever get to go. It was as if he had never left and it felt good.

After a few seconds, Eddie opened his eyes and returned instantly to reality. If this was his legacy, destiny, or whatever, he was all in now. As he turned around, he saw Jimmy standing just off to his left, staring at him with that goofy grin.

"You went there, didn't you? I know you did. I spoke to you twice and you didn't even hear me."

Eddie just grinned at him and replied, "Okay, let's get to it. I ain't getting any younger."

Jimmy had his tablet in hand and began showing Eddie the other custom modifications to the truck and trailer. They walked to the back of the trailer and Jimmy opened the doors.

"Now, tell me what you see," said Jimmy.

Eddie looked inside and saw what appeared to be cargo stacked on pallets.

"Okay, cargo with no brace bars or tie-downs."

"Right. Now, watch this." He tapped an icon on his tablet and a sound emitted from within the trailer. As Eddie watched, the walls and ceiling slowly started to swell. Within minutes, a thin membrane-looking material seemed to envelop the cargo and cover it completely. The noise stopped automatically. Jimmy nodded to Eddie and told him to touch the material.

"It's hard. Very cool." Then, the recognition came. "So, no more having to secure cargo?"

"Exactly! It's a super strong elastic material we call Flexo-Buytl-Stylene, or FBS. An experimental hybrid rubber/plastic compound sealed in a framed system that inflates kinda like a balloon as you just saw. You set the pressure according to the type of cargo and a high-speed air compressor does the rest, stopping automatically when it hits what you set. Once the cargo is sealed, it essentially becomes part of the trailer providing complete stability. After you reach your destination, you reverse the compressor and it retracts back to a flat surface.

"Cool. No more load bars or worrying about stuff sliding around and creating instability."

"Right. FBS—you'll get used to all the acronyms—works in tandem with the gyroscopic stability control system. GS..."

Eddie held up his hand. "Just explain that one to me some more and leave the geekisms with the guys in the lab coats. Now, you said I should be able to go into a turn and not worry about the momentum throwing me into a ravine?"

"Essentially, yes. You know how you can feel the g-forces in a race car when you go into the turns?"

"Yes. The only things holding me in the seat are the safety harness and the seat brace."

"Pretty much the same here. The stability control is the truck and trailer's safety harness. Its job is to keep the g-forces in check when you go into turns, and is also what's used in spaceships and airplanes to keep the instruments stable in flight." They walked around to the wheels and Jimmy pointed to the wheel covers. "The gyros are housed inside the wheel covers in the tandems on both the truck and trailer. The computer automatically compensates the g-force by calculating how much resistance is needed."

"Hopefully that works here on earth?"

"In theory, yes. Like I said, some of this needs to be tested in the field."

"So, if it doesn't work, I'm the one in *that* field finding out first," Eddie said

Jimmy frowned. "We're not going to let that happen. We will start you out slowly and build up momentum, going faster each time."

"Okay, gotcha. Next."

Jimmy pointed out where the cameras and sensors were, and how they worked through the GPS. He explained about the ultralight frame and panels, and how all the wiring and components are hidden in the frame. He knew from experience that giving Eddie too many details would be pointless and overwhelm him, so he kept to the basics. There was much more he would ease him into later. Although Eddie was expecting to get the truck to 200 mph, Jimmy's goal was actually 300. That was the optimum speed for what he had envisioned for this future truck. He would keep that to himself for now.

"Okay, time to fire this bad girl up."

They both climbed into the cab with Eddie in the driver's seat and Jimmy in the passenger's. Eddie noticed the technicians that had been milling around scurrying off to the control room with everyone putting on ear protection. *Curious. What's up with that?*

After a brief review of the icons on the screen and the gauge package, Jimmy instructed Eddie to fire it up. As he did, the monster engine dubbed CatZilla came to life.

"Nice rumble," Eddie commented.

"I thought you'd like it." Jimmy replied. They sat for a couple of minutes watching the gauges settle down while the engine came up to temperature. "Okay, just start off like you normally would and up shift like you are getting onto the interstate and up to highway speed."

Eddie complied. He watched the tachometer and speedometer, and once he got up to 75 mph, Jimmy told him to hold it steady, while explaining how to engage the turbo system.

"Here are your controls for the turbos." Four icons appeared on the screen in the middle of the dash labeled, T-1, T-2, T-3, and T-4, with an "on-off" button below each. "Now, to date, 75 mph is the optimum speed to engage the first one. Tap the button and step on the accelerator and keep in mind that this is without the hyper-electric drive. We want to test that one in the field. Ready?"

"Ready."

Eddie tapped the T-1 button, stepped on the accelerator, and what happened next startled him so much he lost track of his thoughts.

There was a bright flash of light above him that briefly lit up the whole area. The torque was incredible. The truck felt like it was literally trying to break the chains holding it to the platform. The exhaust emitted a sound like a lion roaring. Once the initial sequence of things was over, Eddie could hear the Dyno track spinning wildly and his speedometer jumped to 125 mph. He looked over at Jimmy, shocked.

Jimmy nervously replied, "That's one of the quirks I was talking about. We had to make a special exhaust to compensate for the back pressure when the turbo kicks in. It has modified injectors to accept a larger amount of fuel and the first shot of fuel produces a flame out of the stacks which is the flash of light you saw. Fortunately, it burns off quickly. We're still working to fix that, though." He grinned.

"That's one hell of a quirk! Good Lord, man. That's gonna clear out some neighborhoods. That scared me and I was inside!"

"Yeah, well, it's temporary. We need that initial boost to get to the speed we need and while we learn how to program the electric hyperdrive system. Once the engine part gets broken in, we can use the electric drive system to launch and get up to speed, and then use the diesel part to boost it to the next level. That way we can program the entire system to work in sequence. Like I said before, eventually the whole system will be totally electric, but we're not there yet."

Eddie let off the accelerator, slowing the machine so he could stop it. He pulled the parking brake and shut it off. "Damn! That was intense." Eddie looked at Jimmy for a minute. "Okay, what's next?"

Jimmy had been holding his breath but now breathed a sigh of relief, hoping Eddie wasn't going to bail on him. He tapped on the screen and a graph appeared showing the results of the engine's performance. "This is where we check how the engine is running and performing. All this information is sent back here to us and can be adjusted as needed."

Eddie watched and listened as Jimmy went over the entire system again. The night vision, the GPS, reading the heat sensors, accessing the fire suppression system, the braking system, the aerial and 360-degree view cameras, and backing sensors.

"There are some other things, but we will get to them later on. Right now, we need to get it on the road and do a shakedown run. You good?"

Eddie was still regaining his composure from the Dyno run, but was ready to get back on the road. That is where he felt more comfortable. He would work out the kinks and get to know the truck there. The highway makes or breaks all men and all machines.

"Yeah, let's get to it before I change my mind. About the electric drive system—you did say it was battery powered, right?" Eddie asked

"Yes, why?"

"I don't have to stop and plug this thing in somewhere, do I?"

"Oh, no. It has a self-charging setup. It can essentially run indefinitely."

"Indefinitely? Really? Interesting. And this is not on the market yet, why?"

"Because, like the rest of this stuff, it needs to be tested in the field and proven. I figure, if all these things can take the abuse of being used in the world of an 18-wheeler, it can survive the average person."

"Okay, makes sense. What's next?"

"Here's what I was thinking," Jimmy said. "Let's get it unchained and out on the road. I have a road test in mind that I programmed into your GPS. Come in the office and let's go over it while the crew gets the truck outside." They climbed out and Jimmy gave his tech crew instructions.

Eddie walked around to the front of the rig and looked at it again. From all appearances, it looked like a normal truck. But he knew now that it was much more than that. Aside from being a high-tech marvel, this thing truly was a beast. He wasn't sure yet just how much of a beast, though. All he knew was that one little demonstration told him there was a lot more there. Now, it needed a name worthy of that status. After some thought, he remembered back when Kate got angry with him. Her eyes looked like they could shoot fire out of them and burn him to a crisp. She later said that person was "Morgana," her alter ego. He tried to never let that person out of the bottle, if he could help it. It was one of the few things that truly scared him.

"So it is, then," Eddie said, speaking directly to the truck. "From now on, your name is Morgana. Just don't hurt me and I will do my best to return the favor. You and me, we are going on an adventure to parts unknown. You have to trust me and I have to trust you."

Jimmy came over to where Eddie was. "Well?"

"Her name is Morgana.

"Ooooh! I know where that comes from." Jimmy grinned. "I remember making a couple quick exits from the house back in the day when she got on a tear. It fits. I think Kate would approve."

"Me, too."

Okay, you ready?"

"Lead the way," Eddie replied and they went back into the office where Jimmy laid out his plan.

"Here's what I need you to do," he began. "Like I said, we need to see if these things really work. According to the weather intel, there should be a good fog rolling into the valley and mountain areas tonight. The cargo in the trailer represents thirty thousand pounds. That should be a good enough load to test the stability control and takeoff capabilities. It will also get you used to the night vision and mapping screen." He brought up a map on his tablet. "I mapped out this route. It's 169 miles to Rocky Gap, Virginia, up I-77." Jimmy looked at the time. "If you leave here at nine p.m., that should put you up there around midnight. Then just turn around and head back.

"There are plenty of twists and turns to see how she handles. Start at the speed limits and let us monitor how the trailer reacts. If everything works, we can gradually increase the speeds. Remember, we are monitoring everything the truck is doing in live action, so we can alert you if we see something you don't."

"Okay, what about cops?" Eddie asked

"Got that covered. We have satellite view, scanners, and radar jamming, if need be. Can't use the stealth just yet. Still working some bugs out of it."

"Well, I'd like to get my gear and Radar and settled in the truck. By the way, any quirks I should know about before I head out?"

Jimmy just grinned. "Not at the moment. You have enough on your plate for now."

Eddie eyed him for a couple of seconds. "Yeah, that's code for, 'Yes, there is more, but I don't want you to freak out right now.' I can read you like a book, buddy. That's okay, though. I've got my eyes wide open. Let's do this."

"Right on, man!" They fist bumped and shook hands to seal the deal.

Jimmy hadn't seen Eddie this motivated in many years. He was glad to see some of the old spark back in his eyes again. He hoped it would bring some healing and maybe a little joy back into his old friend's life. Eddie certainly had paid a heavy price and gotten a raw deal. The man was due. Jimmy was determined to see his friend rise from the ashes and live again. This truck just might be the ticket.

They went outside where Eddie loaded up Radar, then he and Jimmy walked around the truck one last time watching the technical assistants doing their last-minute checks. Neither spoke. When they came back around to the driver's door, Eddie broke the silence.

"Look, Jimmy, I'm sorry I yelled at you earlier. I guess with everything that has happened, I've been kind of on edge lately."

"Hey. Forget about it, man. You forget I know you. I know what you've been through. No big deal."

"No, really, I mean it. You have done an amazing thing here with the facility, the technology you have come up with, the staff you put together, everything. I wasn't seeing the big picture. This is a big deal, my friend, and I will do my best to help you any way I can. I'm going to take this thing and straighten out the kinks for you, and hopefully, it can do what you say it can do."

"Listen. Relax. Just go have some fun, buddy. You do what you do and we'll take care of the rest. Also, there is a little button under the right side of the console. I hid Bertha in there. You know, just in case."

Eddie smiled. "Thanks. I feel better knowing I got some backup."

They hugged each other and then Eddie jumped into the truck. As he fired it up, he surveyed the interior and then came back to the dash. It wasn't his long nose, but it was sufficient. "Not a horrible interior. A little more modern than I like, but I could get used to it. What do you think, Radar?" The dog glanced over at him but made no reply. "Okay, I'll take that as a whatever."

The truck had a nice throaty rumble sitting there. Eddie eased it into first gear and let out the clutch. The rig started rolling forward leaving its sterile garage behind. After he got out of town and onto I-40, Eddie noticed how easily it shifted and how well it drove.

"These boys did their homework. Doesn't get much smoother than this," he said to Radar. They continued heading toward I-77 and Eddie focused on the task at hand.

Back at the complex, Jimmy and his crew were glued to their monitors, seeing the road as Eddie saw it. The casual observer would think it was a big video game, but this was very real and very intense for everyone. Bobby Chu was focused on the computer monitoring the engine and transmission hyperdrive activity. Marcy Graddick was at another monitor watching the turbo activity. Danny Wong was watching all the brake and axle activity, and Steve Decker was on the gyroscopic stability control monitor. The others were watching several other screens and checking their notes.

Everybody was excited, but waiting patiently now as they watched the product of their collective talents head out on its maiden voyage. They had poured their heart and soul into this project in the hopes of not only changing the future, but finally getting a chance to exercise their gifts and perhaps, along the way, make a difference in the world. Each one was handpicked by Jimmy for their ability to think outside the box and their willingness to do whatever it took. Once Jimmy gave them his vision, each was given a choice: They could leave and do other things, or stay and make the impossible a reality. Those that stayed were at the monitors tonight. After all the failures, heartbreaks, disappointments, and the many times Jimmy had to encourage them not to give up, here they finally were, watching, waiting, hoping, and praying that all went well. A coffee run was in order. Nobody was sleeping tonight.

****

CHAPTER NINE
REDEFINING 'BAD ASS'

As Eddie cruised up the mountain through Fancy Gap with ease, he marveled at how well the truck accelerated under a load. Even though it was only 30,000 pounds, it was still impressive. Jimmy came on the com checking on him and Radar.

"We're good. So far, it feels pretty good. Just wish I had more hood, that's all. Radar thinks you should have built in a couple of dash-mounted dog dishes, though."

Jimmy laughed. "I'll get the team on it right away. Hey, when you get up to the 77-81 merge, lean into it a little when you start the turn, just so we can check our setup to make sure it registers."

"Okay. Will do." Eddie was feeling better being back on the road. Nowadays, it was where he was the most comfortable. He tolerated people for just so long, and then he would retreat to his truck. It seemed the only one he didn't mind being around lately was Radar. Eddie felt like they had a kindred spirit. They only associated with certain people, avoided most others, kept to themselves, and didn't require much else. Still, the animal was a bit of a mystery in the way he showed up in Eddie's life and how he seemed to be so regimented in his behavior. "Time will tell," he supposed. For now, his mission was the task at hand.

Once he made his turnaround in Rocky Gap, he would see what the truck was made of. Pushing machines to their limit was what Eddie McVane was good at. Although this rig was the most-high tech and complicated thing he had ever piloted, at its core it was still just a big hot rod. He would use all his skill and abilities to push it to "the zone."

Cruising along, Eddie would normally be checking out his new sound system and all the other things you naturally do in a new truck. But this wasn't just any truck. This was a technical work of art and his friend's blood, sweat, and tears on wheels. He had been replaying Jimmy's impassioned plea and mission statement in his head. His friend had been with him all these years, and until today he never saw him for the genius and visionary he was. He felt embarrassed and somewhat ashamed of himself. He thought back to the facility Jimmy had built, all the equipment, and the staff he had assembled to build the high-tech marvel he was piloting now. Not just anybody could do that, no matter how much money you gave them. No, he might be a little on the eccentric side, but his heart certainly was in the right place. On top of that, he handed him the keys to this thirty-million-dollar marvel and told him to go have fun. Who does that? No, tonight Eddie was all business. He was focused and determined to help his friend's efforts be a success.

As the signs for the 77-81 merger came into view, he tapped the com and Jimmy was already waiting.

"Gotcha, buddy. We're ready. Just use your judgment on the speed and we will see how she does."

"Copy that." Eddie looked over at Radar. "Brace yerself, buddy. Hard left coming up." As if on cue, Radar adjusted himself on his seat. As they approached the turn, Eddie made sure it was clear of traffic and then started at the posted speed and pressed the accelerator a little to about twenty mph above that. Although he could feel the g-forces, the truck and trailer stayed planted. He exited back onto the highway, accelerating more as he went. It was smooth and effortless.

Jimmy came back on the com. "Perfect! The gauges showed that the gyros are working as planned. Our monitors only showed a three percent resistance adjustment. "How'd it feel?"

"Like a sports car. Stayed planted and no roll. Felt kinda weird, but I could get used to it."

"Cool. How's the truck feel so far?"

"Good. Still getting used to it. It'll come. Just have to spend some time with her. There are a couple more turns up the road. If it's clear, I'll press the throttle through them as well."

"Okay. Talk again when you get to Rocky Gap."

"Ten-four."

Eddie continued up I-77 and began to feel the truck out some more. It had excellent throttle response and shifted smoother that anything he had driven to date. He had no need, as yet, to shift past sixteenth gear. The rig felt well planted to the road, and really did feel like a sports car and not at all like an 18-wheeler. He also had to admit that the leather seat Jimmy chose for him was very comfortable. After a while, he cut on the CB just for a little chatter to set the mood for being back on the road.

Jimmy and his team were still at their posts watching everything. They were pleased to see the gyroscopic stabilizer system register on the graph. That meant it worked. Now, the question was, how fast could Eddie push it through the turn? As would be expected from a roomful of nerds, they took the information they had so far and tried to calculate a speed.

****

Eddie jumped off the exit for Rocky Gap and looped back around to jump back on I-77 heading south to Morganton, North Carolina. He checked the time. It was 12:09 a. m. He had made it a leisurely drive deep into the Virginia mountains, with just a few modest tests through the turns to check the gyro stability system. Going back, he would push it harder. The fog rolling in was gaining in intensity and would surely thin out traffic. He checked in with Jimmy for weather and traffic reports.

"Fog is showing as extremely heavy all down the corridor, and traffic is light. Should be perfect conditions by the time you get to Fancy Gap."

Eddie continued his run back down I-77, testing and checking the truck's responses as he went. He was getting used to the feel of the wheel and how the truck rode. He liked how tight the handling felt when he went into turns and switched lanes. It felt as if the trailer was one with the tractor. There was no fishtail feel when he yanked it back hard. *Doesn't even feel like there's a trailer back there*, he thought. As they rode along for a while, Eddie was focused on the road more intently now as the fog intensified. He chatted at Radar while glancing back and forth from the touchscreen to the road. As he was coming past the exit sign for Hillsville-Galax, he hit Jimmy up on the com. "Hey, bud, ready to try out that night vision."

"Okay. Remember the icon with the binoculars. Tap that."

Eddie did so. The windshield changed to a blue/green tint and it was almost as if someone blew the fog away and brightened up the night. He could still see faint wisps of fog, but everything was more visible. "Wow! Check it out, Radar. It's like somebody changed channels and we got a better signal. Very cool." Radar looked at him with no comment. Eddie picked up his pace and was back at 75 mph. "Now that's what I'm talking about. Jimmy, I like it. It works great."

"Awesome, man! Good to hear. We checked the traffic ahead. Except for a few trucks down the road and some four wheelers scattered mostly on secondary and town roads, you have a clear shot to shoot the Gap."

"Copy that. Any cops?"

"Not ahead of you, according to what we have found. Got a 'Smokey Bear' behind you about ten miles and a couple of 'City Kitties' prowling the local towns, but nothing else."

"Good deal. How are the kids?" Eddie grinned, while asking about the group of eager technicians he knew were huddled in front of their screens, wide-eyed, watching the activity.

"They are well. Anxiously waiting for Dad to get back home, safe and sound, and hoping he doesn't break their pride and joy. Almost there, guys. Just a bit longer."

"I'll let them know."

Eddie was checking all his gauges and enjoying the new experience of being able to see plainly while driving in a totally fogged out mountain pass. He was becoming more comfortable with Morgana, and was looking forward to going out west and stretching her legs out on some long highways. As they were coming down through Fancy Gap, Radar starting making some funny grunting noises. Eddie looked at him and noticed the dog staring at him and grunting. Based on what happened in Louisiana, Eddie's senses went on full alert and he became totally focused on everything within his view.

"Okay, what's up, dog?" The dog barked at him directly twice.

Suddenly, the CB came alive with a driver asking for help finding a runaway ramp. *"Hey! Anybody out there know what mile marker the runaway ramp is? I'm losing my brakes fast and picking up speed. Don't know how much longer I can stay in control of this thing."*

Eddie looked at Radar who was just staring at him intently. A couple of other drivers tried to offer advice to the out-of-control trucker, but to no avail.

Eddie raised Jimmy on the com. "Got a driver up ahead that lost his brakes and is picking up speed. I know that stretch and if he doesn't get to that runaway, he's gonna crash. Hard!"

"What you got in mind?" asked Jimmy.

"If I can get ahead of him, I figure I can let him get up against the back of my trailer and slow him down enough to get to the ramp.

"Sounds risky. Think you can do it without wrecking?"

"All I know is I can get there. If this thing is as solid as I think it is, I believe she will get the job done. This is supposed to have them bigger brakes you were telling me about. Well, here's a good test."

Jimmy agreed. "If anybody can do it, you can. It's your call, buddy."

"I just know if I don't try, this guy is dead for sure. I don't want that on my conscience knowing I had the power to get to him and didn't use it."

"Okay. We're here if you need us. Go get em'."

The team looked at one another and then back at Jimmy. Danny Wong spoke up.

"Boss, you sure this is a good idea? I mean, what he's talking about doing? We don't know how this technology is going to work yet."

Jimmy looked at his team. "Listen up. This is one of the best drivers on the planet and if the truck has what it takes, he'll pull it off. You just keep on top of those screens and keep me posted on what it's doing." Reluctantly they all complied.

Meanwhile, Eddie noticed that Radar was still looking at him. They stared at each other for a moment. Finally the dog grunted at him.

"Okay, we're a go. Jimmy, find me that mile marker where that runaway is and get it to me fast."

Eddie got on the CB. "Breaker 1-9. How about that driver with no brakes? Give me the next mile marker you see."

He waited a few seconds and the driver replied, *"I just passed the 199.5 and picking up speed. Got any ideas?"*

Eddie saw the 198-mile marker.

"Okay, driver. I just passed the 198. Stay in the slow lane if you can and I'll be right there."

"Okay, but I'm not sure how much longer I can hold her," the driver nervously thought.

Eddie looked at Radar who was still staring at him. "Okay, dog. Let's do this." Radar grunted again.

He reached over and pulled up the icon for T-1. He prepared himself and hit the button then the accelerator. As CatZilla roared, the fire lit up the night sky and the truck launched like a drag car coming off the line. Eddie held on with his heart pounding in his chest, focusing all his skill on the road in front of him. He shot down through the pass in the fast lane and the truck handled like a corvette. He was rounding the turn hanging on for all he was worth when he passed the out-of-control driver's rig like he was parked. Eddie immediately shut off the turbo and got on the brakes.

Whoa, horsey! Damn! That didn't take long! He never did look at the speedometer so he had no idea how fast he went. He grabbed his mic. "Okay, driver, when my trailer comes into view, aim for the back of it and I will match your speed, then when we touch, I will get on the binders."

"Copy that!" came the reply.

Eddie switched on the rear camera. He could see the driver's lights in the distance behind him. He checked his speed: 135 mph. He got on the brakes some more and the truck started getting closer. He watched the rear camera until the other truck got to his rear bar and as soon as he felt him tap it, he started applying the brakes harder. He got on the com and shouted while watching the road and the cameras and the struggling driver behind him.

"Jimmy!"

"Got it! 1.2 miles ahead. Hold her steady."

"I'm good. Truck still feels solid. Not sure about my friend back there. Don't know what he's haulin', but between us, I'm guessing 180 to 200,000 pounds of weight. We're at 125 mph right now. This is gonna be close. She's starting to slow down some. I want to try and get him as slow as possible before the ramp. Hopefully, take away some of the impact when he hits the stones."

As they rounded the next few turns, he could tell by the way the front of the other driver's rig was weaving, that the driver was doing all he could to keep his truck under control.

"Hang in there, buddy," he whispered watching the road and the camera.

The control room was thick with nervous anxiety. Jimmy and his crew were watching the cameras as the drama unfolded. Most of them felt like they couldn't breathe and wondered how Eddie could let alone drive like that. Danny Wong was on his monitor watching the temperature on his brake system steadily climbing.

"How we doing, Danny?" Jimmy asked

"Temperature is rising fast. Didn't design them with this scenario in mind. I don't know how much longer he can hold him back."

"Just keep me posted."

Jimmy was nervous, but confident in Eddie's skills. There is no one else he would rather have in that truck right now.

Eddie could feel their two trucks slowing, but knew this new brake system was not going to hold much longer. He hoped it was strong enough.

Just then he saw the sign for the runaway ramp ahead.

"Okay, driver. Get ready. When I tell you, make a slight right and you will be at the ramp. Good luck."

Finally, they were at 60 mph. Eddie readied himself and tried to gauge the timing as best he could.

Back in the control room, Jimmy checked with Danny. "How we doing?"

"So far, so good."

Eddie saw the start of the runaway and shouted into the CB mic, "*Now!*"

As he watched, he felt his truck wiggle and saw the runaway rig disappear from his camera view. Morgana started slowing more now without the added weight. Eddie's heart was racing and his palms were sweaty on the wheel. He had never done anything quite this crazy before. Sure, he had heard of it, but never thought he would be the one doing it. He finally slowed down enough to pull over on the shoulder and stop. As he did, a cloud of smoke and the smell of scorched brake pads wafted past and into the cab area.

The control room erupted in a collective cheer with high fives all around. They were relieved when they saw on the satellite feed of the runaway trucker get out of his rig and their experimental rig on the shoulder of the road, all in one piece.

Radar was still looking at Eddie from his passenger seat.

He started quizzing the dog. "Did you see this coming, too?" Radar offered no response. They looked at each other for another second. Then Eddie grabbed the CB mic. "Driver, you make it okay?"

After a few seconds the driver came on the radio, all excited.

"Brother, I am more than okay. I am great! You just saved my life, man! I want to buy you the biggest steak you ever had. Anytime, anywhere. What's your handle?"

"No need, driver. Just lucky I was passing through and happened to be in a bit of a hurry. Just be more careful next time and get on home to the wife and kiddos. Gotta go. Catch you on the flip side. We're outta here!"

And with that, Eddie pulled back onto the highway and decided it was time to get out of there before the cops and emergency personnel showed up. He quickly got up to speed and then hit the turbo to put some distance between him and the runaway truck. The driver was still talking to him, trying to get more information. He just cut the CB off. No way he could give out his CB handle after that little episode because he knew once the fellow settled down, he would start asking questions. He was just thankful the guy was okay. Eddie tapped the screen and checked in with Jimmy.

****

The mood in the control room was elation now instead of worry.

"Hey, man!" Jimmy said excitedly "We were watching the fore and aft cameras. That was some piece of driving, dude. We checked the satellite images and it looks like your guy will be okay."

"Yeah, I spoke to him. Hell of a ride, for sure. Truck did great. I've never driven anything this heavy that handled that well. That takeoff is gonna take some getting used to, though. I overshot him a little."

"Um, yeah. By a quarter mile or so. You passed him at 155."

"Seriously? Damn! I wasn't watching the speedo. Had my hands full of steering wheel. It didn't feel out of control at any time, though. And it was fast as hell! I was just glad the brakes held. Haven't had a rush like that in years."

"Yeah, Danny said the brake temperature went way beyond their testing numbers but held. Much longer, and I don't think they would have. That new material we used made the difference, I'm sure."

"Well, whatever it is, it's got my vote. Okay, Radar and I have had enough excitement for one night. Tell the children they did good and I will be home shortly."

****

"Wow! That was better than any test we could have come up with," said Danny Wong. Steve Decker was all smiles as he showed Jimmy his numbers from the gyro stabilizer readouts.

"He went into that last turn before he started slowing down at 155.4 mph! The resistance was only fifteen percent! That is way better than I expected. Those gyros rock!" Jimmy was all smiles.

Bobby Chu was all smiles too. "Engine and twans numbers good too, Boss. Eddie the man!"

Marcy Graddick said her turbo numbers were good, but could still use a little more tuning.

"I don't think Eddie is going to complain," Jimmy began. "He said he was hanging on for dear life when it kicked in. I actually think we overbuilt this thing a little, but we will make those adjustments later. Better to have too much than not enough. For now, I think we can all be proud of what we've accomplished here tonight. Good job, people. Now, why don't you all go get some rest? You've earned it."

They looked at one another and then back at Jimmy. Marcy spoke up first. "If it's okay with you, Boss, we would like to stay until Eddie gets back. We all agreed earlier that if all went well, we wanted to meet and thank him in person. You've told us so much about him, we were beginning to wonder if this guy was even real. Well, after what we witnessed here tonight, you were right. He is The Man."

"Right on," Danny replied. "I mean, who else on the planet would risk their life driving an experimental truck at a buck fifty plus, down a mountain highway in the dark, in fog, not knowing how or if it would work, to save a total stranger? The dude just rewrote the definition of badass, in my book." The rest agreed.

Jimmy was proud of his team's skills and abilities, but he was even more proud of the respect and appreciation they just paid his best friend.

"Absolutely. I don't think he will think it's a big deal, but I believe he will also pay you all respect for what you have accomplished, and, of course, enabling him to do what he did and live to tell about it. Eddie respects hard work, honesty, and results, even though he may not understand this world we live in. He is a bit rough around the edges sometimes, but he is straight up, the real deal. No better person to have as a friend. Not many like him left around. We'll all greet him at the door."

****

As Eddie and Radar cruised quietly through Morganton toward the facility, Eddie kept eyeing the dog and reviewing the evening's events. Radar was watching the road ahead as if anticipating going back to the shop. *Did he know again that something was about to happen? How is that possible?*

140

As they pulled up to the bay door, it was already going up. Eddie opened the door of the cab and let Radar out. For whatever reason, he just did not want to go into any building and instead, took up his usual spot by the door. Eddie pulled inside and parked on the markers. As he got out, Jimmy and the team were there waiting.

"Hey, guys. Here it is. All back in one piece. Except for a few scratches on the rear bar, I don't think I broke anything." To Eddie's surprise, they all started applauding and whistling. Each team member came over, shook his hand, and thanked him for doing an awesome job.

Danny Wong spoke up first. "It is an honor, sir. You took what we built and pushed it beyond anything we could have hoped or asked for. To take a completely new and experimental vehicle and push it to the limits that you did, well, that's just amazing. We can only imagine what it must have taken for you to risk your life for that man tonight."

Eddie was feeling humbled and a little uncomfortable with the attention.

Danny looked around at the others and they nodded. He looked at Jimmy for approval.

"If it's okay with you, Boss, we would like to be Mr. McVane's official team from now on. Whatever and whenever he needs us."

Jimmy grinned and looked over at Eddie. "They grow up so fast, don't they?"

Eddie chuckled. "Yes they do." He looked over at the group.

"Seems like only yesterday they were just little cubicle hatch-lings, running around, getting underfoot, chewing on their iPads, and asking all manner of annoying questions. Now look at them. All grown up and building badass super trucks with all kinds of gadgetry. Who knew?"

They all laughed.

"Sounds good to me, guys," Eddie said. I feel a little more at ease knowing there are real people behind all that's going on with this thing. I'm good with that. Now go home and get some sleep."

They thanked him again and headed home. He waved them off.

As Jimmy and Eddie watched them leave, Jimmy put his hand on Eddie's shoulder. "You just made some young people very happy, my friend. They saw for themselves tonight what I have been trying to tell them about you, and they were blown away. You have a new fan club, buddy, whether you want one or not."

Eddie just shook his head. "You know I hate this."

"I know. Next thing you know, they'll have posters of you in their cubicles, toys, games, bobbleheads. But, what ya gonna do?"

"Okay, I've had enough of you. I need some sleep." Eddie turned and began to head out. "I'll call you tomorrow, Jimmy."

"Good night, Eddie. We'll get the truck unloaded and go over every bit of it before you get back on the road. Same time tomorrow night. Love you, man!"

Without turning around, Eddie waved his hand over his shoulder as he went out the door. "Yeah, yeah."

****

He woke up the next day thinking about all that happened the night before. He wished Kate were alive to share it with, although he wasn't sure she would have approved of him risking his life. Eddie

142

hoped the man got home to his family okay. Speaking of which, he figured he would check in with Jr. before he set out again.

Then Eddie started thinking again about the dog and his behavior. *What is his deal? I know I call him Radar, but did he really sense something? Nah, can't be. There's nothing to see. Just another coincidence.*

As he was getting dressed, Eddie looked out the window to where Radar was sitting. If anyone else were looking, that's what they would see—a dog sitting. But Eddie felt there was more and his thoughts returned to Radar and his odd ways. *What is he doing? Watching? Waiting? Guarding? For what? Maybe I'm overthinking this thing too much. Maybe I should just go with the flow and not worry about it.*

His phone started ringing. It was Mike Jenkins, his freight broker.

"Hi ho, Eddie. Got a nice run for ya, if you're interested? I mean, you okay? You back in a truck? All good?"

"Yeah, I'm good. Got a new truck and trailer. Ready to work. What have you got?"

"Good, glad to hear you're okay. I got a load from Charlotte going to Rapid City, South Dakota. You'll have run empty from there to Hill City, South Dakota. Then that load goes to Fort Worth, Texas. I'll call you after that," Mike assured him.

"Okay, Mike. Sounds good. Text me the info and email the paperwork. I'll let you know when I get loaded."

"Thanks, man. Good to have you back. Later."

Eddie hung up and continued getting ready. As he went outside, Radar jumped to attention and assumed his post at Eddie's right side. He looked down at the dog who looked back at him.

"Don't know what to make of you, dog. Is this a regular thing with you?" Radar just grunted. "For some reason, I get the feeling that response is more about food than anything else." Radar gave a low woof. "Okay, then. A late breakfast it is."

They headed off to the restaurant and while there, Eddie called Jimmy to see where they were with the truck.

"She checked out okay, but the brake rotors were pretty toasted so we changed them and put on new pads. Everything else is good. Should be ready by seven. All systems go," Jimmy reported.

"Good. Mike has loads for me from Charlotte to the Dakotas and down to Fort Worth."

"Cool. We'll check out some roads to do a few more tests. You ready?"

"Ready as I'm gonna be."

"Um, *your team* is waiting patiently to send you off. I think they got you a gift."

"Seriously? Did you not tell them?"

"I tried to. But they really like you and wanted to do something nice. Just go along with it and let them have their moment. They really look up to you."

Eddie sighed. They did seem to be a good group. After all, they were his eyes and ears for this truck, plus it was their life's work. He never was much for attention, but he would make an exception in this case.

"Fine. Tell them I'll be there at seven."

"Roger that. See you then."

Eddie had been out of the social scene for three years now, and except for the occasional conversation here and there, hadn't really had much interaction with people. He preferred to keep to himself and had grown used to the idea. Now, it seemed as though his quiet world was being invaded by people again.

Radar was another story. Although Eddie enjoyed his company and felt like he and the dog had a connection, he wasn't quite sure what that was or what it meant. Did it mean anything? He certainly was an original. Eddie was starting to see a pattern of sorts, and seemed to be able to understand Radar's ways. Time will tell, he supposed. For now he just wanted to get back on the road and back to the world he felt more comfortable in.

****

Later that evening, Eddie pulled around to the back of the complex and parked by the bay door where the truck was. He would put on his best face for his new admirers and hoped it wouldn't take too long. He grabbed his gear and Radar followed behind him, taking his usual place at the entrance door. Eddie went in and found the crew already at their stations with the truck pointed out toward the door, ready to go.

Jimmy came out of the far door toward him. "You ready to light the fuse on this thing?"

"Got my Bic ready." This was an exchange they used for years right before getting ready to race. Racers and truckers develop their own code over time to set the tone for the moment at hand, and just like their racing days, there was the same anticipation and excitement in the air because now was the time for the real tests. Although the initial run up and down I-77 last night was a success in many ways including some unexpected ones, it was only a single shot. This trip was going to be an endurance run. The truck would be pitted against a host of situations and scenarios that could only be guessed at on paper. Now all the hypotheticals and *what ifs* would be put to the test. Would their experimental future truck, with all its technology, survive in the real world? They were about to find out.

Jimmy coaxed Eddie to check in with his team.

"I don't have to feed them or change their litter boxes, do I?" Eddie asked.

Jimmy cracked up. "Stop! Go be nice."

Eddie eased over to the control room and went inside.

"Good evening, people. Everybody ready to rock and roll?"

"Yes, sir!" came the collective reply. "Before you head out, we have something for you."

"Oh?" They gathered around and presented Eddie with an engraved plaque. On it was a picture of the truck and trailer with the number *71* on the doors. It was Eddie's old race car number. Underneath was engraved:

Racing To The Future

Driver

Fast Eddie McVane

Crew chief

Jimmy 'The Hammer' Wagner

Crew

Bobby Chu

Marcy Graddick

Danny Wong

Steve Decker

Co Pilot

Radar

Eddie was overwhelmed by the gesture. He looked at the team, trying not to choke up.

"It was Bobby's idea," said Danny Wong. "It's just our way of paying respect for what you accomplished in the past and what you are doing for us today. We hope that's okay? Jimmy told us you're not much for this kind of stuff."

Eddie looked at the plaque again and then back at the team. "No. It's all good. I am flattered. Really. Wow. I don't know what to say. Thanks, guys. This is very cool. Actually, better than any trophy I ever got."

He was speechless for the first time in a long time. He was also telling the truth. Eddie was more flattered with this gesture than any trophy or accolade he had ever received. To be recognized by anyone from this generation today was indeed a big achievement.

Jimmy came in to save him. "Okay, people. We are on a schedule, so let's get back to it."

Eddie was relieved. Everybody said their goodbyes and wished him luck. As they went out the door, Jimmy whispered to Eddie, "You okay?"

"Yeah. Thanks for getting me outta there. Did you know about this?"

"Yup. They had me look over the final design. I think it's cool. I told ya, you got a fan club again."

"I guess so. Not sure what to do with all this new attention."

Jimmy looked at him when they got to the truck. "Look, just go with the flow, man. It's time to start living again, don't you think? I mean, you've beat yourself up for three years now. When is enough, enough? You got people who believe in you and need you. That must account for something, right?"

Eddie thought for a moment. He looked back toward the control room, then back at Jimmy. "Maybe you're right. Maybe it's time to move on. I'll work on it."

Jimmy patted him on the back.

"You got this, brother. Go have some fun for a change. We got yer back."

"Okay, let's go see what this thing is made of."

As the door rolled up, he eased the truck outside, got out to let the dog in, and then headed toward Charlotte to get his first load with the new rig. He showed his new plaque to Radar who grunted his approval, then set it where he could see it. Eddie McVane was feeling a new sense of pride and purpose.

Purpose. A reason for being and doing something. Not just existing and waiting to die. Eddie would ponder these things over the next several days. For now, he was glad to be back on the road and back to his own, private little world. Trouble was, he was no longer alone. Not really. The truck had eyes and ears, and the dog was a constant presence and mystery. It was getting a little crowded again in his otherwise singular lifestyle. Time would tell if it was good or bad.

Chapter Ten
When God Speaks, He Doesn't Stutter

Sitting at the Flying J Travel Center truck stop in Sioux Falls, South Dakota, Eddie was eating breakfast at Denny's and looking forward to a restful day. Although the truck drove and handled well over the past couple of days from Charlotte, it would take time for him to get the total feel for it. Every vehicle has its own personality of sorts, and learning each one is not immediate. It certainly was impressive on its maiden run on I-77 under an extraordinary circumstance, but out here in the real world, it was a whole different story. There are a lot more variables to contend with.

Deep down, Eddie also admitted to himself that he was excited about the prospect of having a crew and going that fast again, especially in something this big and heavy. Being part of a team and thinking about something other than the past was a welcome change. It was the first time in a long time that he felt good about anything.

Eddie wanted to keep moving but it was the Lord's Day and he refused to run on Sundays if he could help it. He did it partly out of respect and partly because he could hear Kate in his ear reminding him that Sundays were a day of rest. She made sure he learned early on that Sundays were *off limits* and it was rare that he ever violated her rule. Her words, her voice, running through his head just as clear as if she were standing there, *"God gives you six days to do what you gotta do and he only asks for one day of your time. You can manage that! We don't need the money that bad."*

He smiled, remembering how she would stand flat-footed in front of him and poke a finger in his face, leaving him only one response, "Yes, ma'am!"

Eddie knew not to argue with that finger or that look of determination. That's when he started slowing down and stopped working all hours of the night, and started going to church. Kate even made him wear a sport coat and tie, and absolutely, *"No boots!"* Although the service was usually good, and he and the pastor got along well, it was still the most uncomfortable hour and a half of Eddie's life. Thinking back now, it really wasn't so bad.

As he lingered over his coffee and the memories of church and Kate, his thoughts drifted to the pastor's eulogy for Kate. It barely scratched the surface of the woman Eddie knew, but it was all that the time given would allow. Now more of that day flooded back and Eddie's once-bright mood left him. He remembered the condemning looks people gave him through their fake heartfelt apologies for his loss. *Hypocrites*, he remembered thinking. *Guess they forgot the part about not judging others.* They not only made a hard day harder, but took away his time to grieve and replaced it with resentment and bitterness toward everybody, especially Russell Cortland. Not surprisingly, Eddie hadn't been back to church since.

Firmly in the abyss, he felt the pain of his son still blaming him for what happened that day. It was always there, but he couldn't hold it against Junior. He wanted to tell him the truth, wanted to explain how it was all Russell Cortland's doing, but that would go against Eddie's duty to preserve Kate's memory. He wasn't going to do battle with Russell in the off chance that it would look bad on Kate and have people think bad of the boy's mother without knowing the facts. Eddie knew how quick people could be to pass judgment. No, he would gladly carry that burden to his death.

****

Somebody taking the seat in the booth behind him brought Eddie back to reality. He brushed aside the memories and finished his breakfast. After he got through, he paid his bill and eased out the front door of Denny's. Walking casually back toward his truck with Radar heeling at his right side, he noticed the "Trucker's Church" trailer parked not far from his rig. They were holding service outside today and a contingent of worshipers was already gathering in the chairs provided as the music started playing gospel songs. The guitar player was singing, "Leaning on the Everlasting Arms," one of Kate's favorites. It brought back a few of the better memories of happier times, but still, it wasn't the same. As the two of them walked along, Eddie was deep in thought while they were going by the church setup when the dog started easing left in front of him. Eddie almost tripped over him.

"Hey!" he yelled and stopped short, while Radar kept walking to the left. Eddie was perplexed by the unusual move. The dog had always heeled at his right side. Standing there, he watched as the animal casually walked over to the area toward the chairs, where church was being held, then sat about three feet behind the last chair. Eddie stared at him, dumbfounded and confused.

"Now what?" he exclaimed. He was definitely not in the mood to go to church, but was stuck in place, not really sure what to do with this sudden turn of events. The dog just sat there attentively, as if waiting for the preacher to start his sermon. As Eddie watched him, he was reminded of how the dog had saved his life. He was also reminded that he had told God he would check in soon. Looking up at the sky, he studied it for a long moment.

"Today you're calling in my marker? Today? Really?" Eddie looked over to the chairs where the dog was sitting. Finally, he gave in, but not quietly.

"Okay, Okay. I get it! I guess I should be happy I don't have to wear a tie," he grumbled.

Eddie walked over, took the chair in front of Radar and picked up the bulletin. The dog eased up and sat at his right side. Eddie glanced over at the dog and sarcastically said, "Next time, please use your signals when turning."

Radar ignored him.

After a few songs, the pastor got up from the chair where he had been sitting behind the singers. As he stepped up to the podium, he opened his Bible and said a prayer. After he was done, he looked around at the eclectic crowd of drivers in front of him and began his sermon.

"Thank you all for coming today. I want you to open your bulletins and follow along with me as I read."

Eddie opened his bulletin and looked at the scriptures sectioned off for today's message.

Matt 6:14: "For if you *forgive* men their trespasses, your heavenly Father will also *forgive* you.

Matt 6-15: "But if you do not *forgive* men their trespasses, neither will your Father *forgive* your trespasses."

As he read it, Eddie felt a host of emotions well up inside of him. Again, all he could see were the faces of the people at his old church judging him. He could also see Russell Cortland's face—his once trusted friend who violated their friendship and deceived him with photos and texts trying to break up him and Kate. Eddie went from anger to conviction and back again.

He had replayed that day in his mind hundreds of times over the past few years. He went through as many scenarios, cursing himself for not seeing the clues, not paying attention to who Russell really was, most of all, for not listening to Kate's pleas to let her explain. Eddie knew Kate loved him and would never be unfaithful, but his jealousy got the better of him that day.

A lot of good any of this was doing him now. He felt like a fool. He felt guilty. Most of all, he felt loss. Deep down, Eddie blamed himself more than Russell. The long weeks on the road, the late nights, the missed dates, dinners, and games all to make sure his family would have what they needed and be taken care of for the future. He didn't realize until it was too late that life was about living it. Just like at breakfast, Eddie was again feeling resentful for being here, reliving all those memories and the awful feelings running through him.

Stupid dog! Eddie thought. But he stayed...and he listened...and he stewed. The pastor continued.

"And here is another important thing we all need to understand. God knows better than any of us about hurt and loss and deceit. Jesus, His Son, was sold out for money. He was lied about. He was mocked. He was beaten, and ultimately, He was killed! Now...don't you all think God was mad about that? Don't you think He, at that moment, wanted to destroy those who killed His only Son? I know I would have.

"If I were Jesus, when I got back to Heaven, I would have been so angry and upset that the very people I tried to help and teach did all these things to me instead of accepting my message. I would have told God to forget about it, wipe them all out, and let's start over. We can do better. But He didn't do that. Instead, He forgave a thief that hung on a cross next to him. He asked God to forgive the ones who crucified Him. And He told us to do likewise.

"Now, notice, when God speaks, He doesn't stutter. He doesn't offer alternative solutions in this department. No, He speaks very plainly."

Eddie was hearing plain enough, but he wasn't liking what he was hearing. The message was clear and unmistakable, aimed, Eddie felt, right at him, but the weight of it was more than he could bear. The pastor was finishing up with one last point.

"The reason He asked us to do such a hard thing is because of the change it brings to us. Forgiving someone who has hurt you is one of the hardest things you will ever do. But until you do it, that person will have control over your mind and your life. It will eat you up inside, it will consume you, and it will keep you from enjoying a better life. Until then, in a sense, they own you.

"Remember, forgiveness isn't about letting them off the hook for what they've done. No, it's about breaking their hold over you and letting God deal with them. Paul says in Romans 12:20: 'But if your enemy is hungry, feed him, and if he is thirsty, give him a drink; for in doing so you will heap burning coals on his head.' "

Eddie was in full conviction mode now. He knew he was being dealt with spiritually, but wasn't sure he was there yet. He could not argue a single point the pastor made, but he also fully understood the responsibility of a truth heard. Despite his misgivings, Eddie did like the "heaping burning coals on his head" part. That sounded more appealing to him than just forgiving and forgetting. He was contemplating the message when the pastor was ending the service.

"Let us pray…"

Afterward, everybody stood up and helped put the chairs back. They chatted a little with each other and then went their separate ways. Eddie and Radar headed back to the truck. He looked down at the dog as they walked along, thinking about all he was experiencing here lately. It was a new kind of strangeness he wasn't used to.

"Not quite sure what to make of you, dog." Eddie walked over, to the passengers side to let him in, and closed the door. As he walked around the front of the truck, he muttered to himself,

"I really need a vacation…or maybe a new hobby. Cliff diving into shark-infested waters maybe. That could be fun."

CHAPTER ELEVEN
BE OHÍTIKA!

Eddie had just picked up his load in Hill City, South Dakota, and was heading back up Highway 385 to pick up I-90 and eventually on to Texas. The second preliminary test run from Reliance to Murdo, South Dakota, yielded good time and performance numbers. Traveling at 150 mph, he covered fifty-seven miles in just about twenty-three minutes.

I could get used to this, he thought. The screen dinged with an update from his crew via text message that CatZilla and all the other systems had performed flawlessly. Every gauge was green and no adjustments were needed. Although Eddie was happy with that, he still wasn't used to the roaring sound it made when he engaged the turbo.

"I'm not convinced Jimmy didn't do that on purpose because of the cat motor. Special exhaust, my butt!" he rambled at Radar. "Him and those crazy movie car sounds. It's like working with a damn teenager sometimes."

It was only 7:30 a.m. and already they were well ahead of schedule. Coming around the curve, Eddie decided he had time to stop at the Country Store at Three Forks. After parking his rig, Eddie and Radar strolled across the lot and headed for the store entrance. Taking in the sights of the morning, he saw a clear and beautiful day shaping up.

There were not many people around this early. A few people at the pumps getting gas, a group of bikers getting ready for a ride, and an old Indian man sitting off to the left side of the store on a picnic bench. Eddie glanced over at him as he went inside, but didn't think much about him. In this part of the country, he had grown used to seeing Indians on a regular basis.

Radar assumed his usual position at the entrance while Eddie browsed around the store looking for snacks and drinks, and, of course, a souvenir for the grandkids. He hoped they would one day have a nice collection of items to remember him by and at least some type of a positive memory. When Eddie got to the cashier, he looked toward the door entrance as he always did to take a peek at Radar, and noticed the dog wasn't there. *Okay. Where did he go? Usually stays there until I come out. He wondered.* Puzzled, Eddie finished paying for his stuff and went out to look for him. Squinting in the bright sunlight, he finally saw the dog sitting in front of the old Indian at the picnic table.

Maybe the dog was just curious? Maybe the Indian reminded him of his old master, the WW2 vet? Who knows? He wondered.

As he got closer, he could see that he was very old, almost ancient. He had coal black eyes and skin that looked like worn leather. His cheeks were sunken in, and his hair was pure white. A collection of beads hung around his neck, along with feathers and beads braided in lengths that hung down from his headdress, which was full of feathers. His clothing appeared to be a tanned hide of some sort with teal, white and some red stitching. He was holding a staff in his right hand that also had feathers at the top and markings carved into it all the way down the sides. Now he could hear the old man chanting something. Radar just sat in front of him as if he were listening to a concert.

This is new, he thought. Although he was still learning the dog's nature and habits, this was totally out of character for what he knew to date.

As Eddie got closer, the old man stopped his chanting. He wasn't sure what to do, so he offered an apology for the interruption. "Hi, sir. Sorry if my dog is bothering you. He usually doesn't have much to do with people. He must like you."

The old Indian just sat there without any response. After a moment, Eddie looked down at Radar and said, "Come on, buddy. We have to go now."

Suddenly, the Indian started speaking in cryptic sentences, pausing between each one.

"You are the one who goes swift, like the great wind across the prairie…many seek to catch the wind, but their hands will be empty."

Eddie was caught off guard. "Huh, what?"

"You are his chosen. Follow and he will show you the way… His spirit will guide your spirit—follow him."

Now Eddie was frozen in place with total bewilderment.

The Indian continued, "Your heart is heavy with much sorrow. What was done in darkness will be brought into the light. When this happens, you will no longer drink from the cup of bitterness, but you will drink from the stream of peace.

"The sign of the wolf is good. Do not be afraid. It will be well with you. There is a great battle coming…the evil ones must be stopped. Some braves will die…you must be swifter than the eagle in that day. Do not let fear keep you from going higher…you must be ohitikA!"

Pausing one final time, he finished with, "Wakan tanka kici un."

Then silence.

Eddie just stood there for a moment, bewildered, and wondering what just happened. He had no idea what or who the old man was referring to.

"Follow who?" Eddie asked. Without answering, the old Indian went back to his chanting.

With that, Radar got up from his position in front of the old one and heeled at Eddie's right side like he had always done. Eddie looked down at the dog, then back at the Indian. Totally perplexed and not wanting to be rude, he offered a farewell.

"Um, okay. Thanks. I think? Nice chatting with you…sir." The Indian offered no response. Eddie stepped back a little then turned to go back to the truck. He walked away with the old Indian's words echoing in his head, glancing back one last time muttering to himself as he crossed the parking lot.

"Okay. That was about as weird as it gets. Just my luck," he thought, *"an Indian psychic. Great!"*

When they got back into the truck, Eddie settled in and set his GPS to the delivery address in Fort Worth, Texas, but he continued to look over where the old Indian was sitting. Taking a few moments before doing anything else, Eddie tried to remember what he had said. *"Wind? Guiding spirit? Great battle? Some will die? Sign of the wolf?" What's all that supposed to mean?"* One thing he did pick up on the "heart heavy with sorrow" part.

As a God-fearing man, Eddie wasn't much for spiritualism, but he did respect the Indian culture. He had heard many stories over the years, but typically didn't give much credence to them, believing it was a cultural thing. This was different, though, and Eddie was somewhat taken aback by what happened and how he felt. Maybe it was just because he was personally involved.

Continuing to go over things, Eddie saw it was more than his involvement in this odd encounter that had him unsettled, if you can call standing there being chanted at, involvement. There was the accident. The rescue. The incident at the trucker's church, and now this with the Indian.

What had been a nagging, but fleeting back-of-the-mind thought was now front and center, and could no longer be pushed away. There was a common denominator to all this and it wasn't Eddie McVane.

He looked over at Radar who was staring out the window at some other activity in the parking lot. Eddie finally said, "When we get home, young man, we are going to have a serious discussion about talking to strangers."

For the next day and a half as he drove to his destination, Eddie chewed on the words of the old Indian. He had 1,100 or so miles of road to Ft. Worth and he spent most of them—when he wasn't being interrupted to do a speed test or go over the results with Jimmy and the team—trying to remember as much as he could. He began jotting down notes, at first just to preserve what he remembered, but increasingly to keep track of when something along the way connected to what the Indian said.

After Eddie dropped his load in Fort Worth, he headed for the nearest Waffle House for a quick breakfast. Waiting for his food and sitting there looking at Radar in his usual place—or as Eddie began to call it, his post—questions about the dog swirled in his mind.

Why did Radar wander over to the Indian that day instead of waiting at the entrance like he usually did? Actually, he didn't wander, come to think of it. The dog went directly to him. Did Radar pick up on something? He isn't called Radar for nothing, but that's just a fun name I gave him. Still, why does the dog only go to certain people, and it's never someone who's, well, an average person. There's always something different about them.

Eddie shrugged and took out his notebook. He wasn't going to figure out the dog anytime soon, but he did have some new notes to add from something he remembered. In between bites of his eggs over-easy and a few coffee refills, Eddie was writing away when his phone rang. It was Mike Jenkins, his freight broker.

"Eddie! My man. My favorite freight dragger! How ya doin', buddy?"

"You mean, the guy who makes you look good and makes you great commissions? The guy who always pulls your ass outta the fire? That guy? I'm doing great. What are you selling today and what kind of jam are you in now?"

"Come on, don't be so cynical. You are my favorite driver. Seriously."

"Yeah, yeah. Cough it up. Who stiffed ya?"

"Damn it! Jerry Higgins. He jammed me up with a big client and now they're threatening to go elsewhere. Claimed he had truck issues or something."

"More like partying issues," Eddie joked.

"Whatever. If you can do me a solid, man, there's a big payday in it for you."

"What's the load and where does it have to go?"

"Dry box, Ventura, Cali. Pick up in Dallas."

"Next big question. When's it gotta be there?"

"Three days from now."

"What? Good luck with that one. One thousand seven hundred fifty miles in three days? Are you nuts? You don't need me, you need David Copperfield."

"Who?"

"David Copperfield. The magici…never mind. How in the hell am I supposed to pull that one off, Mike?"

"Look, I know it's a lot to ask. But you're the only guy I know that would even have a shot at making it happen. This is my job on the line, Eddie. At least think about it. I got a load going from there to Portland that I would gladly pay you full shot, and waive my commission, just to get my ass outta this jam. This is a big one for me, buddy. If I can't fix this, I'm in a serious pickle."

"Well, I will do some calculating, but in the meantime, I'd start polishing my resume if I were you. Call you back in a while."

"Thanks, man. You really are my favorite driver. Let me know. You're the best."

"Yeah, yeah." Eddie had heard it all before. He seemed to recall three other times over the past two years that Mike was about to lose his job. The guy should be selling cars. He'd make a fortune. Mike wasn't as bad as some freight guys he had dealt with in the past, though. At least he did get Eddie good paying loads and not try to push the bottom-of-the-barrel stuff off on him, or argue rates.

Eddie would make Mike sweat for a while and then call him. He texted Jimmy about this next load and waited for a call to see where he would set him up for more tests. Meanwhile, it was back to making more notes while he was eating and checking on the dog.

Eddie never had a dog he didn't have to train, or worry about wandering off and getting hit by a car or something. Radar didn't seem to bother anybody and other than occasionally introducing himself to people of his choosing, seemed self-sufficient and low maintenance. It was just that he was a little weird. Then there was that Indian. He had Eddie questioning a lot of things.

His phone rang again. It was Jimmy.

"Hey, man. So, yer goin' to California, eh? Perfect. I got a route all mapped out for you when you get loaded. I will send it to the truck. Now we get to test out the electric hyperdrive takeoff and the stealth mode. This is gonna be awesome." Jimmy sounded like a kid at Christmas.

Eddie, however, had other things on his mind.

"Yeah, cool. Hey, do you know any Indians?"

CHAPTER TWELVE
THE TIMES, THEY ARE A-CHANGING

Jimmy didn't know any Indians, but gave Eddie some websites to check out. He thanked Jimmy and would spend more time on that later. Right now, though, he was in Dallas, Texas, getting his paperwork from the shipper and a load going to California. Despite being somewhat preoccupied with the Indian as well as the message from the truck stop pastor, Eddie was still focused on the task at hand. There was a job to do—two jobs, actually—and people were counting on him to use all his skills and talents to put this truck through its paces, while others were counting on him to pick up and deliver items.

While they were loading his trailer, Eddie accessed the truck's computer to learn more about the different systems. He was never one for high-tech gadgetry, but this setup interested him. After that run down I-77 the other night, he was impressed with the truck's capabilities and more intrigued at the possibilities. The night vision, the gyroscopic stabilizers, the fore and aft cameras, the expanding walls, all of it had massive potential. Forget the speed. Just those items alone would change the industry and make truckers' lives much easier and safer. As Eddie was checking out the icons, he saw one that read, "Trailer Tandems." He tapped on it and a diagram of the trailer came up with a description of the tandem's function:

1. Slide fore----aft 1-2-3-4-5-6-7-8-9-10, indicating that the tandems slid at one-foot increments.

"Interesting. That's a pretty good slide. Wonder why so far? A very unique setup. So, I can access these functions from right here without pulling pins and locking wheels? Cool." It also had a diagram showing the trailer with a load and how to slide the axles or spread them to balance the different loads according to their weight. When the weight balance was just right, a green light would signal. "The axles spread? A multi-functional tandem setup? Also cool. Another great idea. These guys definitely did their homework."

He tapped around the screen on the other icons, the stealth, night vision, infrared sensors, cameras, fire suppression, and CatZilla. There seemed to be an icon for just about every part of the truck. He passed over the Doomsday icon. "Don't need to review that one." There were other icons he didn't recognize, he tapped on them but they didn't respond. "Must not be activated yet. Wonder what they are?"

Just then there was a rap on his door.

"You're all set, driver." Eddie got out and went inside to get his paperwork. Once finished, he pulled away from the dock and closed the doors. He thought about all the technology in the trailer alone, and still felt a little guilty for not listening to Jimmy earlier. This was indeed some great technology and would definitely benefit the industry. Eddie looked around at the other truckers in the yard. He watched some using load bars and checking their tie-downs. All he had to do was close the doors and press a few buttons. Kind of felt like cheating. They would have this same setup one day, though, and he felt good about helping make that happen.

While he was getting ready to head out, Radar was watching him and seemed eager to get rolling. He gave a low grunt as if impatient. "Relax. We're on our way. Stop nagging." Eddie eased out of the distribution center and onto I-20 headed west. Jimmy had a route set up for him going through Weatherford, Texas, for a nighttime test, but it was only about an hour's drive so he had some time to kill before it got dark.

He decided to hang out at the Driver's Travel Center in Fort Worth until Jimmy gave him the go-ahead. While there, he would study the information his crew had sent him and make sure he didn't hit any wrong buttons. Tonight, they were going to test the stealth and hyperdrive system. *This should be interesting*, he thought. The truck already had monster power takeoff, what more could they possibly need?

As he rode along, Eddie thought about his life for the past three years—the solitude, the long roads to nowhere, the lonely nights with only his thoughts about all he had lost and what had happened. He had given up all hope of a life, leaving him to feel like a failure and resigned to living out his days alone. He'd almost gotten used to it or at least convinced himself he was.

Now, for the first time in those three years, Eddie was inspired to rise above his own misery and think about someone other than himself. Jimmy was firmly back in his life and he brought along his team which was really Eddie's team. Junior seemed to be coming around, and of course, there were the grand kids. Then there was

Radar, mystery and all, who nevertheless was becoming a fixture in Eddie's life. He had to admit he did feel safe with him in the truck and genuinely liked his company. "The times, they are a-changing," he softly sang to himself.

The sign for the truck stop came up and he turned off the exit. Eddie idled into the parking lot and found a spot in the back lot to hole up for the next few hours. Jimmy said that 2:00 a.m. would be an optimal time to do the next test. The team texted him a collective "good luck" and said they would be there for whatever he needed. That was still all new to Eddie and he wasn't yet used to it. Being a self-sufficient individual and a loner when he was on the road all those years was a strange feeling. After thinking about it, he realized that maybe he had let some of his past hurts harden him and he shouldn't take it out on these young people who seemed eager to work with him. He promised himself he would work on that.

He checked the time. It would be a few hours before test time, so he decided to take a nap and prepare for the long drive ahead. As he laid there, Eddie mulled over the preacher's words from South Dakota about forgiveness. That was a tough one. Russell Cortland carried on with his life as if nothing happened. How was that fair? He hated thinking about it and wished he could wash that part of his mind clean. He switched back to what the old Indian had said: *"What was done in darkness will be brought into the light. Then, you will no longer drink from the cup of bitterness, but from the stream of peace."* Was that in reference to this thing with Russell? How was that supposed to work? As he slipped off to sleep, Eddie tried to remember better days and happier times.

****

The sound of the phone ringing woke him up. It was Jimmy.

"Time to rock and roll, old man. Get yer game face on."

"Okay, all systems are a go. When you leave Fort Worth, take I-20 to Weatherford. We have been scanning the area, and it should be clear by the time you get there. Danny is ready to test the stealth, and Bobby is ready on the hyper-drive system. Once you get through Weatherford, there is a road you will cross under called Ric Williamson Memorial Highway. That's where we plan to test it."

"Okay, got it. I'm gonna grab some coffee, and then we'll be on our way." Inside the truck stop, it was coffee first, then his customary wander through the gift section looking for something to take back to the grand-kids.

Sipping his coffee and clearing the cobwebs, Eddie began focusing on the route Jimmy laid out and the tests they'd be running. He walked back to the truck, breathing in the cool night, Radar at his side. After reaching the truck and letting the dog in, Eddie did his walk-around, checking for anything out of place. As he climbed in and fired Morgana up, there was a nagging sensation in his spirit. Something felt out of place. But what? He still didn't know all the ins and outs of this beast, so, for all he knew, he could be looking directly at something wrong and not even know it. Maybe that was it—the opposite of how he felt when he was around his race cars and "normal" trucks. Back then, he knew everything about them. But this technology was all new to him, leaving him nothing but doubt about what he was checking. Still, the feeling wasn't going away, and it was more than just unfamiliarity. He decided to check with Jimmy and his crew before he pulled out.

"No, sir. Everything checks out here," came the reply from his crew.

Jimmy sat forward in his chair. "What's up, Eddie?

"Not sure. Just a feeling."

"You want to postpone till another time?"

Eddie thought for a moment and decided to carry through.

"No. If something is going to break, I'd just as soon it did it on a deserted highway with no one around. Let's get to it. Just stay sharp."

"Will do. Be careful."

Having heard the entire conversation, the crew looked at one another and then at Jimmy. "What's up, Boss? We don't see anything here. What's he talking about?"

"Listen, guys, I've been with Eddie long enough to know if he has a feeling about something, I listen. Y'all just keep at the ready for anything."

Everybody did a re-check on their calculations and reset the testing data. All looked good.

Eddie jumped back onto I-20 and set a pace for Weatherford. He glanced over at Radar, who didn't seem to be concerned about anything, just facing forward, looking at the road. *Maybe I'm just off tonight.* He thought. *Maybe that accident got me spooked or something.* Talking at Radar, he asked, "I'm sure if there was something to worry about, you'd let me know, right?" The dog looked at him but didn't respond. "Okay, then. I guess we're a go."

They continued and waited for further instructions from Jimmy and his team. He checked and scanned all the gauges, screen monitors, and anything related to the test. All good.

After twenty minutes, Jimmy came on the com. "Okay, Ric Williamson Memorial Highway is coming up. We have been checking the sat feed and scanning the area. All there is a Trooper car at a tow yard but he's far enough away that I don't think he will be any problem. We should have about six to ten miles clear to test. When you cross under the bridge, you'll see the hyper-drive system activated on your screen, but don't worry, it doesn't engage until you reach 125 mph. We need you to turn on stealth mode and cut all the lights before that though. So, make sure you do that when you see the activation message. Then, once you hit seventy-five mph, fire up CatZilla and accelerate just like you did before."

"Okay, then what?"

"Like I said, the system takes over at 125 mph, and the diesel part goes on standby. The acceleration you feel after that will be the hyper-drive system."

"Okay, got it." As he crossed under the bridge, Eddie switched over to night vision mode, cutting off all lights, and activated the stealth. The icon for the truck and trailer showed a green outline around it, indicating that the stealth was activated. The road ahead looked clear. Eddie looked over at Radar. "Time to light this candle, buddy. Let's see what she's got."

He accelerated to 75 and then hit T-1 to engage the turbo. Fire lit up the night sky, and CatZilla roared to life. The truck jumped forward and quickly reached 125 mph. Suddenly, blinking on the screen caught Eddie's eye. The green stealth outline around the truck and trailer icon flickered. Eddie was accelerating faster now as he felt the electric drive system kick in, and the engine went quiet. Just then, Radar barked a warning. Eddie shot him a look. "Now what?" He was looking out the window to their right.

Back at the compound, while everybody was busy watching their computers, Danny happened to glance over to the monitor showing the satellite feed just in time to notice that the trooper car had been on the move and was in close proximity to Eddie. He shouted out a warning to Jimmy. "Boss, that Trooper car is right at Eddie's exit."

"What!? Jimmy looked over at the satellite monitor and, sure enough, the Trooper's car was just about to cross over I-20 when Eddie hit T-1 and put on a light show for him. Jimmy watched in horror and frustration as the Trooper slammed his cruiser in reverse backing up to line up with the ramp and was smoking his tires forward as he took off down the exit ramp to go after Eddie.

"Awe, shit! Dammit! Just what we don't need. Bobby, hack that car and shut him down. Danny, scramble his communications. We can't let him get to Eddie and we sure don't need the advertisement."

"On it boss!"

Jimmy was pacing back and forth now, rubbing the back of his neck and watching the drama unfold. Taking a deep breath, he tried to calm himself down before calling Eddie.

He tapped his ear piece. "Eddie, we've got a small problem."

"Yeah, I'm guessing the stealth, right?"

Jimmy shook his head. "Yep. What did you see?"

"The outline blinked. A short, maybe?"

"Don't know for sure, but it gets worse."

"What? How so?"

"It must have shown up on that local Trooper's radar and now he's coming after you."

"What?!" Eddie turned on the back cameras. Sure enough, in the distance, he could see the lights of a patrol car. His heart started racing. "Crap! What now?" he shot back at Jimmy.

"We're working on it. Just keep your foot in it."

"Seriously? You want me to outrun a cop? This is not cool, Jimmy. Not cool at all!"

"Ya gotta trust me, Eddie. You can't let him catch you. That will be big trouble for both of us. We are hacking into his patrol car right now. Don't worry. We will shut him down and reroute you. He can't see what kind of rig you are, nor any markings so, just keep going. We got this."

"I hope you're right. I'm too old to go to jail." Eddie watched the camera and gauges. Now, he was at 155 mph and climbing.

Back in the control room, it was a flurry of activity, the sound of fingers hammering on keyboards was almost deafening while Jimmy was pacing back and forth.

"C'mon, guys, we're running out of time."

Danny and Bobby were using all their hacking skills at a breakneck pace to shut down the approaching patrol car.

Finally, Bobby Chu sang out, "Got it! I'm in!" He tapped a few more keys. "There! You done!"

Jimmy came over and looked at his screen. "Good man, Bobby." He watched as the diagnostics on the screen showed a catastrophic engine failure. Suddenly, Jimmy was alarmed. "What did you do?"

Bobby explained, "Once I got into the OBD, I shut down the first thing I could see. The oil pump."

"You blew the cop's engine up? Oh, no. Not good! You were just supposed to shut it off. I hope nobody checks that OBD system."

"Sorry, Boss. I panicked."

Jimmy paced back and forth. "Not cool, not cool."

Danny piped up. "Okay, he is scrambled for now but he was able to relay the pursuit to his dispatcher."

"Okay. Keep him scrambled for now until we can get Eddie off the highway and onto a secondary road. Bobby, try to scrub any sign that we were there on that OBD system."

"On it boss."

Just then, Eddie was on the com. "Guys? What are we doing? I'm at 160, and the cop is getting smaller. Did he give up? Gonna be running out of road here soon. I see some headlights in the distance. Talk to me." Jimmy took a deep breath to calm himself down so as to not sound worried to Eddie.

He tapped his ear piece again. "It's okay, Eddie. We shut him down. Don't worry. We will find another route here shortly. You can back it down to highway speed and put your lights back on now. Sorry, man, we definitely have a glitch. It must be something in the connection on the truck somewhere."

"Well, it took a few years off me that I can't afford. Let's try not to let that happen again, okay? Will the cop be able to track me?"

"No, we jammed his signal, and he didn't really see anything to identify you. You're safe."

"I hope so. Don't need that worry hanging over me."

"Roger that." On another note, how did it feel?" asked Jimmy.

Eddie was still a little unnerved by the episode but managed to muster a grin. "Like driving a bullet, only quieter. It was like nothing I've ever experienced before. Once it got to 160, I was starting to get tunnel vision. I could feel the suspension working and adjusting to the speed, and I saw a little diagram on the screen showing what looked like spoilers, maybe?"

"Yes. Those are air deflectors that help stabilize the unit as you go faster. They activate automatically, as needed."

"Well, except for that little glitch with the stealth, it all seemed to work well. It was an incredible feeling. Amazingly smooth ride, too. It felt like it wanted to go faster. I don't think 200 will be a problem."

Jimmy smiled knowingly. He knew that 200 was doable all along. They already hit that mark on the Dyno a month ago. These sprints on the open road were just a shakedown run to confirm what they already knew. Once the computers were calibrated and Eddie was more comfortable with the truck, they would push it even more. Way more. But today wasn't the day to discuss that.

"Okay, buddy, that sounds good. Something for you to look forward to. Meanwhile, let's get you another road where you can be anonymous."

Jimmy and the team went to work steering Eddie through the back roads of Texas to safety for the rest of the night, jamming radar signals as they popped up and monitoring police bands for any news of the evening's event. After a while they were able to get Eddie back to I-20 and merge into traffic with other trucks so as not to stick out in case there was anybody looking for a suspicious truck on the back roads.

While riding along, Eddie picked at Radar, chiding him about being off his game. "What's up there, dog? You slacking on me? You're supposed to warn me before a problem occurs, not during."

Radar grunted a reply and looked out his window as if trying to ignore him. Eddie smiled and poked at him a little more. "It's okay, we all have an off day once in a while. You hang in there, sport. You'll get your mojo back." Radar continued looking out his window as if Eddie wasn't there.

They drove through the night with no more incidents and headed to California. After dropping his load in Ventura a day and a half later, Eddie picked up a shipment going to Portland, Oregon. For now, it was all about staying off anybody's radar and making himself as small and unnoticeable as possible. He directed his thoughts toward Radar. "A trip to Oregon should be nice and uneventful. Nothing ever happens up there."

CHAPTER THIRTEEN
GOT NOWHERE TO GO AND
ALL NIGHT TO GET THERE

Destiny or Fate; according to most definitions, are closely related in meaning. The first suggesting that our path in life is pre-destined while the other is considered to be more of a result of our own life choices, whether good or bad. The latter being the most used referred to as *"Well, I guess it just wasn't meant to be for me. That's my fate and it is what it is."* But, sometimes the two, 'Destiny and Fate', cross paths in a most unexpected way that presents the participants a *'second chance' or possibly, a different outcome,* if you will. Case in point;

Rodney Cecil Cooper is a fourth-generation lawman. His great-great-grandfather, Royce Cecil Cooper, was a Texas Ranger who served with Captain Jack Hays in 1841. In June of 1917, his great-grandfather, Dub Cecil Cooper, was part of the first deployment of US troops to France during WWI. After serving through the end of the war, Dub came back home to Fort Worth and joined the Texas Rangers, where he served with distinction until he retired as Captain in 1947. Rodney Herbert Cooper, Dub's second son and Rodney Cecil's grandfather, continued the family tradition and joined the Rangers, eventually leading to his firstborn becoming the fourth of the Cooper family to wear the famous star-in-the-wheel badge.

Unfortunately, Rodney Cecil, the third son of Rodney Herbert Cooper II, better known as 'RC' or 'Coop to his friends and Officer Cooper to his coworkers, hadn't quite measured up in his father's eyes and what was expected of such a lineage. RC just didn't seem to have the same qualities as his forebearers, despite being taught about his heritage from an early age and surrounded by so many photos and memorabilia throughout the Cooper home that it was like living in a mini-Rangers' museum. Not for lack of trying, though. doing all that was asked of him, but always falling short. Disappointing, to say the least, to his proud father. But RC made the most of his situation and was determined to be the best lawman he could be in spite of his failures. He would try again later. In his mind, he was still a good lawman and that's what mattered. Tonight however, his life was about to change in ways he could never have imagined. He had just left a local tow yard after following up on a drunk driver tow-in and was about to cross the bridge over I-20 on Ric Williamson Memorial Highway when three bizarre things happened back-to-back. A loud roaring sound off to his right, two bright fire balls of light and then his radar unit briefly showed 125 MPH! For a brief moment he saw the outline of what appeared to be an eighteen-wheeler and it was moving out at a rapid pace.

"What the Hell?" He stammered out.

Startled to say the least, instinct took over and he slammed on his brakes while putting his cruiser in reverse, he smoked his tires backing up and then repeated the process putting it back into drive as he floored the cruiser taking off down the exit ramp and onto the interstate to pursue the, what was now just a dark, barely visible, outline of a tractor trailer. There were no lights or distinguishable markings so it was hard to make out what exactly was going on with it. All he knew was that he was not going to let it get away.

"So, ya wanna play, eh? I'll be right there, Big Boy!" RC bellowed with four generations of Texas lawmen's blood rushing through his body. This guy wasn't getting away.

Picking up speed, he called in the pursuit. G-12 to dispatch, I'm in pursuit of an 18-wheeler, westbound on Interstate 20. Vehicle is traveling at...at... ah....RC looked down at his speedometer to verify his speed, and for a moment, he hesitated, dumbfounded at what he was seeing.

After the dispatcher heard his unfinished report trail off, she responded, *"G-12, what is the speed of said vehicle?"*

RC stammered for a second when he realized he was doing 135 mph now, but the truck was pulling away from him at a rapid pace. Pulling away at 135 mph!

"Dispatch, I am at 135 mph. I repeat, one, three, five and accelerating. Subject is believed to be traveling at 150 plus!"

"G-12 can you repeat that, please? Offer Cooper? Officer Cooper! Can you repeat that, please?"

RC was trying to get his head around the fact that as fast as he was going, the dark shape of the 18-wheeler was leaving him far behind. "How can that be?" he said in amazement.

Finally, he responded to the dispatcher, "Dispatch, I am in high-speed pursuit of an 18-wheeler that is believed to be supercharged or something. I am at one-four-five, repeat one-four-five miles per hour, and he is pulling away from me. I cannot keep pace with him."

Totally focused on the road ahead, RC squinted to see if he could see any distinguishing marks, but he saw nothing. He was now at 150 mph with his foot pressed hard on the pedal, willing it to go faster, but still the dark shape kept getting further away.

Just then, his patrol car started making unfamiliar sounds from under the hood that he'd never heard before but knew were not good.

"*No, no, no, no*! Don't do this! You can't do this to me! C'mon!"

Then suddenly, a loud rattling noise came from the engine, followed by smoke billowing from under the car. There was no doubt his pleading was to no avail.

"*Nooo! Damn it*!"

Immediately, despite having his foot still planted on the floor, the vehicle started slowing down. Pumping the gas pedal, he tried to revive it, but to no avail. Now there was no engine sound, just the wind and road noise built up from reaching 150 mph that, now, was working its way back down to nothing.

Beating on his steering wheel in defeat, he cursed his fallen cruiser, "Damn it all, the luck!"

He rolled as far as he could and then eased over onto the shoulder after about a mile and a half and stopped.

"*G-12, are you still in pursuit?*" came the voice of the dispatcher into his moment of broken vehicle hell.

Not replying, he just sat there for a moment, staring after the nothingness, trying to remember any details of the ghost-like apparition that eluded him. *Eluded*. That's not even close. No, elude is when someone gives you the slip by trickery or just gets away. This guy didn't elude. He blew through like he knew there was no one and nothing that could catch him or stop him.

Finally, having cursed his vehicle for the last time, RC responded, "Negative, Dispatch. My patrol car has expired. Repeat. Unit G-12 is 10-7." As he sat there staring into the nothingness, he was still trying to get his head around what he just witnessed. Although he had dealt with some crazy truckers running fast in the past, this was way out of the norm. Something that sounded like a Lion roar, two flame flashes out his stacks and then, gone! *How is that even possible?* He wondered.

After a moment he realized he did not get a reply back from dispatch. He keyed up his mic again. Only this time, all he got was static. "*What the hell?*" He wondered. He tried again. Still, just static. Throwing his mic down, his voiced his frustration.

"Well, this sucks." As he sat there with his lights flashing, and just the darkness surrounding him, he reached for his cell phone to call in. Now,his phone wasn't responding. Even after repeated attempts. He looked at his phone and began to wonder what was going on. He had been up and down this highway a million times and used his phone countless times and never had any problem with reception, ever.

"Okay, now I have no way to communicate. Perfect."

As he sat there thinking about that, his conspiracy theory side was kicking in. He looked around and at the moment there was no other traffic on the highway, especially at this hour of the night so it would take at least twenty minutes before someone came looking for him. "Well, now I've got nowhere to go and all night to get there." He said to himself. As he sat there for a few more minutes he began wondering

Just what is going on here? Shaking the thought off, he finally decided to set out a road flare and triangles to add to his visibility on the roadside. After doing so he walked around to the front of his cruiser and stood there, waiting and looking down the empty highway, shaking his head in disbelief, as he muttered under his breath. "Who the hell are you and where did you come from? In added frustration at it all, he yelled into the darkness. *And who the hell needs a 150 Mile per hour truck, anyway?"*

But, just like the ghostly truck that eluded him earlier, his words disappeared into the darkness and no answers came back. For R C, this was going to be a tough one to explain. Even he had a hard time understanding it. But he determined right then and there that he was going to get answers, no matter what it took. As he turned to get back in his car, he could see flashing lights in the distance coming his way so he knew help was coming. Just then, while he stood there waiting, his radio came alive with dispatch calling for him to respond. Now he knew, something wasn't right. There was definitely something more going on here than meets the eye. He reached in and grabbed the mic to let them know he was okay.

For Officer Cooper, his journey for answers was just beginning.

Fate, meet Destiny.

Chapter Fourteen
Add Matchmaker to His Resume

It was a nice, sunny Saturday morning in June. Eddie and Radar were on their way to drop his next load in Portland, Oregon, when he decided he would chill out for the weekend. That little episode in Texas still had him looking over his shoulder the entire trip and he was feeling the stress. Eddie hoped Jimmy and the crew had the problem with the stealth worked out. No SWAT team had shown up yet, so that was a good thing. Still, he kept an eye out.

They were way ahead of schedule and didn't have to unload until 7:00 a.m. on Monday. Coming into Central Point, Oregon, he jumped off the exit and headed to the Pilot Travel Center there to fuel up and check everything over. Even though the truck performed well and he was comfortable driving it, Eddie was still getting used to the idea of something so big going so fast. The hyperdrive system would definitely be a game changer for the future of trucking once they got the bugs worked out. That said, he needed a break from it all. Eddie looked over at the dog.

"What do you think, buddy, time for a little sightseeing?" Radar sat up from his lying position on the seat and assumed his post stance.

"I'll take that as a yes." They turned into the plaza and headed for the fuel islands. Once there, he and Radar jumped out. Eddie gave the young attendant instructions for fuel only and that no other service was needed. He certainly didn't want anybody looking under the hood at the heartbeat of this monster lurking beneath its skin. Even with the hood having an internal locking system besides the hood straps, Eddie wasn't taking any chances. The last thing he needed was some Nosy Nellie seeing something odd, and there's more odd than not under there, and asking a bunch of questions, or worse, taking a picture and posting it on the Internet.

After walking around and checking the truck and trailer unit over for anything out of place, he and Radar headed over to the restaurant area. The dog veered off to the grassy area across the parking lot to do his business while Eddie continued inside. Once he was seated in a booth by the window, Eddie glanced over to check on Radar and saw him heading toward the front entrance. *Back to sentry duty*, Eddie thought with a smile. He knew the dog would sit there patiently until he came out just as he had done everywhere else they stopped except for Three Forks.

Three Forks. The Preacher. The Indian. He was no closer now to understanding any of that than when they happened. As he rolled those around for another spin in his head, a glimmer of insight came to Eddie. Maybe he wasn't any closer to figuring it out, but he was closer to one part of it. Could that be the key?

With that, while waiting at the table to be served, Eddie began looking up all the information he could on Briards. He felt a touch of excitement at this development.

Briards: protective, fearless, faithful, intelligent, loyal, obedient, smart, confident dogs; French heritage; Used for herding and protecting flocks. The French also used them extensively during WWI as sentries, messengers, and search and rescue.

There was even a story in one article in the 14th century, about one of these dogs getting into a life-and-death duel with a guy who had killed his master. The dog won.

Wow. Seriously bad ass stuff right there, he thought. *And now I get the sentry thing.* It was starting to come together, but before Eddie could pat himself on the back for his brilliance, another thought about Radar hit him. *Well, sure, he is as advertised, but am I his master now?*

More than that was the way the dog seemed to have a sixth sense or something. There was a mention that if a Briard was sent out to search for survivors during the war and the dog passed by you, you were as good as dead.

Interesting. That could be explained, but this was more of a forewarning before anything happened. Eddie was running out of explanations for how the dog knew they were about to be hit head on by the truck that day. Plus, there were the other times when he distinctly made a noise right before something happened. In fact, Eddie was beginning to recognize that there were different noises the dog would make depending on the situation. Suddenly, that glimmer of insight turned into a fog of questions.

Why does he only choose certain people to be friendly toward? How is it that he especially chose that Indian? What about when he pretty much pushed me to the trucker's church? For that matter, why did he pick me—a complete stranger—to follow that day at the truck stop in Louisiana instead of all the other people who passed through there before? And those noises he makes. What do they mean?

Struggling to keep his thoughts on track, Eddie recalled what the waitress told him about Radar. The dog used to come in with an old man who was a WWII vet. Another glimmer.

Maybe the dog had military training. It would explain a lot of Radar's regimented behavior along with the Briard traits he'd read. A lot, but not all. There remained far more mystery than fact about the dog. Nevertheless, he was glad to have his company. It made the rides less lonely. He had to chuckle at that one. Three months ago, being lonely wasn't even a thing.

The waitress came over and broke the spell. He ordered breakfast and coffee. As she poured his first cup, he briefly surveyed the room and didn't see anyone he recognized. *Good*, he thought, *not really in the mood for idle chatter today*. Although he had met and made some acquaintances over the past few years, he still preferred his solitude.

His food arrived and Eddie set about enjoying a quiet meal. When he finished, he tossed back the last sip of coffee, dropped some money on the table for the waitress, and headed to the cashier. Glancing out the entry door, sure enough, Radar was at his post. He mentally checked off some boxes and nodded to himself. Sentry trait of the Briard. Possible military training.

Wandering over to the store area, he picked up some food for Radar and a couple of bottles of water, then headed out the door. The dog jumped to attention as Eddie got up to him and heeled along his right side as they headed back toward the truck. He was wagging his tail now because he knew there was food for him. They got into the truck and moved it over to a parking space at the back of plaza area.

Eddie always looked for a safe spot for the dog to eat his meal and drink his water out of a set of dog dishes he had picked up for him.

He was still getting used to the idea of having someone else to care for again. Another change from three weeks ago. Now Eddie checked off a box on a different list. He put that aside for now and looked at the dog in front of him eagerly devouring his meal. All things considered; the dog was pretty low maintenance. The animal seemed to be content with being his companion and didn't seem to have any interest in wandering off anywhere, so he didn't have to worry about him bothering anyone or getting lost. Definitely different from previous dogs he had owned, but it seemed fitting somehow.

As Eddie sat on the curb next to him, his arms propped on his knees pondering the events of the past three weeks and what came next, Radar finished up his meal and then came and sat next to him. He was still deep in thought when Radar took his nose and nuzzled it up under Eddie's right arm as if to say thank you. Somewhat surprised, he reached his arm over his side, gave him a pat on the head, and a good rub on the side. The dog leaned into him. It was the first time the dog showed any real affection toward him.

Bonding behavior, maybe? he wondered. Whatever it was, he felt honored. It was as if Eddie had passed some kind of test or something.

"Yeah, you'll do to ride the fences with," he said, rubbing Radar's head some more. After a few more minutes Eddie decided it was time to go.

"C'mon, dog, let's go find a sight to see." Radar jumped up and seemed happy to hear that news.

When they got back in the truck, Eddie looked up local attractions on his phone and saw that Valley of the Rogue State Park was just up the road about twenty miles. It also had a dog park. He decided that was the place they would stop. He planned to let the big dog have a run for a while and maybe just wander around himself and clear his head. So, they jumped back onto I-5 and headed north for a short 15-minute cruise to the 45B exit to the park. As they idled into the campground entrance, Eddie eased his rig into the parking area and shut the truck down. He sat there for a moment and listened.

"Quiet. Peace and quiet. It's a beautiful thing. Okay, dog, let's go wander." Radar was already at attention ready to do just that.

Eddie decided he would get a room for a couple nights in Grants Pass. Still feeling the effects of the accident, his shoulder and back were feeling old today. He looked over at Radar. "Don't bounce as good as I used to, buddy." The dog just grunted as if in agreement. They both emptied out of the truck and Radar assumed his heeling position on the right. They wandered through the area toward the dog park which seemed empty of other dogs at the moment so he figured this was a good spot.

Eddie thought he would see if the dog responded to commands so he stopped. Motioning, he pointed toward the park and gave him a command.

"Okay, buddy, go on. Have a run and get some exercise. You've earned it." Radar looked up at Eddie as if to say, *are you sure?* Eddie motioned again for him to go and off he went.

"Okay, then. He understood that well enough."

Radar ran in a full gallop, hair blowing back from the wind, down to the park and around the trees and back again around Eddie, and then back to the park and up and down the tree line. He was in his glory. Eddie just watched with a smile. What a regal animal. He walked along with his hands in his pockets, his sunglasses shielding his eyes from brightness and the warmth of the day all around him. The best part? There was no one in his ear talking about this, that, or anything else. Just quiet. It was a good day. A very good day.

Radar came back at his side, tongue hanging out and panting from his romp. He looked thankful for the exercise. From what Eddie remembered reading, these dogs were built to run, work, and protect a herd. It also said they could cover up to fifty miles a day. This romp was barely a warm-up for him.

As they strolled over to the restrooms, he found a beverage machine where he stopped to grab a drink and a water for the dog. Eddie took in the scenery and surveyed the people and surroundings, something he did everywhere he went. "Have an exit strategy in mind and keep an eye out for suspicious activity or people," was his motto. He learned that long ago in the Army and it served him well in a few bars over the years, as he recalled.

Several campers and motor homes of various sizes were parked in their designated slots. Some people had tents and little cook stoves going, others were at picnic tables with kids running around. One lady was by herself at a picnic table reading a book. Other folks were riding bikes around and a couple were backpacking. Going for a day hike, he guessed. There were also a few travelers from the road who stopped to take some pictures and walk around.

One thing that did catch his eye, though, was what appeared to be an all original 1963 Split Window Corvette parked under a shade tree. As an old hot rodder and gearhead from birth, Eddie knew these cars well and enjoyed seeing them whenever he got the chance. The stats started rattling off in his head. *Small block 327, 360 hp, Rochester four-barrel carburetor, four-speed Muncie, independent suspension and Daytona Blue to boot. You don't see that color often. I would love to take that bad boy for a spin. Sucker's got to be worth a fortune. Oh, well, must be nice.*

After getting his drinks, Eddie looked down and was surprised not to see Radar at his side. Now where's he gone off to? He looked around and didn't see him.

At first, there was no sign of the dog anywhere, but then his eyes were again drawn to the picnic table where that lady had been reading a book. Now, though, instead of reading, she was petting and talking to Radar whose tail was happily wagging.

What? Odd behavior indeed for a dog who was usually antisocial.

Curious, Eddie eased over to where they were and heard her talking to him. A good sign. Most animals have good intuition about people. As he got closer, Eddie noticed she was nice looking. Brunette, shoulder-length hair, pretty features, and rather nicely shaped. He also noticed she was not wearing a ring on her left hand. In his age range maybe? He shook the thought off and tossed it aside. Where did that come from? He hadn't looked at another woman since Kate. Besides, he was just passing through.

She noticed him coming up and asked, "Hi. Does he belong to you?"

Eddie smiled broadly. "More like I belong to him."

"Really?"

"Yes, it's a complicated relationship. He just kinda showed up one day and has been with me ever since."

"Interesting," she said.

"Yeah, still trying to figure him out. You know, you must be okay because this is only the second time I've ever seen him go up to anybody and be all happy and tail waggy. He usually tries to avoid people."

"Is that so? Sounds like a pickup line to me."

Eddie stumbled for a second when he realized it did sound like a pickup line.

"Oh, no, ma'am. Not at all. He's only been with me for a month or so now, and besides you and one other person, I'm the only one he seems to have anything to do with. Still not sure why."

"Really?"

"Really. Most antisocial animal I've ever seen. Shies away from everyone even when they try to give him a treat, pet him, or whatever."

"That is unusual," she replied.

"Makes these funny noises, too."

"Oh yeah?"

"Usually for different things or situations. It's weird. And he's got this, this...thing."

"Thing?"

"Yeah, a thing. Like a sixth sense or something."

With that, she marked her place and put her book down. She had noticed Eddie and Radar earlier when she heard the truck pull in and park. She saw the two of them get out together but shrugged it off and went back to her book. Now, though, this story sounded much more interesting. Besides, this fella wasn't half bad-looking and he seemed harmless enough. She was intrigued.

Eddie noticed that she put her book down and realized he had probably invaded her quiet time.

"Look, I'm sorry. I've just been blathering on about silly stuff, not thinking you just came here to get away for some peace and quiet, and here comes some yahoo and his weird dog interrupting your day. I apologize."

"No need. I'm intrigued and would love to hear more. Tell me, Mr...?"

Oh. Sorry. Eddie. Eddie McVane. And this here is Radar."

"Debbie Patterson."

He reached out and they shook hands. She reached over and patted Radar on the head.

"Hiya, Radar. Pleased to meet you." She motioned for Eddie to sit down. "Please, sit with me." As he did, she continued her inquiry. "So, Mr. McVane…"

"Please, Eddie."

"Okay. Eddie. So…you have this dog with a sixth sense, makes funny noises, seems to like only you, and now me. What do you think that means?"

Eddie was sure his dumbfounded look made a sound. Feeling embarrassed now, he looked at her sheepishly and said, "Well, when you put it like that, it does sound kind of like a pickup line." She looked at him with a devilish grin and one eyebrow raised.

"Ya think?"

"Yeah, it is pretty corny, huh?"

She just smiled. It was a pleasant smile and made him feel like he wanted to talk to her some more.

"Look, you'll have to forgive me, I'm a little out of practice here. I haven't had a real conversation with a woman in over three years, other than some of the dispatchers I deal with or to order a meal. I'm a little rusty."

"And why is that?" she asked. Debbie could tell Eddie was a little uncomfortable, but he seemed like a nice enough guy, so she decided to give him a chance and let him collect himself.

"Look, relax. Yes, I came here to get away from the store I run and for some peace and quiet to read my boring book. But it's rare that I have the chance to meet somebody and engage in meaningful conversation especially about such a unique dog as yours. Usually, it's just the local gossip and politics. There has to be a good story there. So, let's hear it. What *is* your story, Mr. Eddie McVane? It has to be better than this book I'm reading. At least, I hope it is."

She put her hands on the table, looked him in the eyes, and jokingly said, "Please tell me it is."

Eddie rocked backward a little and chuckled. *Well,* he thought, *she has a great sense of humor. Sounds like she can hold her own.*

"Wow, no pressure there," he began. "Well, it all started when I asked my friend Jimmy to hop up my truck a little bit and then..." Eddie went from the immediate present to the distant past, telling Debbie all about his growing up in North Carolina, his and Jimmy's racing days, and back to the present. Of course, he left out the part about Morgana, the fire-breathing truck, Jimmy's green diesel energy scam, and some of the more colorful situations he had been involved in recently. That might be deal breaker.

But what was he doing here anyway? He wasn't looking for a girlfriend or even a relationship. Still, she was fun to talk to so far. Actually, as he told her, she *was* the first woman he had been this close to in almost three years.

Debbie listened intently as Eddie told her about himself and finally, how he lost his wife of over thirty years. She could tell it bothered him to talk about it and could see his mood darken somewhat when he mentioned Russell Cortland's name. Unbeknownst to Eddie, Debbie understood that mood very well.

She steered the conversation back to his son and asked how he was doing. Eddie perked back up. She found herself enjoying his company and his story. Eddie had a gentle and easy way about him. He seemed like a genuinely nice guy, something Debbie didn't think existed anymore, and she found herself feeling unusually comfortable with him.

"He's doing great!" Eddie exclaimed. "Junior works at a computer tech company in Charlotte, North Carolina, and the grandkids are also doing great. My granddaughter wants to be a model and my grandson wants to be a professional fisherman."

"Really. That's great," Debbie replied. She could see him swell with pride at that.

"Oh, yeah, that boy fishes every chance he gets."

Eddie noticed he was talking more to this woman today than he had to all the people he had met in the past three years. Oddly, he felt very comfortable talking to her. Come to think of it, she was the only other person he had shared his story with about Kate besides Jimmy.

He noticed how sincerely Debbie offered her condolences when he told her about Kate. She also seemed to understand and respect his reasoning for not telling Junior about the incident with Russell Cortland, but still thought Eddie should tell him at some point. It didn't hurt matters at all that she was amazed at the story of Radar saving them both and how they had come to be at the park today.

Finally, Debbie sat back and said, "Wow. You certainly did not disappoint me, sir. You have been through a lot. My book is not nearly as interesting."

"Yeah, it's been a wild ride, for sure." Eddie took a moment to look around for Radar. "Did you see where the dog went?"

"Here he is," Debbie said and motioned sideways and down with her head.

"Huh?" Eddie said and then looked under the table where she was looking. Sure enough, there was Radar, passed out and sound asleep. "Well, we must be boring to listen to."

Satisfied that Radar was accounted for, Eddie turned to her and said, "Okay, your turn. What's Ms. Debbie Patterson's story?"

"Well, mine isn't nearly as colorful as yours, but here goes," Debbie replied and set out matching Eddie in depth and coverage of her life.

As she talked, Eddie found himself taking in all her features. Her hazel eyes, her soft complexion and auburn hair, and how it bounced on her shoulders when she moved her head. She laughed easily and had a great smile. He liked how animated she was as she described her childhood growing up in Arkansas with three brothers and a younger sister, and their antics. Debbie told him of her dad's lumber business, her mom's great cooking, her grandparents, and the large

Patterson family gatherings. She has two children—a son and a daughter—both grown and with families of their own, and they visit often.

She had her share of hard times as well. losing one brother in an industrial accident. After that, her family grew even closer with Debbie's sister moving next door to her parents, while the other two brothers took over the family lumber business which they run to this day. They, like Eddie, also raced cars when they were younger. That made him perk up a bit and smile which Debbie noticed. She paused for a second and said, "Yeah, I figured you'd like that part."

Eddie kept smiling because now he knew she would not be put off by his likes and interests. Plus, he had an in with her brothers. Always a good thing for the family to like you. Then he caught himself. What am I doing? None of this matters. I'm just passing through, and in a week, this chance encounter will be no different than exchanging pleasantries while standing in line at the next diner we hit. Then he looked again at Debbie and thought how maybe it did matter.

With that, Radar stirred and made sort of a cooing sound. Debbie and Eddie both stopped, looked at each other, and then leaned down slowly to check under the table. All they saw, though, was a dog peacefully sleeping like a perfect angel.

They shared a quiet laugh and Debbie resumed. She told Eddie how her husband took a job in Oregon and moved the family here twenty-some years ago. Although she wasn't keen on the idea in the beginning, she went along anyway, doing her "wifely duty" to make the best of it.

After the kids got married and moved out, she started a knickknack/souvenir shop in Grants Pass. By this point, she was happy enough until one day she discovered that her husband had been having an affair with a younger woman at his company. For four years!

"Uh-oh," said Eddie. "Not good."

"No, not good," she snapped.

He could see the fire in her eyes as she told her story. Eddie understood that feeling well. "So, what did you do next?" he asked

She softened a little and looked away for a moment, then said, "Well, I cried. A lot. Felt stupid. A lot. Cursed. A lot. Broke stuff. A whole lot."

Eddie grinned at how even through this she kept her sense of humor.

"Cried some more. Broke some more stuff. Then I just sort of shut down. I literally could not get out of bed for almost a month. I just laid there and felt sorry and miserable."

"And then?" he asked.

Debbie leaned in toward him and her brow furrowed. "And then I got pissed!"

Hoo boy! Eddie thought. *One would do well not to get on this girl's bad side.*

"So, is he still breathing?"

She eased back and grinned. "Oh, yeah. Lord knows, I wanted to choke the life out of that two-timing SOB, but I did him one better. I got the best lawyer I could find and cleaned out his wallet to the bone!"

"Touché," Eddie said.

"Not only that," she added, "I took his most prized possession."

"Yeah, what was that?"

"See that old Corvette over there?"

Eddie glanced over at the Vette he'd noticed in the parking lot.

"No way!" he exclaimed, then gave her a high-five. "Way to go." She smiled with that mischievous smile Eddie already loved seeing.

"I drive it every chance I get, right by his office," she proudly told Eddie.

"Good for you."

"Yeah, he still tries to buy it back from me through other people, but I tell them I will be buried with that car." She gave Eddie a knowing look.

"Well, serves him right." Eddie laughed. Then he got serious. "I'm sorry that stuff happened to you. It must have been hard, for sure. But I can see you're a fighter and not one to stay down for long. A rare quality these days. Ya done good," he concluded.

Debbie smiled. "Why, thank you. That's very sweet of you to say."

Wow! Eddie thought. *This girl has some moxie.* He liked that. A lot.

They chatted for another hour or so exchanging stories and a few laughs. Finally, Debbie looked at her phone and realized she still had errands to do.

"Oh, my, I forgot all about a hair appointment," she said with a more than a trace of disappointment.

"Oops. My bad," said Eddie.

"No, no, that's okay. I have thoroughly enjoyed our conversation. It's been very refreshing, actually."

"Same here," said Eddie.

"Well, you did very well, Eddie McVane. For someone who hasn't talked to a girl in three years, you did good. I was very entertained."

"Cool! Can I use you as a reference?"

She laughed out loud and lightly touched his arm.

"C'mon," Eddie said. "I'll walk you to your car."

"Sure," she said cheerfully.

Radar assumed his position at Eddie's right side. The three of them strolled leisurely in the warmth of the day toward where the Corvette was parked while Debbie and Eddie chatted some more along the way. Eddie wasn't sure what he was doing or feeling now. He had mixed emotions about being this close to another woman. It somehow felt natural to be with her, though. Was this right? Could he possibly care for someone else again? He didn't know. He still felt broken inside, but for some reason, he liked being with her. He didn't understand what he was feeling, but couldn't seem to help himself.

When they got to the car, he looked away and then back at her, smiling sheepishly.

"Um, look, I'm not very good at this sort of thing, and again, it has been a long time, but I sure would like to take you to dinner. I mean, that is, if you don't think I'm being too forward?"

She looked at him thoughtfully for a moment, then replied, "Not forward at all. A little soon maybe but…"

Eddie held up his hand before she could finish.

"I know, we just met and all, but I don't know, sounds weird maybe, but I thought maybe, you know, just a nice dinner. Besides, I don't know about you but at my age, courtship times have narrowed quite a bit in recent years. Time is definitely not on my side. Besides, you wouldn't want to disappoint the dog. I mean, after all, this meeting was kind of his idea."

Debbie laughed and smiled a wondering smile at him.

"Well, when you put it like that, how can a girl resist? Besides, I didn't know I was being courted."

Eddie smiled sheepishly again.

"Yeah, it was kind of a surprise to me, too."

Pausing for a moment, studying Eddie, who looked totally out of his element, and somewhat panicked, she replied by looking at the dog, "Well, we wouldn't want that to happen now, would we, Radar?" Kneeling down, she cupped his face in her hands and rubbed his cheeks. He was wagging his tail and very much enjoying the treatment.

When Debbie stood up, she looked at him with that mischievous smile and then asked, "You like steak?"

Eddie looked at her with an incredulous stare. "Seriously?" he replied "I'm a guy. We kill things and burn them to perfection on the grill, so yeah, I'd say I like steak."

She chuckled. "Kinda figured that out about you. There is this nice little place in Grants Pass called One Fifteen Broiler. It's at 115 Northwest D Street. Think you can find your way there by seven o'clock?"

"If I can't, I'll sell this truck off and buy me a cab company so I can."

She shook her head and smiled at him. "You are a piece of work, Eddie McVane. Okay. Seven it is. I'll be waiting."

"It's a deal."

She got in the Corvette and looked up at him with that smile he couldn't get enough of.

"No, it's a date."

"Right. Date. Got it."

She just shook her head, chuckling as she drove off.

He and Radar watched Debbie as she drove out of the parking lot. She waved and Eddie waved back. He wasn't sure how or what he was feeling, and wondered what he was doing, but compared to all the craziness he had been subjected to over the past several weeks, today was by far the best he had felt about life in a long time. He was going on a date! He looked down at Radar thoughtfully for a moment.

"Well, I guess we'll have to add 'Matchmaker' to your resume as well." The dog looked up at him, still wagging his tail, and grunted.

"Well said, my newfound weird companion, well said." They turned and strolled back toward the truck. Halfway there, suddenly it dawned on Eddie that he didn't have any dress clothes for such an occasion. He hadn't been out of jeans in years. And why would he be? He hadn't any inclination for such a thing until just moments ago. A little panic set in, but he pushed it back.

"No, I can do this. It's just a dinner date. Dog, I need to upgrade the exterior. This lady deserves a little class, wouldn't you say?" Radar grunted again.

"You're right. A trip to the men's store it is then, Matchmaker. Good advice, for a dog."

Chapter Fifteen
It's Okay to Be Okay

On the drive to the salon and throughout her hair appointment, Debbie was somewhat nervous and strangely excited at the same time. She hadn't been on a date in a very long time and here she was getting ready for one with a man she only met a few hours before. She couldn't recall ever doing that. Truthfully, she had not met anyone recently who even sparked mild interest and the few dinner dates she had early on with some of the local men after her divorce were basically non-events.

Sure, she had gotten over her husband's infidelity long ago, but Debbie also knew that everybody around had heard the story and formed their own opinions, and not always with her in the best light. She briefly considered moving back home to Arkansas with her family, but aside from leaving her children who were settled in the area, Debbie Patterson refused to be intimidated or shamed for something her husband did. He may have thought he was getting away with something at the time, but in the end it was she who won the day. It didn't feel like a victory at all to her, but then, vindication rarely does.

The sting of deceit and the pain of heartbreak lingers long after such episodes in one's life and Debbie still felt traces of it. She was disappointed in some of her friends who she felt had to know or at least had heard something about her husband and could have passed the news on to her. As a result, Debbie's circle of friends had gotten considerably smaller since that time. So, too, had her capacity to trust people making it somewhat—no, extremely—puzzling to her why she accepted a dinner date from a total stranger.

Eddie McVane seemed like a nice enough guy and he was certainly pleasant to talk to. Debbie felt oddly comfortable with him almost from the start. That was something she hadn't felt in many years. Of course, she being an animal lover, and Eddie having such an interesting dog didn't hurt, either.

She decided to keep an open mind about it for now. No sense in judging this man for something her ex-husband had done or herself for jumping into the date. For tonight, she would just try to enjoy an innocent dinner and some agreeable male company. She hadn't really been looking for anybody anyway and had resolved to be single the rest of her life, so she didn't have anything to lose. Yes, she resolved they had hit it off, and that should mean, if nothing else, a nice evening out.

Then, remembering their conversation earlier, a few things stuck in the back of Debbie's mind like, for one, Eddie used to race stock cars. Her brothers used to race back around that time as well. Maybe they knew of him. *Slim chance*, she thought. They did do some traveling to race, but she couldn't remember where. She would call her brother Danny another time and ask him. Also, Eddie's partner was into research and development. She wondered what kind.

Debbie tossed all that aside. Right now, it was about the most important thing—what to wear. Well, he doesn't seem to be a fancy kind of guy, so maybe something middle of the road. A white camisole blouse with a black jacket? Black slacks? She fussed over what shoes to wear and settled on black ankle boots. Now, jewelry. Not too much, just some earrings, a bracelet, and that broach Grandma Patterson gave me.

She laid out her outfit for the evening and felt it was appropriate. Satisfied that her clothes were set, Debbie puttered around the house for a while and did some chores trying to take her mind off things, but mostly anticipated the evening. She called her daughter and decided to share the news with her. Debbie's son was a different story because he continued to be upset with her thinking she should have tried to work it out with his father. She would forgo that conversation for another day.

The voice on the other end of the phone was excited. "That's great, Mom. I am so happy for you. It's about time you got out and enjoyed yourself." Debbie's daughter had worried for some time that all her mother did was work and act as a recluse. She couldn't blame her for burying herself in the little knickknack shop and rarely going anywhere after the divorce, but that didn't mean it was okay.

"Well, he is a truck driver," Debbie explained, "and just passing through, but I believe he is a good guy. He lost his wife three years ago and has been alone ever since. Anyway, it's just dinner. I'm not sure I'll ever see him again."

"Just dinner, huh? Seems like Mr. Just Dinner must have made some impression on you to get you out of the house. That says something right there. And you never know. So, what's he look like?"

"Well, he's in his sixties, but still looks good. Salt-and-pepper hair, mustache, well groomed, nice tan, still has a good physique, I mean, a little paunch but solid looking. Seems easygoing and has a good sense of humor."

"Jeeze, Mom, you're not buying a horse." They both laughed. Jenny was glad to hear her mother laugh so freely for the first time in a long time. She was truly happy for her. "Mom, just go have a good time. You deserve to be happy. But call me with the details."

"I will. Love you."

Debbie was excited but cautious. She didn't want to get her hopes up too much, but she knew she'd be disappointed if their chemistry didn't carry over into the evening. They clicked and she liked the feeling. *Wait*, she thought, *what am I doing? Why am I fussing so much? Am I wanting more than a date?* She scolded herself. "It's just dinner. Nothing more. He's a nice guy but just passing through. Go have a few laughs and relax. Don't make a big deal out of this."

She checked her phone. It was 4:30. "What am I going to do for two and a half hours?" Now, she was anxious for the time to go by. Debbie Patterson couldn't remember the last time that happened.

****

Eddie found a Men's Wearhouse in Medford, Oregon, and while Radar posted himself outside, he went in and began browsing. Suddenly it occurred to him that he'd never gone to a men's clothing store without Kate. Now Eddie started to panic, not knowing where to begin. Fortunately, a middle-aged classy looking salesman with graying hair, glasses, and a British accent came to his rescue.

"May I help you, sir? My name is Robert."

"I hope so, Robert. I haven't had to dress up in years. Now, suddenly, I not only have to dress up, but it's for a dinner date tonight with a really nice lady and frankly, I don't have a clue where to start." The salesman looked him up and down, taking in his rugged features, plaid shirt, jeans, and cowboy boots.

"Well, I've worked with worse," came the reply. "Come with me, I will see what I can do."

Eddie frowned while following the salesman to a desk. "Thanks, I think."

Robert grabbed a measuring tape and began sizing him. First his chest, then arms and neck, and finally his waist and inseam. He stepped back and looked at Eddie again. With one arm folded across his chest and the other arm resting on it, chin in his hand, Robert tapped his index finger on his lips just studying Eddie. Finally he asked "Can you describe this woman to me and what she was wearing?"

Somewhat taken off guard, Eddie tried to respond as best he could remember. "Um, well, she's pretty, shoulder-length hair, brunette, tan complexion, hazel eyes, nice smile. Looks classy, actually. She had jeans, a very nice pink shirt, a polo I think."

"Shoes?"

"Sandals." Eddie put his hands in his pockets and smugly smiled at the salesman, feeling proud of himself for remembering so many details.

Robert returned Eddie's smile with a frown before responding. "Do you remember what kind of jewelry she was wearing?"

Eddie thought for a moment. "Um, a bracelet and a watch, I think. Also, earrings and some kind of necklace."

"Mmm," came Robert's response. "So, if she is wearing that much jewelry casually, she obviously cares very much about her appearance and balances her outfits out. She will, no doubt, do the same with a dinner outfit. You are going to need a complete makeover. Let's see if we can smooth out some of those rough edges for her."

Motioning for him to follow him, Robert took Eddie over to the pants, then the shirts. Once done there, he fitted him with a blazer. Then a belt, socks, and shoes. Eddie waved off the idea of a tie.

"Not happening, Sport."

More frowning. "One can always hope, sir."

When he was done, Robert, the British salesman, had transformed Eddie, the North Carolina trucker, into a respectable-looking gentleman. Glancing in the mirror, Eddie saw a stately looking business-type guy. Dark-blue blazer, light-blue small checked button-down oxford shirt, gray slacks, black belt, and black loafers.

"Not too shabby, Robert. I barely recognize myself. Think she'll like it?"

"With all due respect, sir. You came in here looking like an extra from your *Dukes of Hazzard* TV show. Even at that, she accepted your offer for a dinner date so there must have been something she liked behind that rough exterior. Yes, sir. I think she will be impressed."

Eddie gave him a squinting glance. "That's a sideways compliment if ever I heard one. But...I'll take it. Sold. Bag it, tag it, and ship it, Robert."

"Very good, sir. You have truly made my day."

After leaving the store, Eddie gathered up Radar and headed to the motel for a shower and a chance to plan out his evening. As he was shaving, he took stock of his appearance. He didn't remember looking that old. Grayer, more wrinkles, a little more paunch. "When did that happen?" He tried sucking in his stomach. "Maybe an extra notch on that new belt." Eddie was nervous and anxious at the same time. He wasn't sure what he was doing and felt a little uncomfortable going through all this fuss to have a dinner date with a strange woman he just met. Albeit a very nice-looking and very pleasant woman.

He also felt a little guilty, almost like he was cheating on his late wife. It had been three years, after all. He should move on. But how does a person do that? Eddie hadn't really thought about it much till today. He figured he was going to be alone for the rest of his life so why spend time thinking about it? Yet, suddenly, here he was a couple of hours away from more than thinking, and he was starting to feel like it was too much, too fast.

The only way he was able to break his doubts and relax was to tell himself that no matter what he was feeling, dinner was, at most, a first step. He convinced himself that it didn't mean anything more despite how great he felt when he was with Debbie before, and how many butterflies he felt swirling around his stomach now. Clearly a case of overthinking it all when he really just wanted to enjoy some pleasant female company for once, and have a nice dinner.

Besides, he already got a new suit of clothes out of the deal and they had to be worn somewhere. Satisfied he now had everything under control, Eddie hung up his new outfit and finished what he was doing. He threw on a T-shirt and a pair of jeans, and got some food and water together for the dog.

He went out and sat down on the curb next to Radar as he ate. Eddie chatted at him as he thought about the events of the day. He also thought about all the events leading up to this moment and how Radar fit into them.

"So, you have a sense about people, do ya? How do you do that? How do you know?"

The dog ignored him and kept eating.

"Trade secret, eh? Don't blame ya. Probably best I don't know anyway. I've got enough to deal with." As Eddie sat there, he again thought about what the old Indian said:

"The sign of the wolf is good."

"What does that mean?"

"His spirit will guide your spirit."

"Whose spirit?"

He looked at Radar. "Was he talking about you? Are you my guide or something? And if so, where are we going?"

Radar did glance up at him briefly then went back to eating. Watching the dog, Eddie pondered some more out loud. "Well, you did save my butt in Louisiana. And you seemed to know about that guy losing his brakes on the mountain before he came on the CB. And now this. Never in a million years did I plan on meeting a woman and dressing up like this for a dinner date. As a matter of fact, there are a lot of things here lately that seem to be out of the norm."

He thought back to the sermon at the trucker's church. *Was that a sign as well?* It was all kind of weird and puzzling to Eddie. He had heard stories of such things happening, but never really thought much about them. Not that he didn't believe they were possible, just that none ever happened to him…that he could think of.

That reminded him that the Indian seemed to be predicting things about the future in some parts:

"There is a great battle coming. Some braves will die."

"What kind of battle? Who are the braves that die? I must not be afraid to go higher? I must be swifter than the eagle in that day. What does all that mean?"

He did understand the *"heart heavy with sorrow"* part. But what did he mean by, *"What was done in darkness will be brought into the light."*

Finally, he shook his head. "Enough already. As of right now, I am officially off duty. I am going to do my best to enjoy the evening and not think about any of this stuff. I need a break. I have to remember to not say anything stupid, not bump into the furniture, and try to remember which is the salad fork."

"I can do this," he said looking at Radar. The dog just grunted a reply. "Okay, I'll take that as a 'No sweat, Eddie, my man. You got this.' Thanks, buddy. I feel inspired." He looked at his phone. It was 4:30. Two and a half hours suddenly seemed like an eternity.

****

Eddie called the cab company and asked for a car to be at the motel at 6:30. It was a short drive to the restaurant so that should be perfect timing. As he was getting dressed, he looked in the mirror and thought about the moment at hand and the past three years leading up to tonight. All he did for those three years was live in his memories and the pain of all he had lost. He finally capitulated by realizing—

211

more like resigning himself—that his life was as good as it was ever going to get and nothing more.

Then, out of nowhere came the past three weeks where suddenly he's driving the truck of the future designed by his best friend, has a team of computer nerds to look after the truck, picks up a dog (or the other way around) and now, a dinner date with a woman he met just hours ago. Eddie could only shake his head at himself in the mirror.

"Not at all what I had in mind this weekend. I must be crazy. But, *at the moment,* it feels pretty good. Maybe Jimmy's right. Maybe it's time to move on."

Eddie wasn't sure how to do that but he would give it a try. *Besides,* he thought, *what harm could come from having dinner with an attractive woman?* Admittedly, he was more comfortable driving at 150-plus mph in an oversized hot rod than getting ready for this date.

He checked the time: 6:15. "Taxi should be here anytime now." He checked the mirror for a final fit-and-finish look before going outside. As he stepped out the door, Radar stood to attention and cocked his head at Eddie, seemingly not sure what he was seeing.

"What's the matter? Never seen a guy in a suit before?" He walked up to the dog who seemed curious about his wardrobe, sniffing and making sure it was him. "So, what am I supposed to do with you? I don't guess you would stay here and keep an eye on things?" Just then the taxi pulled up. As Eddie moved toward the car, the dog moved with him. When he opened the door Radar got in and Eddie followed.

Guess that answers that, he thought. The cab driver looked at the two of them and smiled. He seemed amused at the pairing of Eddie, all dressed up like a business executive, and Radar, shaggy-haired and taking up a majority of the back seat.

"Where to?"

"One-fifteen Northwest D Street."

"Ah, One-Fifteen Broiler. Good food, nice atmosphere."

"Good to know." As they drove along, the driver kept looking in the mirror at Radar. Finally, his curiosity got the best of him. "Is he some kind of service dog or something?" Eddie smiled mischievously.

"No, he's my wing man. Helps me get girls."

That got a laugh. "Really?"

"Oh, yeah. Best chick magnet I've ever had. Look at that face. Women swoon over him. He's like Elvis with fur. Got me a date for tonight."

The driver cracked up. "That's awesome, man. I need to get me one of them. You wouldn't rent him out, would ya?"

"Hadn't thought about it but maybe. Let me consult with my associate." He looked at Radar. "Whadda ya say, buddy? We could make some extra money on the side? Get you that new high-tech dog dish with the automatic dispenser you've been wanting." Radar just looked at Eddie, grunted, and gave a low, "Erph."

"Ah, yeah. He says thanks, but he is currently engaged in prior commitments."

"I understand. Well, if he ever gets freed up, tell him to call me."

"I'll make a note." Eddie grinned. They chatted back and forth on the way. Eddie was trying his best to not be nervous, but the truth was, he felt like a teenager on a first date.

****

Debbie finished getting ready with the last few swipes of the hairbrush and a couple of adjustments to her blouse and blazer. She looked once more in the mirror, then at her phone, and decided it was time. She grabbed her purse and headed out the door.

Driving to the restaurant, the butterflies in her stomach would not quit and she scolded herself for being so nervous. "Relax. It's just dinner. You've had dinner out before. You can do this." She found a parking spot and headed toward the entrance. Checking her watch, she was ten minutes early and stopped to wait in the lobby.

A few moments later, the taxi carrying Eddie and Radar pulled up. The driver turned to Eddie and said, "Here you go, pal. One-Fifteen Broiler."

Eddie nodded and paid him the fare plus a good tip.

"Thanks, man," said the driver. "Don't forget me if your friend decides to expand his services."

Eddie pointed at him and then reached across Radar for the door handle.

Inside, Debbie was taken aback—pleasantly—when they got out and she saw Eddie dressed in a sport coat, shirt, and slacks. He looked like an entirely different man. *Very nice*, she thought and watched with amusement while Eddie was talking to Radar as if giving him last-minute instructions. For a second, she was sure the dog had tossed his head toward the door as if to say, "Stop stalling and get in there. I know what I'm doing out here." Then she shook her head, blinked quickly a few times, and told herself to calm down and stop imagining things.

214

As they stood outside, Eddie looked down at Radar and said, "Okay, I suppose you will find a spot that suits you, so do what you do. I guess I should be glad you're not my mother, otherwise, this would be a very awkward first date. I look good, though, right?" The dog seemed to nod his head slightly before he grunted which stopped Eddie for a second before he finally said, "Well, wish me luck."

He turned and headed in. As Eddie went through the door, Debbie was there like she said, waiting for him in the lobby. She looked at him with a welcoming smile.

"Wow!" she exclaimed. "You do clean up well. You look very distinguished and handsome."

Eddie, too, was quite taken by Debbie's appearance. She looked very classy and seemed even prettier than at the park. He took a deep breath and smiled back at her.

"Thank you," he said. "You look very nice as well. And very striking, I might add. Shall we?"

He motioned toward the door and offered his arm. Debbie blushed a little, smiled, and accepted the offer, putting her hand under his arm. He felt solid and secure.

As they walked along toward the dining room, Eddie was trying not to be overwhelmed with the moment. He had not been with another woman in thirty years since he first dated Kate, and after she was gone, had not given any thought to seeing anyone else let alone having dinner with a complete stranger. That is, until today. He still wasn't sure what he was doing but for some reason he felt compelled to follow through, and Debbie's arm in his did feel gentle and caring.

The waitress showed them to their table. Eddie thanked her and moved to pull out Debbie's chair for her to which she said sweetly,

"Thank you." She was still cautious in her mind but did admit to herself that she liked being fussed over and treated like a lady. It had been a long time.

"I must admit, I am really impressed. I didn't expect this," Debbie said once they were both seated. Eddie knew she wasn't talking about the restaurant.

"Well, admittedly, I am a little rusty and maybe just a little nervous. As for the clothes, I did have some help from a snooty guy with a British accent named Robert. We won't be going to the races together anytime soon, but he did seem knowledgeable about what it takes to groom a Neanderthal like myself and make me presentable."

She laughed. "Well, it was very nice of you to go to all the trouble. I would have had dinner with you either way, Caveman."

Eddie was taking in all her features and enjoying the moment. Debbie was a good-looking woman—no, a *beautiful* woman—with class, grace, and an easy way about her that made him feel comfortable. Her confidence and strength showed in the way she carried herself. He began to relax some, feeling more like he could be himself.

"Well, thank you, but be advised, I am still just a regular guy under all this and I drive a truck, so I apologize in advance." Smiling, she gave him a look that let him know he need not apologize for anything.

"You forget, I grew up in the country with three brothers in the lumber business, and their race cars and their trucks and all that goes along with that. I doubt there is much you can surprise me with or make me run off in the opposite direction. How about, let's just enjoy the moment and pick up where we left off in the park? Like you said earlier, at our age, time is not our friend."

Eddie sat back in his chair and looked at her with an amused smile. He liked her direct approach and honesty. He found it refreshing and reminded him somewhat of Kate, although he cautioned himself in making comparisons. Debbie had just the right amount of sass for him.

"I agree," he told her. "I think sometimes we get so caught up in the preparation of things that we tend to overlook the moment. Now, about that steak."

The waitress returned and they ordered their drinks—wine for her and beer for him—along with salad, steak, and baked potato. Then it was more talk about each other's marriage and kids, the ups and downs, and all that goes along with life. They had indeed picked up where they left off earlier.

While Eddie was listening to her at one point, his eye caught the broach on the lapel of her jacket. It was the likeness of a wolf. Just then the old Indian's words echoed in his head: *"The sign of the wolf is good. Do not be afraid. It will be well with you."* Eddie leaned forward a bit and looked again at the broach. He felt almost drawn to it. The question formed in his mind. He wondered if this was what the old Indian was referring to.

When she paused, he commented on it. "That's an interesting piece of jewelry."

Debbie looked down at the broach and touched it. "It was my grandmother's," she said proudly. "She gave it to me when I was little girl. She was part Indian and had all these saying and beliefs. She used to tell me all kinds of stories about spirit animals and how they would guide and protect you. She said this one would protect me. I never did think much about all that, but I wear it because it reminds me of her. I have always been fascinated by wolves. They have such a mysterious quality about them and an amazing social structure."

As Debbie was telling him of her grandmother and her interest in wolves, Eddie found himself enjoying listening to her talk and watching her eyes sparkle while describing certain things. He didn't realize how much he missed conversations like this. He also marveled at how this woman, this strange beautiful woman he barely knew yet felt such a connection with, happened to have a grandmother who was part Indian and gave her a wolf broach that she just happened to wear on their date.

With that, a sound reached his ear that he swore was one of Radar's mysterious grunts. Eddie slightly turned his head, half expecting to see the dog had somehow found his way into the dining room. Instead, he saw that someone at a nearby table had just picked up his phone. Must have an odd ringtone, Eddie concluded.

Debbie was curious why Eddie seemed so interested in the broach, noticing he kept glancing at it while she spoke to him. Aside from that, he was charming, funny, and refreshingly honest. Although she put her head in "protection mode" as a fail safe to not be taken advantage of, her heart was not listening very well. She was mentally scolding herself to remain aloof and be objective. *He's a nice guy, but he is just passing through. Don't get yourself in a tizzy.* Unfortunately, her defenses were failing miserably.

****

After a while, the conversation came around to Eddie talking about his partnership with Jimmy and the high-tech truck he built.

"Yeah, this thing is crazy. I mean, I am still learning how everything works."

Debbie seemed genuinely interested and asked him to tell her more.

"I didn't look very hard at it when I first saw it either, so it seemed pretty normal to me. I mean, you saw it at the park. Looks like a lot of other trucks you see on the road. Maybe a bit newer and shinier, but not like it's something from outer space. The thing is, though, it is definitely not like other trucks. Jimmy went through a lot of trouble to keep it stock-appearing for that reason."

Eddie then shared with Debbie a few of the truck's innovations, but left out the speed and stealth part. She may have grown up with racing brothers, but there's no telling how she would respond to him doing 150 mph+ on the highway let alone doing that kind of speed while being invisible to radar. Those aren't things you just throw out there to the casual listener. At least not on the first date.

"Wow. Those things sound like science fiction. That's amazing," She said and then started listing what Eddie did tell her. "Gyroscopic stability control? Night vision glass? Inflating walls to keep the cargo in place so you can whip through turns like you're in a sports car? And they all really work?"

"Oh, yeah. They work great." Now it was Eddie's turn to be proud.

"Pretty much my role at the moment is to see how this stuff works in the real world. The goal is to perfect these things for the future of the industry. I have this team of nerds that monitors everything going on with the unit and tells me what needs adjusting. A lot of it is geek speak to me, but we manage to work it out. They're good kids and they worked hard to build all this technology into this thing for the future."

Debbie was curious, but didn't want to seem intrusive. "So, is this what you do now? Test drive experimental trucks?"

Eddie thought about that for a moment. He shifted in his seat a little, not sure how to answer the question, but he felt like he could be up-front with her.

"You know, to be honest with you, up until Jimmy talked me into driving this thing, I hadn't really had a plan for the past three years. I just drove to put the bad behind me. I went from here to there and back again, not really caring what day it was or what was going on in the world. About the only non-driving thing I did was go see the grandkids for a bit and then get right back on the road."

Debbie understood that feeling well. No longer caring or feeling or having a direction. Just trying to find a reason to get up in the morning. But she was determined not to let her ex or the past beat her down and make her miserable. She was going to live life to the fullest despite those people and things. It sounded more and more like she and Eddie had a lot in common.

"Well," she said, "it sounds like driving this truck is a chance at a new beginning. Is it something you want to do?"

"Yes, very much so. It is exciting, definitely not boring. Plus, this team of tech nerds seems to have adopted me. Gave me a plaque and everything."

"Really? That must have made you feel pretty good." She enjoyed how Eddie was obviously quite fond of the team.

"Yes, it did, actually." Eddie beamed. "Not sure what to do with all of it yet. I guess I'm still getting used to the idea of having a team of people involved in driving a truck. Not to mention having a new sidekick. I'm still not sure what to make of him."

"It sounds like you got your hands full for somebody that was just trying to coast along. So what's next do you think?" Admittedly, and despite herself, Debbie was fishing for what he had in mind for the future.

Eddie looked down at his drink for a couple of seconds and then back at her.

"I honestly don't know," he said carefully, understanding all the good so far between them could be crushed here. "I didn't really plan for or expect any of it. I guess I'm kind of going with the flow."

She turned her head slightly as she looked him in the eyes.

"I think you still have more life left in you than you think, Eddie McVane. I think you love the challenge and the excitement that goes along with it. I understand some of what you're going through. I didn't think I would ever be able to face people again after what my husband did. I lost friends. I felt ashamed and foolish. But I refused to let it beat me. I didn't do anything wrong and neither did you.

"You reacted honestly to a situation that somebody else caused. If you don't mind me saying, I don't know anything about your wife other than what you've told me, but I have to believe she wouldn't have blamed you if she lived. Deep down, I think you know that, too.

"Look, I can see you're a decent guy. I think you've been given a second chance and I believe you should take advantage of it. Not everybody is that lucky. I know it's difficult, but learning to forgive yourself is the first step. That's the hardest part."

Eddie sat motionless as he pondered on what Debbie said. He had seen there were a lot of signs pointing in that direction, but couldn't seem to be able to get through the door. Now, she opened up that door a little more for him. She was also 100 percent correct: Kate would be right there, in his ear, telling him to get his head out of his butt and get back in the game. Still, it was hard to let go because he felt letting go any of it also meant letting go of Kate.

As this ran through his head, Eddie looked at her and realized something was different inside him. He felt it as she was finishing her thought, but then pushed it away so he could think. Now it was back and couldn't be pushed away. For the first time since, well, since before Kate passed, Eddie felt comforted. And he liked it.

Snapping back to reality, Eddie was again drawn to the wolf broach and just as before, the Indian's words echoed as clear as the day he said them: *"Do not be afraid. It will be well with you."*

Debbie noticed he was quiet. "I hope I wasn't out of line," she said hopefully.

"Not at all. Thank you for that insight. It's just that I have not really talked with anybody else about this besides Jimmy." Now Eddie was concerned he may have allowed matters to get the best of him.

"I'm sorry, this was supposed to be a fun evening and here I go and throw a wet blanket on everything." He was visibly distressed.

Debbie countered and reassured him he was doing a good thing by talking about it.

"No, I think it's good that you are talking about it. I know from my own experience that being able to finally get it out and off your chest is best. It's a good thing, Eddie. You're not throwing a wet blanket on anything. You and I have both been broken and beat up a little by life but we're still here and we're still kicking. Aren't you tired of carrying that baggage around? Don't you think it's time to let the wound heal and stop picking at it? It's okay to be okay, you know. There is nothing wrong with that."

Eddie looked at her thoughtfully and was thankful for the moment. He couldn't remember the last time he felt that kind of peace about the subject.

"I know you're right," he replied "I just haven't taken the time nor had the opportunity to sit down and do that. Thank you for understanding and for your insight."

Debbie knew she had to continue while she had his attention. "It takes time, and some days are better than others, but you keep moving forward. I think, deep down, we all know what we have to do, but it helps to hear it from someone else. I had someone tell me the same thing one day and it set the wheels in motion for me."

Eddie was thinking how happy he was for this dinner date. It was indeed eye-opening. He wasn't sure the wolf prophecy had anything to do with it, but he was glad nonetheless.

They sat a while longer, but the restaurant was thinning out and they knew it was time to go. Eddie made the observation. "Well, I guess it's time. Looks like they are running us out. I have enjoyed the dinner and the company, very much."

"Likewise. It was a very nice evening."

He paid the bill and they headed out. He held the door for her and followed her out. As they went outside, Debbie saw Radar stand at attention and wait patiently for them. She went over and gave him her now customary cheek rub and pat on the head. "Such a good boy."

She turned and looked at Eddie. "Seems our chaperone is ready to escort us to our next adventure." Radar wagged his tail though neither noticed.

Eddie looked at her with his hands in his pockets, not sure what to do except that he wasn't ready for the date to end. He finally asked, "Um, want to go for a walk? I mean, if you're up for it?"

"Sure. I'll give you the tour," Debbie replied with a big smile and slipped her hand in his arm. She wasn't ready for it to end, either.

With Radar heeling at Eddie's right side, they began up D Street into the quiet June evening. They strolled leisurely through the streets of Grants Pass looking at the different stores and buildings as Debbie told Eddie what each one was along with the history of the town. It was nice out and they both walked and talked as if they had been doing this together their whole lives.

Eddie was interested in what she was telling him about Grants Pass, but he was more interested that her hand was again inside his arm. He was a little surprised at first that she did it on her own this time, but admitted to himself he liked the feeling. But what was he supposed to do next? He hadn't thought that far ahead. Correction, he hadn't let himself think that far ahead. Now here he was enjoying the moment with no clue where it was headed. He liked her very much and felt comfortable being with her, something he never saw coming, but did she feel the same? He thought maybe her arm in his was a pretty good indicator.

After a while they came to where Debbie's car was parked. She detached from his arm and they both leaned back on the car without saying much for a few minutes. Radar sat a few feet away, watching them and waiting.

Finally, Eddie broke the silence, "Nice little town you got here. I've been by a few times going north but never stopped."

Debbie noticed he was trying to keep the conversation going but was struggling. She was definitely breaking protocol for the rules she had set for herself but there was no denying what she felt. She believed he felt it too, but didn't know how to say it.

She decided to give him a little help. "So, Mr. Eddie McVane, what are your intentions? Are you just passing through, or do you have something else in mind?"

Somewhat caught off guard, Eddie looked down at his new shoes for a moment and then back at her. He also heard something he was sure was a grunt from Radar's direction (and not someone's odd ringtone this time), but chose to ignore him for the time being.

"Well, Ms. Debbie Patterson, as of this morning, I was just passing through with my only problems being of the truck variety. Oh, and that occasionally noisy traveling companion of mine." Eddie raised an eyebrow toward Radar who turned his head away. "As of this evening, though, I seem to have a new problem."

She gave him a mischievous smile. "Oh, and what would that be?"

"Well, ya see, there's this cute girl I've kind of taking a liking to and suddenly, I find myself distracted from my current activities of becoming a famous super truck test pilot. Can't seem to focus. That's my new problem."

Sheepishly she cocked her head at him and asked, "My, that does sound like a problem. What do you think you're going to do about it?"

Eddie looked around as if he could see into the future. He was still somewhat nervous and felt out of his element, but decided to take a shot.

"Well...I was thinking I might ask her if I could see her some more and maybe we could spend some quality time together. Get to know each other, and I don't know, see where it goes from there."

She gave him a sideways look and decided to mess with him a little. "Well, it took you long enough to spit it out. I thought I was going to have to send in a tag team partner for you."

Eddie chuckled, "You're not going to cut me any slack, are you?"

She smiled back. "Not a chance. Just letting you know what you're in for."

Debbie looked at him for a moment. "Look, I know you have some unfinished business with this truck thing. That is a very big deal and I know how important it is to you. I also know you have some personal things to work out and that takes time. But I think you're worth waiting for. That is, if you're interested. I would like to see more of you, too. The sooner, the better. I would like that very much. But, for now, you go and do what you must do and I will be here when you're ready."

With that, she stood there with her arms folded just smiling at him, waiting for his response.

Eddie was blown away. He looked at her with complete amazement. Here was a woman whom he barely knew and she just told him she was willing to wait for him. Was this real? It was a little overwhelming. As a matter of fact, the past several weeks were overwhelming to be honest. Tonight just topped it off.

Eddie just shook his head as he looked at her. "Man. You are somethin'. I don't think I've ever met anybody quite like you. If you don't mind me saying so, your man was a fool for cheating on you. He obviously didn't know what he had. And yes, I'm very interested."

"Why, thank you. That's the nicest thing anybody has said to me in quite a while." Debbie blinked a few times to keep a tear at bay.

Eddie looked away for a second and saw Radar staring at him. He was definitely having a talk with that dog later.

"Well," he began slowly, "it's the truth. A man should know what he has and treasure it as such. You never know what tomorrow will bring."

Pausing for another moment, he looked back at her. "You're right. I do have some unfinished business to take care of and I am still coming to terms with all of this. I did not expect to be standing here with you tonight and thinking about the future again. A lot has happened in the past several weeks that I can't explain. I feel like I am being prepared for something to come."

Debbie quizzed him on that. It was unexpected.

"What do you mean? Prepared for what?"

"Not sure yet," Eddie said simply. "I'll tell you more when I figure it out."

"Please do. Now my curiosity is piqued," she said and dropped the matter.

"Will do. For now, thank you for saying yes to dinner and for being so gracious. This is probably the best I have felt about life in a long time and I have you to thank for that."

Debbie blushed at that comment. "You're welcome. I just say what I think. Some people have a hard time with that."

"Well, I don't. I like honest talk. Takes the guesswork out of where you stand with a person," Eddie said.

They talked for a few more minutes and then she looked over at Radar. In a very serious tone she asked, "You think dogs know things?"

"What do you mean?" Eddie cautiously replied.

"Do you think they can sense when people are hurting or need help? I mean, Radar did introduce us."

Now Eddie looked at him, too.

"Never gave it much thought before, but lately I am beginning to believe. Like I said, he usually doesn't have much to do with people, but he liked you straightaway, so in my book, I'd say he is a good judge of character."

She smiled as they stood silent for another minute. Again, Debbie had to break their silence.

"Sooo?" She was looking at Eddie who looked somewhat puzzled.

"Sorry, it is getting late. I guess it's time to go."

She put her hands on her hips and squinted at him. "No, goofball. Aren't you forgetting something?"

Eddie still looked perplexed. "I'm not sure I..."

"A good night kiss, dummy. Am I going to have to retrain you all over?" Debbie shook her head. "Jeeze. I've got a lot of work ahead of me." She reached over and grabbed his face pulling it gently toward hers, and kissed him passionately.

Eddie felt a warmth flow through him that he had not felt in a very long time. When she released him he felt like he was walking on air. He looked at her with an amused and satisfied grin.

"Oh. That. I was gonna get around to that," he said unconvincingly.

"When? Christmas? Gotta pick up the pace, McVane. Not getting any younger here, ya know. We've got a lot to catch up on," Debbie said playfully but firmly.

He chuckled "Yes, ma'am, we do. I look forward to it."

Debbie walked over to Radar and bent down to rub his cheeks and pat him on the head.

"You keep an eye on him for me, okay?" she said to Radar. "He needs somebody to watch out for him. You bring him back in one piece, you hear?"

Radar wagged his tail and grunted as if answering her. Debbie looked at him for a long second. Then she walked back toward her car and stopped in front of Eddie. She took out one of her business cards and handed it to him.

"And you, Mr. McVane, you take care of yourself. Here is my number. Call anytime. And if you let me know when you are coming, I might be so inclined to make you a home-cooked meal."

Without saying a word, he reached for her and pulled her to him, kissing her deeply and holding her tight.

When he finally came up for air, blushing, Debbie looked at him and smiled.

"I think you're getting the hang of it, McVane. Very good." She put her hand on his cheek. "You be careful out there. Figure it out and come back soon."

With that, she got in her car and started it up. Lowering the window, she looked up at him and said, "Thank you for a wonderful evening. I will be waiting for more. Good night, Eddie McVane."

"Good night, Debbie Patterson."

Eddie stood there with Radar at his right side watching her drive away. *Wow*, he thought. *That was something. Does this mean I have a girlfriend now?*

He looked down at the dog and said, "How ironic is this? I have a wonderful evening with a beautiful and fun lady and I get to go home with you. What's up with that?" Radar grunted in response.

Eddie looked after where Debbie's car had disappeared into the night, reflecting on the evening. Finally, he replied to Radar's grunt.

"You're right, buddy. That there is a very special lady. I need to get my head on straight and follow up. That kind doesn't just come around every day."

He called the cab company to come and get them. Of all the things that had happened here lately, this was by far Eddie's best day in three years. Then he wondered what Kate would think about it all. Should he even think that?

A lot of emotions were flowing at the same time. Hope, elation, confusion, happiness, and wonder. "Is this really happening? I guess sorting all this out is part of the process." Eddie decided to let it rest for now and just enjoy the moment. Tonight, life was good and he had a new woman in his life—one that made him feel alive again. But on top of everything else, he wasn't sure what to do next. For the past three years life had been simple. Now, not so much. He definitely had a lot to think about. It would be a long drive back to North Carolina and he would put it to good use.

****

As Debbie Patterson was driving home, she couldn't deny her feelings. Her attempts to remain totally neutral and simply enjoy a casual dinner with this nice man had failed miserably. Although she didn't believe in love at first sight, she did believe in her womanly instincts. There was something special about this guy and she had a gut feeling this was right.

By the time she got home, she resolved that if it was real, he would be back for round two and she'd see what happened next." She found herself hoping that would be soon.

CHAPTER SIXTEEN
THIS...NONE OF
THIS IS NORMAL

Change is not easy for someone like Eddie, especially after so much heartbreak, loss, and betrayal. The long dark days of not caring whether he lived or died and running from those memories had taken their toll on him. To think he could be happy again was almost a foreign feeling. He was at a total loss.

The next few days were a blur for him. So many things were going through his head and heart he could hardly keep up with them. The range of emotions was like a roller coaster ride. On the one hand, he was excited about the possibility of a new relationship; on the other, he felt totally overwhelmed by all that was happening and almost felt guilty, like he was cheating on his wife even though he wasn't, of course.

Driving back to North Carolina gave Eddie time to think about the past several weeks and all that had transpired. The wreck, the dog, the new truck and all that went with it, the incident at the trucker's church, the old Indian prophecy, and now a new woman in his life.

His head was spinning trying to sort it all out. It didn't seem that long ago he was content to just drive along, deliver his loads, and live in relative obscurity. Now there were all these people and situations in his life. He felt good about it, but it was still change. Change meant stepping out of one's comfort zone. Something he was not used to. He had built a nice comfortable wall of protection around himself and his heart. Now, he felt completely exposed in all those areas and that made him uncomfortable. Glancing over at the dog, he somehow felt Radar had more to do with what was going on than Eddie wanted to admit. *This...none of this is normal*, he thought. At least, not in his world anyway. *"Things like this don't just happen to people like me out of the blue,"* he thought. As much as he tried to ignore it, the old Indian's words were becoming more haunting in his head than prophetic. That haunting, as much as Eddie was enjoying all the good things that had been happening, gave him the underlying sense of something else at play, and that was nagging at him.

Despite all that, he couldn't deny his feelings about Debbie. She had sparked something in him he thought was long since dead. Where it went from here he wasn't sure, but he knew he had to pursue it. Only time would tell. He finally decided to push it all to the side for now and concentrate on the tasks at hand. No sooner had Eddie decided that, he started wondering when would be an appropriate time to call Deb.

After about an hour of driving, Jimmy came on the com to check in.

"Hey, buddy, how's it going? I see you're back on the road. Everything okay? You didn't check in."

"Yeah. It's all good, man. Just enjoying the quiet and the scenery. Me and Radar are good. Everything's great. Just a man and his dog cruising down the road, doing trucking stuff."

Frowning at Eddie's response, Jimmy shook his head a bit and thought Eddie sounded different. Thinking about it for a moment he resisted asking any questions and continued. "Okay, good. Bobby thinks he found the problem with the stealth. We think it's a ground wire or a weak link. They will fix it when you get home. There are a couple of other things we need to adjust as well as some upgrades to the computer. Also, your crew is anxious to do some more test runs."

"Got it. Upgrades. Tests. Great. Sounds like a plan. See you in a couple days."

After signing off, Eddie went back to his thoughts and the road. He was obviously distracted and wasn't up for idle chatter right now. He had important matters to contemplate.

Leaning back in his chair, Jimmy was again puzzled at Eddie's response. "Now that is definitely weird. It's like he was in another world. Wonder what that's all about? I guess we'll find out when he gets back."

Jimmy and his team went back to work planning their next strategy for testing the gadgets they had installed on Eddie's rig earlier. When he returned, they immediately spent those weeks he was back doing more testing and putting the truck through its paces. Along the way, Jimmy tried to read what was going on with Eddie but got nowhere. He seemed fine enough but there was something different about him that Jimmy couldn't put his finger on. Eddie seemed more energized and more engaged with his team, even socializing with them from time to time. For now, Jimmy was glad to see him happy and let it go at that.

****

A Nice Evening for a Healing

Over the next several weeks while Eddie was in North Carolina, he would call Debbie and they would talk about everything under the sun from food, family, and raising kids to garage sales, history, the good old days, and just about everything else you could imagine. After bailing him out so many times, Eddie made a deal with Mike Jenkins to make sure he got all the loads going to Oregon. Eddie was enjoying her company and she seemed to enjoy his as well and the deal with Mike Jenkins was the perfect fit to see Debbie regularly.

After dinner in the evenings, they would set on the front porch swing while she rested her head on his shoulder and they sometimes wouldn't talk but just swing. All the while Radar stood watch at the bottom of the steps. Debbie had learned the dog's routine and accepted it as well as Eddie's. She was content to have him over as often as she could given his schedule. She knew he was adjusting to the new relationship as was she. It was different and refreshing with an air of anticipation for the future, whatever that may be.

Debbie had a new interest in him now after calling her brothers, Danny and Earl, in Arkansas a few days before. She had called to let them know that she had a new man in her life, and in return, she got quite a history lesson that she wasn't expecting. She spoke to them frequently about life back home and what was going on with her. The usual family stuff, but this call was going to be different because she was about to let them know about the new man in her life. They would figure something was up because she intended to tell them on a conference call, but she was still certain they would be surprised. She started slowly, giving them a general introduction.

At first they were skeptical of him being a truck driver, as big brothers who were protective of their baby sister would be. Debbie was holding her own, but that didn't mean they were any happier about it. However, when she brought up the subject of Eddie being an ex-race-car driver, they changed their tune a little, and, of course, they wanted to hear more. But first, as always, they had to bicker among themselves. It was their usual family stuff.

"That doesn't make make him a bad guy," Danny said.

"Doesn't make him a saint, either," shot back Earl.

"Just because you drove a race car didn't make you a race car driver. We knew a lot of wannabes back in the day and most didn't make it more than a year or two. What kind of race cars did this guy say he drove, Deb?" asked Danny.

She wasn't exactly sure, but said he raced on dirt for a number of years and was even considered by NASCAR. That didn't seem to help matters any and now her brothers were back to working together.

"Really?" they both replied.

"Sounds like a sales pitch to me," said Earl skeptically. Now he bored in. "So...what's this big time race car driver's name?"

"Eddie McVane," Debbie answered.

The phone went dead silent. She thought she had lost her connection until Earl quietly asked her where he was from.

"Morganton, North Carolina." Another silent pause. Debbie was starting to get annoyed with the fits and starts of the conversation.

Finally they asked in unison, "Fast Eddie McVane?"

"I guess," she replied, now more puzzled than annoyed. "Why?"

They both started giggling like schoolboys before they responded.

"Are you kidding? Is she kidding? She's playing with us, isn't she? I'm not really hearing this. Are you hearing this?" They went back and forth a bit like that until Earl finally told Danny to shush and turned their attention back to Debbie. He asked as calmly as he could, "Debbie…Eddie McVane. Are you sure that's his name?"

"Well, yeah," she started. "I mean, I didn't check his driver's license but that's what he told me when we met and he does seem to answer to that last name."

The brothers were obviously excited and went back to speaking between themselves, chattering about stats and numbers and championships along with continuing to press her for more information. She wondered if they remembered she was on the other end of the line.

Danny took over. "Our baby sister dating Fast Eddie McVane! This is unbelievable. Tell us more. Tell us everything. How tall is he? What does he look like? What is he driving?"

Debbie was really perplexed now. "What are you two goofballs yammering about? What's the big deal?"

"What's the big deal?" exclaimed Earl. "Only that back in the day, this guy was legendary. He could do things with a car that were unbelievable. We've watched him drive on every part of the track and stick it in places that were impossible, but somehow, he would get through and take the checker. And he did that at every track he went to. He was amazing to watch. He won several championships and still holds records at tracks all around the Southeast. This guy was the real deal! People said he had a gift or something."

"A gift? Like what?" she asked them. Then she asked herself who this man Eddie McVane was. She thought the only thing mysterious about him was the dog and she was getting used to that as well.

"Don't know for sure, but he was the man back in the day. He was almost unbeatable. Him and that crazy mechanic of his. What was his name?"

Danny answered for him. "Jimmy. Jimmy the Hammer."

"That's right!" said Earl. "Jimmy the Hammer. That guy. They were some pair."

Debbie's brothers were indeed pleased and seriously impressed. They were also seriously excited and the questions came like a machine gun. Finally, she had to slow them down, the Arkansas way.

"Hey!" she shouted into the speaker. "One at a time! You guys! Sheesh! Beside the fact that you're asking a million questions a minute, Eddie doesn't really talk about those days that much. Maybe something in a passing comment, but that's about it. As a matter of fact, he actually talks to me about things I like, that we like together. We have a really good time just hanging out doing simple things. It's all good."

"Okay, okay." They backed off some.

She smirked at the phone and chalked up another one for the Arkansas way.

"So anyway, how in the world did you meet this guy, sis?"

Debbie told them the story of how she and Eddie met, their dinner date, and that they had been seeing each other for a while now. She told them how she was happy for the first time in a long time. Her brothers listened quietly.

She continued and told them the story of how he put the racing on hold after his father died and about Kate, Eddie's late wife. Debbie felt it was a chance meeting in the park that day but so far it seemed promising. More than promising, she smiled to herself.

Danny and Earl both expressed their approval and told her how glad they were that she was happy. They had worried about her ever since the divorce and checked on her regularly, though they were sure she didn't notice. She did.

Although they were pleased and now calm, Earl couldn't help himself and asked, "Could you get a couple pictures for us and maybe an autograph? That would be great."

Debbie immediately shot that down. "No. I'm not going to embarrass him like that," she scolded. "But I will tell him that my two goofball brothers used to watch him race and they were fans."

"C'mon, we still are fans," they chided her. But she didn't budge and said no again. Finally, after catching them up on the kids and her business, they said their goodbyes.

She guessed her brothers approved. Albeit more because of Eddie being somewhat of a famous driver from back in the day as opposed to how he treated her. Still, she thought it was a good thing and a vast improvement over her ex whom they tolerated but never really warmed up to. Not to mention the part about them threatening to come to Oregon and do bodily harm to him after finding out how he treated their sister.

No, Mr. Eddie McVane seemed even more interesting now. He didn't come off as having an ego or wanting to brag about his accomplishments. He seemed content just to be in her company, and she liked that.

From her own experience after her divorce, it took time to heal. She knew Eddie was dealing with a different type of healing. Although she didn't ask him directly, she could see him working through the process, still feeling a little awkward at times, though he nervously joked to hide it. The last thing she wanted to do was pressure him. She had a good feeling about him, though, and decided to let it play out. For now.

And so, later that evening comforting one another, her head on his shoulder, his arm around her, they gently swayed in the swing without saying a word. The past, for both of them, seemed to be slowly getting further behind them. It was a nice evening for healing.

****

Eddie sat at the kitchen table the next morning sipping his coffee and watching Debbie cook breakfast while she chattered about whatever was on her mind. He started thinking about the future for the first time since this started. What was next? What was his plan? He hadn't thought much beyond just the moments they shared. It was an odd feeling for him to think about such things. So much to consider. He had been out of touch for so long he honestly had no idea what to do next. He couldn't deny how he felt, but was it love? Was it infatuation? Was it just that she filled a void in his life? She deserved a real answer and to be treated fairly. She was definitely a special lady and deserved a man who would treat her that way. But, was he that man?

Despite how good it felt to be with her, Eddie wondered if he had what it took to go the distance with all the damage that had been done to him and the baggage he was carrying. Did he have enough left in him for one more relationship? On top of that, he still had unanswered questions about the old Indian's prophecy rattling around inside his head and all that had happened since. How would that play into this with her? Did it really mean anything at all? All these unanswered questions were interrupting his otherwise happy moment. Debbie serving him breakfast broke his trance. "Here you go, hon."

"Um, thanks. Smells good."

She noticed him seemingly to be in deep thought and asked, "Is everything okay?"

"Yeah, just got a lot coming up this next couple of weeks with testing," Eddie answered.

She understood but sensed there was more going on with him so she decided to prod a little. "Can I ask you something?"

"Absolutely. Shoot." He began to eat his food.

"Are you okay with everything so far…I mean, us?"

The food never made it to his mouth. Eddie was startled and put his fork down. He thought he gave her the wrong impression and that bothered him. He did tend to brood on things too much and even Kate got on to him about it over the years. He looked her dead in the eyes and replied, "Yes. I'm absolutely okay with us. I apologize. Sometimes I tend to ponder on things too much and it usually gives people the wrong impression. I do have a lot on my mind." Still looking at her, he decided he would just be upfront. If she was who he thought she was, she would get it.

"To be completely honest, Deb, I have no clue what to do next. I mean, yes, I'm happy with us, but I have been in a black hole for so long I think I have forgotten how to live and feel like a normal human being."

She tried to counter with reassuring smile and a joke. "Well, I think you're doing just fine. I mean, for a worn-out race car driver and broken-down truck driver."

He shook his head and laughed. "Thanks."

"Seriously, you are being too hard on yourself. This isn't a race and nobody is keeping score. I told you I would be here when you were ready and I meant it. I told you to do what you have to do."

Eddie studied her for a second and thought, *How did I get so lucky?*

He continued, "I started thinking about the future. Didn't think I would ever do that again. I guess it startled me some. I figure you deserve a man who knows where he's going and has a plan. Right?"

She sat back in her chair and cocked her head at him with that mischievous smile and decided he needed some reassurance. "Okay, let me ask you something."

"Alright." He braced himself.

"Did you plan for us to meet in that park?"

"No."

"Did you plan on asking me out to dinner?"

"No."

"Did you plan on wanting to see me again?"

"Well, no. I mean, not at first."

She leaned in toward him at the table.

"So, that being said, what is it you want to plan for?"

With her locking eyes with his, he felt completely disarmed after that assault and knew he was defeated. Smiling a nervous smile he answered, "Well, I suppose, when you put it like that, I guess I should just shut up and finish this awesome breakfast you prepared and be thankful you aren't a lawyer asking if it was me who robbed that Brinks truck."

She laughed and continued to follow through. "The way I see it, I was living a dull, boring, dead-end life, and you were driving around the country living in a black hole of misery. Sounds like a match made in heaven to me."

Eddie pondered that for a second before she finished her thought.

Finally, she continued, "Look, how about we just take it one moment at a time, one day at a time, and see how that works, okay?"

He looked at her as he took another sip of coffee and reached across the table with his hand open. "It's a deal." They shook hands. Although he was still wondering about all the other things rattling around in his head, he felt that was a conversation for another day. For now, he was feeling very blessed to have such a woman in his life at this time.

Funny, he thought. *In his arena, he was the guy everybody chased and he was in control. But in this one, he was clearly outmatched and outgunned but in a good way.* His confidence level was on the rebound. That feeling he was wondering about earlier, if he dared think it, was it love? He wanted to make sure before he made the jump.

Once breakfast was over it was time to go. Standing on the front porch, they shared a long hug and a "see ya later" kiss. Then Debbie watched as Eddie went down the steps, collected Radar, strolled across the street, and loaded them into his truck. She missed them already as they pulled away, waving as he blew the horn. She would make this weekend last until he returned. Debbie knew she was in love with him but was hesitant to say so, thinking these things had to run their course. *I want him when he's ready.*

Chapter Seventeen
Bama' Bound and Beyond

Back in North Carolina, it was early morning at the compound and Jimmy and crew were already hard at work. They were finishing up some last-minute tuning on the new installments they made to the truck and trailer for Eddie's next round of tests. Everyone was excited about what had been accomplished to date and how well the unit had performed. Their vision for the future was coming true right before their eyes and they were more determined than ever to be the first to make this new technology work. Outside the compound, most thought it impossible and the rest, simply foolish. For Jimmy, the goal was to prove all his detractors wrong.

"A 200-mph cargo transport vehicle? Separate interstate roads for trucks? Gyroscopic stabilizers? Hybrid/Diesel electric? Never happen," they said. Now, he was on the verge of success and it felt good. Really good. Eddie had helped make this happen with him and Jimmy was going to make sure the world knew about it when all was said and done.

****

Eddie was just finishing up his breakfast when Mike Jenkins called. "Hey, buddy, got a trip all set for ya with a slight detour."

Eddie frowned at the detour part. "What kind of detour?"

"Well, I have a load that needs to go to Oxford, Alabama. You will pick that up in Columbia, South Carolina. After that, you grab your next load of frozen fish out of Birmingham and then you are back up to Oregon with a return load back to Charlotte. Sorry, but that's the best I can do this round."

Eddie didn't care much for the detour but he knew Mike was trying to keep him on a steady run back to Oregon to be with Debbie, so he couldn't really complain. "Okay. When?"

"Tomorrow morning. I will email you the paperwork."

"Okay, Mike, thanks." After hanging up with Mike, Eddie called Debbie to give her an update on when he thought he would be there. This was becoming the norm for him now, checking in with her and informing her of his whereabouts. It was his way of letting Debbie know she was an important part of his daily life. She, in turn, seemed to appreciate it and was always interested in not only what he was hauling and where he was going, but also how the testing on the truck was going. Although Eddie would stop short of telling her everything they were doing, leaving aside whether she would actually believe any of it, he told her enough to keep her informed.

Eddie was getting used to being in a relationship again and liked that she was part of it all. He hadn't said anything to Jimmy yet, although he wanted to. They had been best friends for so many years he felt bad not saying anything to him, but this was a private matter and the timing had to be right. Besides, Eddie wanted to make sure it was real. The other problem was, as happy and comfortable as he was becoming with everything, there was still the underlying and nagging prophecy from the Old Indian. How did all that fit into his life? And when, if ever, will that happen? Maybe it wouldn't. Maybe it was all just coincidence and he was overthinking.

Glancing out the window at Radar setting at his post at the edge of the walkway outside the restaurant, he couldn't convince himself of that and it troubled him. He could hear the words of the Old One echoing in his head once again.

As much as Eddie wanted to shake that off, it wouldn't go away. Most frustrating of all was that he seemingly had no one to talk to about this, not even Jimmy. No, Jimmy had his hands full right now and didn't need any other distractions. And he certainly didn't want to jeopardize his relationship with Debbie, although he felt she could probably handle it better than anybody. Eddie toyed with the idea of telling her, but decided against it. No, this was something he needed to work out for himself. The message was directed at him and no one else. If it was real, it was for him to deal with. He put it aside and refocused his attention on the day and tasks at hand.

The dinging on his phone alerted him that Jimmy and his team were ready for him. A welcome respite from his thoughts. "On my way," he replied. As always, Radar snapped to attention when he came out and was ready for action. Eddie loaded him into his pickup. Then they were off to the compound and another round of testing Jimmy's "truck of the future."

After leaving Radar at his post and coming into the garage area, Eddie saw Morgana all shined up and ready for her next run. He watched as everybody was scurrying around finishing up with last-minute stuff. He was still in awe of being a part of all that was going on. *Pretty crazy stuff*, he thought. Never in his wildest dreams did he ever think he'd be involved in something like this.

His team gave him their usual greeting before Jimmy finally noticed him and then waved him over to the truck. "C'mon, man, climb aboard."

Eddie obliged and sat in the driver's seat. Jimmy was his usual excitable self and couldn't wait for him to see the upgrades.

"Okay, here's some things we've added and some others we've activated." He called up a new icon on the screen. Tapping on it, the words "Full Remote" came up. Below it read, "Engage-Disengage."

"Now, this is here for a couple of reasons. At some point, these trucks will be able to be self-driving by AI and driven remotely via someone in a control room from anywhere in the country. Until then, you are in full control of everything. Remember, we are programming your skills into this unit to share with future programmers. Also, worst-case scenario—if something happens to the driver, we can take over and safely handle the unit from here."

Eddie thought about that for a moment.

"Well. I guess that's a good thing. So, if I keel at the wheel, I can die happy knowing my load of fish will still get delivered. Awesome, Jimmy."

He laughed. "Come on, you ain't going nowhere, but yes. Now, check this out." Tapping on another icon, the windshield became what looked like a movie screen.

"We fine-tuned the night vision for better clarity and were able to sync the GPS to react better in real-time to your speed on the screen. Now, as you've learned, heavy, dense fog can still be an issue in some cases, but we think the sensors we've installed along with the new program will give it a new set of eyes and a clearer view."

"Eyes? Really? How will that work?" Eddie asked.

"Well, the sensors are always scanning 360 degrees, reading everything going on around you like sonar. So, because it can also read heat signatures, what we've done here is integrate it with the GPS and programmed it to identify everything it sees. It will project that image onto your screen as you are driving at whatever speed, again in real time. In essence, no matter how bad the weather is—fog, blizzard, hurricane, whatever—what you will see is a clear vision of the road and any obstacles in it. Now, it will take you some time to get used to it because it will look kind of like a video game. I would suggest practicing on a deserted highway until you get the feel for it."

Eddie was impressed, shaking his head while looking at the windshield. "Wow. That would avoid so many accidents. Jimmy vision 2.0 really delivers!"

Jimmy bobbed his head in agreement. "I know, right? Wait…just wait a second here! What do you mean Jimmy vision 2.0? Where did *that* name come from and what do you know from 2.0? You don't talk like that."

"Jimmy. Jimmy. My team talks like that. Which means that I talk like that. You know, all for one, one for all."

In his ear, Jimmy could hear the snickering rippling across the control room. He squinted at Eddie who was grinning broadly and then smiled, nodded his head, and playfully mouthed a few words at him that made both of them laugh out loud.

"All right, let's get back to it. Now, the trailer." Jimmy tapped an icon that Eddie had looked at before but wasn't sure what it was.

"This one you will appreciate. It is for your landing gear. No more crank handle needed except in case of an electrical failure." When Jimmy tapped on "lower", Eddie could hear the landing gear activating and see it per the animated diagram on the screen.

"Very cool," he commented.

"Oh, it gets better." Jimmy tapped the icon next it.

Eddie heard a very distinct *ka chink!*

"Is that what I think it is?"

"Yep," came Jimmy's enthusiastic reply with a wide grin. "You are uncoupled and officially disconnected. You can now roam about the yard, trailer free."

Eddie gave him a puzzled look.

"But I still have to disconnect the glad hands and electrical line, right?"

Jimmy grinned that toothy grin again. "Come check this out." They climbed down out of the truck and he instructed Eddie to look just to the rear of the fifth wheel. In doing so, he noticed three cone-shaped tubes coming from the frame that had detached from three matching fittings under the trailer nose. With his remote tablet in hand, Jimmy tapped on the icons again and while Eddie watched in amazement, the cone-shaped tubes rose up to connect to the matching trailer fittings, while the fifth wheel re-locked, and the landing gear returned to the raised position.

Eddie stood up and exclaimed "Damn, son! That's the stuff right there! You have just made a whole lot of new friends with that one, buddy. Amazing, my friend, absolutely amazing," Eddie replied again. While he was thinking about it, he asked about the sliding action on the tandems.

"Hey, while we're here, Jimmy, I remember a while back I was nosing around the icons and came across the tandem axles and how they split as well as slide. What's the deal with that?"

Jimmy motioned him to the back near the tandems while he explained. "Well, we still have some more to do before it's ready to use full time, but here's the gist of it. The obvious part is for the axles to slide and split to balance out for different loads. But the other part is that we will be able to slide one axle all the way to the landing gear."

Eddie gave him a puzzled look along with the age-old question, "Why?"

"Well, I can show you better than explain." He tapped his earpiece. "Dano. Once I disconnect, move the truck, please."

"On it," came the reply.

Once again Jimmy tapped his remote pad and as before, the landing gear came down, the fifth wheel disengaged, and the lines detached. Then Danny eased the truck forward and out of the shop. After that, Jimmy proceeded to tap some more on his remote pad and again as before, the front tandem separated from the rear one and began its crawl toward the landing gear, only this time it kept going as Eddie watched in anticipation. Once it reached its position, it locked in place. Then the landing gear raised back up. Glancing over at Eddie, Jimmy motioned him to follow, going away from the trailer toward the overhead door to the garage leading outside where now the whole team had assembled. Bobby handed Jimmy a joystick and asked Eddie, "You ready?"

Not knowing what to expect, Eddie shrugged and said, "Sure. Go for it." As he watched in amazement, the trailer began to move and go through the doorway and turn into the parking lot. Once it was in an open area, he watched as the front tandem wheels started turning until they were at a ninety-degree angle. The trailer did a complete 360-degree pivot in place two times before stopping and lining back up where it began. Then the back tandems also turned at ninety degrees. Once in place, the trailer crab-walked all the way across the parking lot until it came to the curb. Then it stopped, paused briefly, and then returned across the parking lot to its original position with the wheels lining back up. Finally, as if on cue, it started backing into the building where it promptly stopped at the exact spot it started from. Eddie stood in silence not believing he saw what he just saw.

After a few moments, he managed to spit out, "Are you kidding me?" Everybody started chuckling.

"So Boss, what do you think?" Danny asked. Everyone was focused on Eddie as he stood there, totally stunned, looking at the trailer and then back at Jimmy and the team.

"Amazing. I mean, that is just out there, guys. A remote-control trailer that can park itself? I guess I shouldn't be surprised at this point, but I still am. That is just out there." Pausing for a moment to collect his thoughts, Eddie asked another question.

"So tell me, what's the end game with this thing? I mean, I have some ideas but I'm sure you guys are way ahead of me on this." Jimmy and the team invited him to follow them to the design room where there was a large screen monitor. Once there, Jimmy had Marcy fill Eddie in on the idea. With a remote in hand, she began her briefing while showing a simulation with a yard full of trailers and trucks waiting to bring more in.

"Well, the tandems were already built as part of the drive system, and the sliding and splitting part was done months ago. But while I was watching the news one day, they had a story on the ports being backlogged and I saw lines of trucks waiting to be unloaded or loaded. And then I got to thinking that at the distribution centers and trailer yards, there is always a need for a yard driver or a crane to move them around. I know some places are using remote tractors, but what if we could go further than just remote tractors? What if the trailers were integrated with their own drive system? That's when I really started thinking about the drive system on the trailer and thought, can that system be modified to be moved remotely and steer as well? That would give you a system that once it's delivered and the driver has processed his e-paperwork, he can separate from the unit and give the yard operator the code for it. With the unit's code, the yard operator can control it with a joystick and move it to wherever he wants in the yard leaving the trucker free to move onto his next load."

Eddie watched all of what she was saying play out on the large monitor and saw the immediate benefit. Jimmy picked it up from there. "After Marcy brought the idea to me, I got Bobby on the engineering of the steering and Steve here designed the program to make it work as a separate unit once it's disconnected from the truck. We haven't tried it yet, but we think the trailer can run at a pretty good clip by itself, seein's how it's part of the overall drive system. We'll try that another day. Pretty cool, huh?"

Eddie was back to feeling somewhat overwhelmed by all of it. Here he was, just a truck driver and here was this team of eggheads who were seemingly reinventing the wheel and everything else in their path. *What am I doing here?* he wondered. *Really, what am I doing here?*

He pushed his doubts aside and spoke to his team. "All I can say is, wow! I mean, this is just incredible stuff, guys. I can hardly believe what I'm seeing, let alone being the one driving this thing. I never thought I would live to see these kind of advancements in my lifetime, for sure. I will say this, though, it seems you guys are just getting warmed up and I see nothing but good things in your futures. Yes, very cool stuff indeed."

After going over a few more things, Danny went out and hooked Morgana back up to the trailer and then proceeded to go over a checklist, making sure everything was ready for Eddie. As the team went back to the control room, Jimmy walked Eddie to the truck for his sendoff on another run. He was still wondering how Eddie was doing and why all his runs seemed to be going to Oregon, though the truck being parked on a particular street every visit was a pretty big clue.

"So, buddy, you doing okay? I mean, all good?" Eddie could tell Jimmy was fishing for information, but he wasn't quite ready to share his newfound relationship just yet so he tried to steer his response in a different direction.

"Yeah, man. I feel better than I have in a long time. I'm still processing all this stuff, but for the most part, it's all good, my friend." He hoped that was enough to get him off the hook for now. When it came to his personal life, Eddie was fiercely protective and private, even from his best friend. He would tell him when the time was right

Jimmy smiled and patted him on the back. "Alright, then. I'll let you get to it. Have fun and see ya when you get back." They fist bumped and then Eddie loaded up and eased the rig out of the overhead door, stopping briefly to pick up Radar. He didn't like not telling him but he had his reasons and it was settled for now.

Jimmy was not completely satisfied with Eddie's answer, but he knew him all too well and decided to let it go for now and focus on the tests and the other inventions they were working on. Nevertheless, he was glad to see him happy and seemingly adjusting well to his new role.

Later that evening, as Eddie was lieng in bed pondering the events of the day, he couldn't help but wonder what was next for him. It certainly was a far cry from being a self-exiled loner drifting from load to load. The last several months seemed to have been a whirlwind of changes in his life that had him contemplating his future. Not something he was prepared for at all. How much longer would he be able to work with Jimmy on this project? How much longer did he want to do this? The real question was how much longer would he be physically able to do this? His budding relationship with Debbie was causing him to think more about wanting to slow down and maybe try living a normal life again. Was he falling in love with her and if they did get together, what next? He wasn't sure if he would want to live in Oregon the rest of his life that far from his son and grandkids. Of course, the mystery of the dog and the Old Indian prophet's words were always present at the back of his mind. As he began drifting off to sleep, the Old Indian's haunting voice echoed once again.

****

The next morning, Eddie and Radar were Bama' bound. By the time they were loaded and headed for Alabama, it was late in the day. The traffic was congested every mile of the way it seemed. Interstate 20 from Columbia to Atlanta gave little relief and trying to get through Atlanta was a crawl-fest. Eddie was beginning to get more onboard with Jimmy's idea of separate trucking lanes to avoid all this. It would certainly make delivering goods easier, not to mention cut down on accidents, road rage, and all the other things that go along with trying to move around the country in a truck. He doubted he would live to see that day, but felt like it was a possibility in the not-so-distant future.

After dropping his load in Oxford, Alabama, Eddie set his sights on Lincoln, Alabama next and the I-20 truck stop for some fuel, a fresh coffee for him, and some food and water for Radar. There was almost no traffic on the highway now due to heavy fog rolling in. After notifying Jimmy as instructed, they got on the com and Jimmy started guiding him through how to adjust to the new screen.

"Like I said before, it will look a little animated but it is all real and you can trust what you are seeing," he reminded Eddie.

"Okay, I'll give it a shot." Eddie tapped the icon as instructed and instantly the view went from night and dense fog to almost a daylight-view movie of the road in front of him. He could see as clear and as far as if it were really clear out. Jimmy wasn't lying: Eddie had a semi-realistic view of the countryside and highway with no obstruction from the fog. Also on the screen were lightly highlighted points of interest along the way—gas stations, restaurants, stores, malls, garages, etc. "Well done, guys," Eddie exclaimed. "A fella could get used to this. It's cool that you can see all what's available in the surrounding areas as you go along that you would otherwise never know was there. Very interesting."

"Yeah, we integrated that part in the program as a convenience for drivers. If you see something you may want to check out, all you have to do is tap on the screen and you will automatically get directions to that location from where you are, right on the lower part of the windshield."

Glancing out the driver's side window, Eddie was a bit surprised for a moment that it was pitch black and fog. "Amazing. Just amazing, guys. This is a vast improvement over the first version." Radar grunted and made a low *woof* noise. "Dog seems to like it, too. He has something more to look at now. Guess he gets bored." Jimmy and the team chuckled, but were glad Eddie *and* Radar approved.

After a short while, Eddie saw the exit sign for Lincoln, Alabama, and adjusted his speed accordingly as Radar sat up in the seat preparing himself for a break in the drive. Eddie notified Jimmy and went on standby.

Pulling into the truck stop and heading for the fuel islands, he shut off the night vision screen and was again shocked at just how bad the fog really was and how packed the off ramps and parking lot was. Steering his remarks at Radar, he said, "Wow. This is bad. These others drivers will really appreciate this new technology when it's available. Look at all these rigs having to wait this out. Can't make any money if you're sitting still."

After giving the fuel attendant instructions, he and Radar headed toward the restaurant where the dog took up his position at the end of the walkway. Eddie liked this place because it used to be one of his favorite stops back in the day, and except for younger faces and newer trucks, it still had some of that nostalgic feel to it. He weaved his way back to the restrooms and then through the souvenir area to pick up his usual gifts. He grabbed some food and water for Radar, and checked out.

Eddie and Radar loaded up and set out for Birmingham where they would spend the night. After they had gotten a short distance down the road, he tapped on his earpiece and reconnected with Jimmy and his team. "Hey, guys, back in action. How about check out the road ahead and see if we can make up for some lost time?"

"Roger that," came the reply. After scanning the area ahead, Danny gave Eddie the all-clear for the next forty miles. Eddie reached over to the screen and hit the icon for T-1. Fire lit up the foggy night and the big cat roared to life launching Morgana forward down I-20 at 135 mph. The adrenaline rush reminded him of the old days of racing and it felt good. Jimmy came on the com and started prepping him on the upcoming tests.

"The bigger test will be after you come out of Guyman, Oklahoma heading to Boise City. It's about a sixty-mile stretch so I'd like to do a ten-mile run on that straight part of US 412 so we can see how the suspension dynamics work with a load at 150-170 mph. According to the trailer gauges, you're hauling 42,585 pounds. We will also see how the aero shields and spoilers work, and adjust at that speed. Without a wind tunnel, everything we've done to date is just computer simulation and our best guesswork. This test will fine-tune our calculations so we can finalize the adjustments necessary to hit 200."

"150 to 170 sounds pretty good if you ask me," said Eddie.

"Well, 200 is the optimum mark we need."

"Okay, well, whatever you say. Me and Radar are going to hole up for the night at that Pilot Travel Center just on the other side of Birmingham on 78. I'll check with you guys in the AM."

"10-4 buddy. Talk then." Jimmy signed off, gave the shutdown signal to the others and sent them home. As he left to go home himself, he reflected that he and Eddie were on the verge of making history. In a little over twenty-four hours, they would be the first ones ever to push a full-size, loaded, diesel/electric hybrid tractor trailer to 200 miles an hour. Getting into his car to leave, he looked up at the massive facility they had built and thought, *Man, who would have thought a couple of racing rednecks could do all this? Ol' Elon ain't got nuthin' on us.*

Chapter Eighteen
Maybe It Was Just a Dream

At the I-20 truck stop in Lincoln, Alabama, young trucker Mickey Davenport sat propped up in the sleeper berth of his truck, eyes wide open with wonderment, his ears straining at the open side vent, listening for any more sounds off in the distance. His mind was racing, wondering if he really heard what he thought he heard. After listening to the trucker's story earlier about a ghost truck that shoots flames shot out of its stacks, roars like a lion and can reach speeds of one hundred fifty miles an hour in mere seconds, he could have sworn he heard that sound off in the distance just moments ago. Mickey sat there staring blankly in the dark with only the dim lights from the parking lot peering through the cracks of his closed curtains. Silence. For ten minutes he sat there, propped up, willing his ears to hear the sound again, but it never came.

"Did anybody else hear it?" he wondered. *"Maybe I could ask one of the other drivers in the morning."*

Shaking the idea off, he slid back down under his covers while positioning his head where he could still hear from the side vent in case the sound came again. *"No, they'd probably think I was crazy."*

He lay there with his hands behind his head, staring at the ceiling of his bunk, still halfway listening for that sound again. His fascination with the idea that there could be such technology out there kept his mind working as he wondered some more. *"If the story is real, what kind of technology would it has to produce those kinds of speeds and to handle mountain roads? And why does it make that sound?"*

Finally, Mickey grew weary of trying to figure it out, rolled over, readjusted his pillow, and closed his eyes. As he drifted off, his mind went back to his college days and studying to get his mechanical engineering degree so he could work on ideas such as these. That training and his inherent curiosity for all things mechanical had become his new obsession.

Like many before him, Mickey had been on a different career path before being bitten by the trucking bug. Originally a native of Pennsylvania, he intended to follow in his father's footsteps by studying engineering at the University of South Carolina and eventually taking over the family business. That was his parents' dream for him and he thought it was his as well. But the need for extra money to fund some of his extracurricular activities changed all that when he got a part-time job at Moe's Truck Garage in the town of Newberry, not far from the college. Mickey had gone to Moe's at the suggestion of one of his classmates who said that his trucker uncle had his truck serviced there and they were looking for a shop helper.

Moe introduced Mickey to a culture and a set of characters that would shape his view of the world for the rest of his life. He was used to working part-time jobs back home to get extra money for his car and to put towards his tuition at college, but this job in unfamiliar territory was his first experience away from home.

When he arrived at Moe's Garage, he was a little intimidated by the shop itself and, truth be told, by the people there. The garage was somewhat cluttered with discarded parts and debris of all sorts scattered everywhere. The thick smell of diesel fuel, grease, and other smells Mickey wasn't familiar with hung in the air along with the stench of cigarettes and the ever-present waft of smoke from the owner's cigar coming out of his small office. There also seemed to be an odd assortment of people working on different things while others just wandered around. Because nobody had anything resembling a uniform, he wasn't really sure who all worked there. A stark difference from the service stations and repair shops he had worked at during his summers in Pennsylvania.

Moe Avery, the owner, was in his office making notes while talking on the phone and said he'd be right with Mickey. He was short and stocky with a bit of a potbelly, wearing a t-shirt and ball cap, and furiously chomping on his cigar while talking on the phone. As he waited, Mickey watched as truckers were either picking one up or dropping one off for repairs. In another area of the shop, there appeared to be race cars with the hoods up and guys working on them. To Mickey, it was an altogether odd collection of things going on all around, for sure. Moe finally called him into his office. As Mickey stood there, six foot two, dark hair, clean cut looking in jeans, a polo shirt and tennis shoes, Moe leaned back in his worn office chair and smiled while looking him up and down.

"Damn, if you ain't the cleanest white boy I've seen in a while. Where ya from, boy?" he declared in a deep southern accent.

Mickey was a little taken aback by the remark, especially coming from another white guy, but he stood firm.

"Pennsylvania, sir."

"A Yankee, huh? Lemme guess. College student. Right?"

"Yes, sir."

"And what is it yer studying to be, college boy?

"Mechanical engineer, sir."

"That so. And what does a mechanical engineer do?" Mickey shifted his stance before answering trying not appear nervous.

"Um, well, some of my courses are in automotive research where we either design or try to improve existing designs on various vehicles like cars, trucks, buses and so on. Things such as aerodynamics, suspension systems, and sometimes new fuels. Things like that. That's why I wanted to work in a truck garage. I wanted to be up close and personal to the things I will be learning to maybe design one day." Moe sat quietly, listening while chewing on his cigar.

"Uh huh. Well, that all sounds pretty fancy and impressive and all, but I don't need an engineer, I need somebody that can clean up, empty trash cans, and help with whatever else we need help with in the shop. You look awfully clean for that kind of work. You ever worked in a garage before?"

"Yes, sir. My friend Ryan, back in PA, his dad has a service station and we worked there during the summers, changing oil, tires, general maintenance on customer cars, and cleaning the shop up." Mickey was dug in now. "Not afraid of hard work, sir."

Moe held a steady gaze on him as he listened. Another puff from his cigar filled the small office with more smoke as he pondered on Mickey's response. He sat there for a minute or so more, letting the silence fill the air along with his cigar before answering Mickey. Finally, he stood up and gave his decision.

"Okay. I'll give ya a shot. We'll see what you're made of. Trucks are a lot more work and a lot more dangerous to work around than cars, that's for damn sure, boy. But understand this: I ain't no nursemaid. I can't be lookin' out for you. Everybody here carries their own weight. And them boys out there, they don't suffer fools very well. If you can't cut it, they'll let me know, and you'll have to find something else to do. Understood?"

"Yes, sir. Got it."

"Alright. Gimme what days and hours you can be here and can you start Saturday?'

"Yes, sir."

"Okay. When you come in, I'll have Daryl show you around the shop and what all needs doin' first. After that, yer to help the other mechanics with whatever they need help with. Hope you got some work clothes, cause it's all dirty work here." Moe looked down at his sneakers smiling, and said. "And them tennis shoes won't last a day, so you might wanna pick up some steel-toed work boots. You drop any of these parts on your feet and, you won't be goin' out dancin' anytime soon."

"Yes, sir. Got it."

Mickey wrote down the days and hours he was available to work and agreed to the wage that Moe offered him to start. He thanked him for the job, and they shook hands to seal the deal. Driving back to the campus, he was a little unnerved by his interview, if one could call it that. But he showed up that Saturday, and from that day on, Mickey worked hard at whatever task was given him. He rarely sat still, always looking for something to stay busy at which did not go unnoticed by Moe and the others he worked around. Mickey seemed to get along with everybody okay even with the gruff nature of some of the mechanics and Moe himself.

They seemed to always be busting Mickey's chops about something, but treated him well otherwise and respected his thirst for knowledge, his eagerness to learn, and thus fed him accordingly. The joking and teasing felt like a bit much to Mickey at times, but he came to learn that it was just their way of initiating you into their circle. If you couldn't take a joke or the harassment or got your feelings hurt easily, you wouldn't last long and therefore weren't worthy of their company.

Mickey also learned that Moe had almost-legendary status in the local racing circles, and everybody who knew him had a Moe story from when he used to run moonshine for his father back in the day. Although he had some rough edges and a storied past, everybody respected Moe, and a lot of his friends and acquaintances could usually be found hanging out at the shop throughout the week. They themselves were a cast of characters who Mickey thought really needed their own reality TV show. There was always some kind of mischief going on whether it was doing a race car burnout in the street in front of the garage, pulling a prank on someone in the shop, or heckling some unsuspecting passerby. Not much was off limits, especially if there was alcohol involved.

Mickey found that he really liked being around the people there and around big trucks. After a while, Moe taught him how to drive them in and out of the shop. When he didn't have much else to do, Mickey was constantly under the mechanic's feet, asking questions and bugging them to show him this, that, and the other thing. How it worked and what it did. He was always analyzing how things were designed and wanted to know what made them '*tick*.'

Over time, he got to know some of the drivers and loved listening to their tales of the road when they came in for service or repairs. They told stories about the things they had seen, the places they had been, followed by a new joke and more stories. Sometimes it was about the great hauls they had made, the accidents they had seen, and, of course, the always-cute waitress story. Mickey absorbed it all like a sponge and memorized every detail. Hearing all this made him want to get his license, so Moe and the others helped him study to get his permit.

They started him out by letting him take certain trucks to the service station to get fuel and gave him strict instructions.

"And don't go on no damn sightseeing tour either! Git ur ass back here and don't grind no gears! Otherwise, yer gonna learn how to swap out transmissions!"

"Yes, sir," Mickey replied.

He did grind some gears in the beginning and was very glad Moe wasn't around to hear it (it was *ugly*!) And yes, there were a few side roads that would take him a longer way back, but Moe never said anything about him taking too long. Mickey came to learn later on that Moe knew what he was doing all along, and that it was Moe's way of letting him figure it out on his own.

Mickey practiced as much as he could in the yard and even started parking trailers out back. He learned how to drop and hook, back in a straight line, and even back around corners. He learned how to do a complete walk-around and check every tire, light, airline connections, leaks, and even things no one told him about. He wanted to know every square inch of whatever he was driving or pulling.

Finally, the day came that Mickey took his driving test and when he passed with flying colors, the news of his success was followed by lots of slaps on the back along with getting his chops busted for being a *"newbie"* or *"fresh meat."* That was by followed the customary shots of Jack Daniels to celebrate the occasion. He felt like he had finally been accepted as one of the guys, and fulfilled a rite of passage.

Soon thereafter, a few of the local drivers offered to let him go with them on some local runs and would even let Mickey drive for short distances. It was an amazing feeling to him. He felt like he could see the whole world sitting up that high and being able to control such a huge piece of equipment was exhilarating to him.

Mickey finished earning his degree two and a half years later. To him, he received two degrees during his time in South Carolina. One from "U S C" and one from "Ball Buster U" at Moe's Garage. During his time at Moe's, Mickey learned just about everything they could teach him about driving a truck, truck repair and service, street racing, and hot rodding. He also learned about taking the ball-busting and giving it back twice as good, and about telling a good joke, honky-tonkin' on Saturday nights, bass fishing every chance you got and knowing the right amount of Jack Daniels it took to wake up in a strange place and forget how you got there.

When he left the sleepy little town of Newberry, South Carolina, and moved back home to Pennsylvania to work at his father's company as he promised his parents, Mickey would remember these people as an adopted family of sorts and carry the memories he had made there for the rest of his life.

****

Two years later, Mickey was sitting at his desk reviewing the renderings on his computer screen of the new design he had been working on recently, checking his calculations, and making the needed adjustments. But lately, he found himself becoming more and more distracted. Working at his father's company was okay and the money was decent enough, but Mickey had become restless, and quite frankly, bored. He had slowly eased away from the gatherings and quit accepting invitations to association functions that his parents were members of, instead preferring to hang out at the local truck stop garage in town on the weekends. Mickey made friends with the owner of the garage who let him work there, much like Moe did back in South Carolina. The smell of diesel, the clang of tools, and the hum of engines felt more like home than any cubicle or boardroom ever could and he was more comfortable there than in his nice office. Mickey did just as he had at Moe's shop, tackling whatever needed to be done and driving anything he could get his hands on.

One Sunday, there wasn't much to do at the shop, so he wandered over to the restaurant next door and took a booth near a group of truckers. From where he sat, Mickey could hear their stories and was reminded of his days in Newberry and all the characters he had met back then. While he was eating and listening to their conversation, his ears caught bits and pieces of a crazy story about a sheriff's deputy calling in a pursuit of an 18-wheeler that shot ten feet of fire out of its stacks, sounded like a lion roaring, and then sped away at over 150 mph within a matter of seconds.

Wow! Mickey thought. *Is that even possible?* He was always reading the latest truck magazines and articles online about new technology and electric truck concepts, but he never heard anything about this kind of speed in a truck. Finally, he turned around and politely asked if he could sit with these truckers and hear more.

"Sure," they said. One driver named John said he read about the story on the Internet. Reportedly, some deputy sheriff out in

Weatherford, Texas, had called in a pursuit of an 18-wheeler running with no lights out on some highway, then took off at a high rate of speed after spewing two ten-foot flames out of its stacks. He said it sounded like a lion's roar or something and blew up his car trying to catch the guy. They all said they didn't believe it, but it was a cool story. Mickey agreed.

After chatting and listening to them for another hour, Mickey went home to mull over the story and other things he had on his mind. On his way out, he grabbed the usual truck trader papers and a couple of trucker magazines. Later that evening, while watching TV, he kept thinking about the crazy story he had heard earlier.

Now, the analytical side of his brain was asking about the validity of the information. Mickey broke down the story:

1. It was reported by a State Trooper in Texas, so there would be transcripts of the incident that are a matter of public record.

2. It was identified as an 18-wheeler.

3. The officer described unusual activity but also gave very detailed descriptions of what he witnessed.

4. There was a vehicle destroyed in the process, so there would be documentation of that as well.

5. Whoever engineered this thing, if it was real, was way ahead of anything he was aware of.

Mickey was fascinated by the possibility of such a story, but, like the others, highly doubted its accuracy. He also had other things on his mind and some big decisions to make, ones he was sure his parents would not approve of. There was no denying the fact that Mickey was not really happy here and preferred to be on the road with the kind of people he met at the truck stop. They seemed to be more genuine and not trying to impress anyone—unlike the people he worked with and even his own parents. No, he had pondered the idea long enough and made his decision.

As he expected, Mickey's parents did not take the news well. His father spewed flames of his own.

"Drive a truck! Are you insane? You're throwing away your career to drive a truck? That's the most irresponsible thing you've ever done in your life, son! I don't understand. I mean, it was a good experience and all, I understand, but not a career."

His mother was a bit calmer. She wasn't so worried about Mickey, but really about what she would tell her friends. The shame of it all.

For Mickey, it was the first time he had ever really stood his ground as a man toward his parents. He had always done as they had predicted and planned for him. This new independent thinking was totally out of character and to them, was obviously the result of bad influences. In reality, he had become a man of his own mind, and he knew what *he* wanted to do for the first time in *his* life.

And that was that.

Three weeks later, Mickey took delivery of his new truck. It was beautiful! A bright-red, shiny new Kenworth T-680 with all the bells and whistles. It had every bit of the latest technology you could get and then some, and it was his. As he sat behind the wheel and took it all in, Mickey's mind went back to his days at that little garage in Newberry, and he remembered how it felt driving around the yard and imagining himself behind the wheel of his own truck, traveling across the country, living out the stories he had heard from other drivers.

Now, it was his turn. He was ready to make his own stories and tell his own tales.

Mickey leased on with a long-haul company that offered multiple routes throughout the lower forty-eight, and it didn't matter where. He just wanted to drive and see the country.

And drive he did. Mickey rarely took any downtime that first year and had the time of his life seeing the sights he had heard about at Moe's Garage and so much more. He met and made friends with nearly everyone he met. The freight dispatchers loved his enthusiasm and dependability. Along the way, he also learned who to trust—and who not to, something every newbie experiences in the trucking business.

Now, lying here in the dark at the I-20 truck stop in Lincoln, Alabama and still wondering about the wild sounds he heard, Mickey remembered Moe's philosophy about life: *"People who know what they're doin' usually messed up a bunch first. In life, ya' don't get old bein' stupid. Ya gotta keep yer wits aboutcha, kid. Listen to the ones who have been there and made the mistakes. If they take the time to give you advice, shut up and listen!"*

Those words echoed in his memories as his final thought for the night was: *"Maybe it was just a dream."*

Maybe so, driver. Maybe so.

Chapter Nineteen
Boss, Can We Get a Raise?

Eddie and Radar had been on the road for just over seven hours now on their way to Guymon, Oklahoma, to start the next series of tests. Wherever possible, Jimmy and his team had managed to have him run at 125 mph to cut the thirteen-and-a-half-hour drive down to seven hours. Eddie didn't really care about the tests all that much; his mind was set on one thing—getting back to Oregon. He had made up his mind that, despite all the chaos and noise banging around in his head about prophecies and what may or may not happen, he was going to tell Debbie how he felt and get on with his life. He knew how he felt, and that was that. He wanted to live again and, frankly, was exhausted from worrying about it.

In the control room back at the compound, it was 3:30 in the morning. Jimmy, Steve Decker, Bobby Chu, and Danny Wong were holding down the fort, managing duties tonight while everyone else took the weekend off. After he checked in with Eddie, Jimmy gave him the green light to activate T-1 and start his run.

"Roger that," came the confident reply. Tapping the icon for T-1, a burst of flame lit up the Oklahoma night sky as CatZilla roared to life, and quickly launched the rig to 125 mph. Morgana had started the first stage of her ten-mile-long run on US 64/412 in Guymon, Oklahoma, and it seemed to Eddie that he had just let the horse, or Cat as it were, out of the barn, ready to stretch her legs. The cab was bathed in the soft glow of the instrument panels, the green lights of the gauges and telemetry blinking steadily as everything registered within perfect parameters. The truck felt smooth, almost alive under his hands, responding to every slight adjustment with uncanny precision. He could feel the rig lowering slightly as the computerized suspension system adjusted to the airflow and speed, hugging the asphalt as it gained momentum. The smell of diesel and warm metal filled the cab, mingling with the faint scent of ozone from the night air outside, adding to the thrill. For him, it was a different, but exhilarating. The feeling was like dancing on the edge of control and chaos all at once.

While listening to Jimmy babble through his earpiece about the engine and other technical details, Eddie began hearing things he hadn't noticed before and wondered if something was wrong. He was still hearing Jimmy, but the voice faded into the background as Eddie tuned into his gift and began to search, scanning the rig and its systems for the odd sound.

After a few seconds of scanning, he determined it wasn't coming from the truck. No, it was something else. What was that sound? A thumping noise, irregular but insistent, yet Eddie couldn't put his finger on it. With his senses alerted, his eyes took another sweep around the cab, but everything seemed in order. He then focused on the screen to see if the tire sensors or any of the other icons were lit up. Again, everything was fine, but now the thumping became more pronounced, almost rhythmic.

Radar also joined Eddie in scanning the cab, then began looking up. *What is that sound? Even the dog hears it. But he didn't make any noises or bark.* The roar of the engine had dropped off, yet it was still difficult to separate the normal truck sounds from whatever Eddie was hearing. He kept looking at the screen, hoping for anything that might give him a clue—tire sensors, telemetry, anything. Meanwhile, Jimmy was still droning on about who knows what, which was actually good in that nothing could be wrong with the truck, otherwise, he or one of his team would have said something by now.

So, what was the thumping? Suddenly, a text came up on the dashboard screen:

MR MCVANE, PLEASE ANSWER YOUR PHONE WHEN IT RINGS.

"What the…? A random text out of the blue? Who would be calling me out here now? And how did they get this number?" Something wasn't right and Eddie was confused.

Then, as promised, his phone went off. Hesitating for a moment, he decided to mess with whoever it was. Surely this was a prank or something.

"Hello. Joe's Pool Hall. Eight Ball speakin'. We rack'em, you smack'em."

After a short pause, a man's voice cut through, calm and authoritative:

"Mr. McVane, this is Matt Taggart with Homeland Security. We request that you please slow your vehicle down to the speed limit. There is a black SUV about two miles behind you with its flashers on. Allow it to pass you, then follow it to a turnoff just down the road where you will be instructed as to your next move."

"*Homeland Security? Seriously?*" he wondered. Eddie checked his cameras and saw nothing. Because they were on a straight, flat road, he was sure he would be able to see some kind of light in the distance, even two miles back. Plus, Jimmy and the team would have alerted him if a vehicle was giving chase. But there was nothing. He wasn't buying it.

Indignant at the request, Eddie shot back, voice rising with defiance, "Zat so! Well, listen up, Sparky. I don't know who the hell you are or what your game is, but this rig ain't stopping for *no*-body and *no*-thing," emphasizing the *no* in both words.

"*Road pirates!*" he thought.

Now, Jimmy spoke up, after hearing the exchange, also puzzled by the interruption. "Eddie! What in the blazes is going on?"

"Dunno, buddy, but I think someone is trying to hijack me! They say their Homeland Security."

"What!?" Jimmy checked his computer screen and saw nothing from the real-time satellite images and frowned.

"I'm looking right at you, and we don't see anything anywhere around you. Can't be possible."

"Well, somebody sure as hell is in my ear."

"How the hell did they hack our communications?" Jimmy asked.

"Don't ask me. That's your department. All I know is they want me to slow down and let some S U V pass and the follow it to, wherever, for what I don't know."

Again, the voice spoke, and this time, it sounded even more like an order.

"Mr. McVane, we—"

Eddie bristled, snapping back, "Listen up, jerk-offs, I don't know what your game is or how you're jammin' our communications, but I don't take orders from road pirates! So you can go pound salt!"

Reaching over to his secret compartment, Eddie slid out the modified Benelli M4 tactical shotgun with Radar watching him intently. The dog stayed silent, alert but calm, muscles tense like a coiled spring.

Eddie boomed into the darkness, voice carrying over the roar of the engine. "I'm warning you right now. I'm armed and I will blast yer asses to kingdom come. So best thing you can do is move on down the road, chumps."

Jimmy came back over his earpiece. "Eddie! You want I should call the cops?"

"And tell them what? It'd be an hour before anybody showed up anyway. Gimme a second. I still got some juice left in this goose. If the bastards want this load, they're gonna have to catch me first."

Jimmy threw out a warning, tension clear in his tone. "Eddie, careful. We haven't tested her under these conditions yet!"

"No time like the present, buddy. Besides, I think this classifies as an emergency." He reached over and tapped the icon on the screen to engage the second turbo and the second phase of the electric drive system.

Fire erupted from the twin stacks, roaring seemingly louder than before. The truck jumped forward violently, with Eddie almost standing on the gas pedal.

"Come and get me, assholes!" he yelled at the voice. The truck was now surging past 160 rapidly.

The animated truck diagram and telemetries on the screen showed the airfoil stabilizers deploying from hidden compartments all around the truck and trailer, compensating for the added downforce, and the side vents on the hood opened to allow better airflow to help cool the engine. Eddie briefly marveled at how smoothly the truck handled even at these extreme speeds before refocusing on the voice in his ear.

The voice spoke again trying to reassure him

"Mr. McVane. Please, we are not trying to rob you. We just want to talk."

Eddie was having no part of it.

"Yeah, sure. I've heard that line before. Tell ya what, leave a number and I'll have my people call your people. See ya." And with that, Eddie focused on his gauges and the road ahead while continuing to accelerate.

Just then a different voice came through, only this one sounded more like the guy in charge, only the background noise sounded different with him.

"Mr. McVane, please comply. We are not road pirates, and we have no interest in your load of frozen fish. We just want to talk to you."

Eddie was startled that they knew what he was hauling. *What the hell? How'd he know that?*

Still, despite the revelation, he continued rebelling against the unknown voice. Eddie shot back at him.

"Sorry, cupcake, but look at it from my seat. Here I am, cruisin' along in the middle of nowhere, Oklahoma, minding my own business, and suddenly, you pop up on my screen and whisper in my ear that you want me to pull over so we can have a chat? Sorry, but ya gotta do better than that, sport!"

"Mr. McVane," came the terse reply, "If we wanted to, we could take you and your rig out at any time but, like I said, we just want to talk."

"Yeah! Sez you! Put up or shut up!" Eddie growled back. He wasn't sure what they were driving and didn't see anything behind him or on any of the screens, but he was going to give them a run for their money.

As he checked his speedometer, he was at 170 mph and starting to climb. Bracing himself, he prepared to engage the next phase and was reaching over to initiate the third turbo/electric drive system when he heard Jimmy over the com.

"Uh-oh!"

"Uh-oh, what? Jimmy! I'm doing 170-plus and all you can say is, 'uh-oh'?"

"Um, Eddie. Listen, there are some serious-looking guys here in tactical gear telling us to stand down."

"What?"

Suddenly, off to Eddie's left side window, the road exploded with light, illuminating everything nearby as if it were broad daylight. If he hadn't been strapped in, he surely would have fallen out of his seat. There, pacing him steadily and ominously, all bathed in the harsh glare, was a fully armed Black Hawk helicopter, its rotor blades whipping the air into a furious roar with its side-mounted machine gun locked and aimed directly at his door. It was a good thing he had two-way glass; otherwise, they would have seen a very startled and bewildered truck driver. As he stared in disbelief, Eddie wasn't sure he was seeing what he was seeing, but he knew it wasn't good. After a brief second, he slowly slid the Benelli back into its hidden compartment, thinking, *I'm gonna need a bigger gun.* As the shock was wearing off, his mind began racing, trying to get his head around the situation.

"Jimmy, what the hell have you gotten us into now?" he muttered under his breath.

Periodically glancing out the window at the helicopter, he eased off the throttle and began gradually shutting down the hybrid CatZilla system. The turbo went silent and the truck began slowly decelerating. Eddie felt bewildered, defeated, and a little helpless now, realizing that whoever they were could indeed take him out if they wanted to. But were they really Homeland Security? It didn't make any sense. *What the hell could they possibly want with us?*

Slowly regaining his composure, he broke the silence.

"Okay, Mr. Voice in my Ear, you've got my attention. What now?"

"Like I said, Mr. McVane, we just want to talk. Please follow the black SUV when it comes into view, and we will explain shortly."

Still trying to maintain his cool-under-pressure persona, he answered back, "Well, when you put it like that, sure, why not? I wasn't busy anyway." Eddie tried to sound cocky, but even he wasn't buying it. While he was slowing down, his mind was racing, trying to grasp why Homeland Security would go through all this trouble. If that's who they really were.

A Black Hawk helicopter with machine guns? They don't just pull you over in the middle of nowhere to have a chat. The night air was still, punctuated only by the faint hum of the truck's cooling systems and the distant whir of the helicopter rotors, creating an eerie contrast to the chaos unfolding in his mind.

****

Back at the compound, Jimmy was both alarmed and pissed off that his facility was so easily breached and his communications were hacked. He and his team were now at the mercy of those he didn't know. Glancing at the two-armed tactical guys with a concerned frown, he asked, "So, what now, guys?"

The one on the left spoke. "Mr Wagner, our orders are to secure the situation and make sure nothing gets destroyed. We are not here to harm you or your operation. Like the Colonel said, he just wants to talk." Jimmy looked startled.

"Colonel? Like a military type Colonel?"

"Yes, sir."

"Okay, what's this all about?"

"He will be forthcoming with that shortly," came the calm reply.

Frowning while looking from one to the other, Jimmy decided to take a wait-and-see approach, but he also wasn't backing down.

"Okay, then. It's obvious you have us at a disadvantage." After a short pause while still staring at the two men, he finished with his own warning. "For now."

Turning his attention back to his screen, Jimmy did just that and motioned to the others to follow suit. He sat there and glanced at the skull-and-crossbones icon in the upper-left-hand corner of the screen. Trying to be inconspicuous, Jimmy casually eased his mouse toward it. The tactical man on the right, though, voiced an equally casual warning.

"Please don't do that, sir. Like I said, we are not here to steal anything or harm you or your teammates, but also, do not attempt to destroy any of your files."

Pausing, Jimmy finally relented. So, he waited, eye darting between the tactical officers and the screens, aware that any misstep could escalate things quickly.

****

Meanwhile, Eddie continued to slow down to a measured speed of 65 mph.

"I'm too old for this crap," he muttered again to himself. Radar kept looking around and making funny little noises, drawing Eddie's attention. He immediately remembered the self-destruct option and wondered if this was one of those scenarios. Grumbling at the dog, he tried to make light of the situation.

"Now you make noises? You losing your edge or what?" Radar looked at him as if apologizing, so Eddie gave him a pat and a reassuring word. "It's okay, buddy. Let's see what these guys want first before we get drastic." He decided he would keep the self-destruct remote within easy reach, just in case.

After a few minutes, the flashing lights of a black SUV appeared in the rear-view camera and then passed his truck. Eddie got in behind it, and after a few miles, it slowed down, signaling him to follow. As they turned off the highway and down a side road, they went for about a half-mile before curving behind an old, abandoned farmhouse. They passed a barn onto a flat open turnaround area that overlooked a long-forgotten pasture where he was instructed to stop.

The SUV then circled and pointed at him nose-to-nose about thirty feet away. In the distance, the Black Hawk glided in for a landing in an open area just off to his right in the field where he just came through. Its rotor wash kicking up dust and debris, scattering shadows in the moonlit Oklahoma night. He could see its silhouette and vaguely discern its details. Radar started making more of those funny noises, prompting Eddie to reassure him once again. "I know, buddy. I'm not keen on all this either."

The black SUV had its lights shining at him, but the two-way feature kept them from seeing inside. Eddie assessed the scene: a black SUV and an armed Black Hawk helicopter. Although they looked like government vehicles, he couldn't be sure. It seemed like overkill for Homeland Security to go through all this trouble just to have a chat with him. But, they really could have easily shot him off the road if that was their intent.

So what's the deal? Eddie wondered. *Seems a bit much to issue a speeding ticket, so that can't be it.* After taking a few more moments to collect himself, he decided that if he were going to go down for whatever was coming, he would do it with style. Eddie reached over to the holder on the dash, grabbed a fresh cigar, clipped the end off, and fired it up. Taking a big puff, he set his mind on the task at hand.

Just before exiting, Eddie hit the "record" button on the com and opened the channel so there would be a recording of the meeting. He also still had his earpiece in so he could hear if anything happened on

Jimmy's end and the self-destruct fob was in his pocket. Jimmy had been quiet for a while now. Whether that was good or bad, Eddie didn't know.

Finally, he braced himself for whatever came next. "Okay, dog. Let's go have a chat with these boys and see what's on their minds." Radar made one of his low funny grunts, as if in agreement.

Eddie climbed down out of the cab with Radar right behind him and eased around to the front of the truck and squared off against the SUV. Casually, he leaned back on the grill, kicked one foot back on the bumper, clenched his freshly lit cigar in his teeth, and waited. Oddly, Radar maneuvered just off to his left, this time at about ten feet, then he sat and watched intently, every muscle taut. Eddie looked over at him, noticing this was out of character for him; to him, it seemed to be a tactical move of sorts. *Preparing a defense, maybe?* He wasn't sure. A new thing to ponder. Nonetheless, he refocused his attention back to the matter at hand.

As he stood there taking in the scene and puffing on his freshly lit cigar, the doors on the SUV opened. Three men stepped out and formed a line in front of Eddie. Although he was feeling pretty taken aback by the events unfolding in front of him, he refused to show it. The men were all dressed in tactical gear, armed with automatic weapons, and looked stone-faced and ready for business.

They approached Eddie and formed a semicircle about fifteen feet away, facing him and Radar. The one on Eddie's far left gave special attention to the dog, but Radar didn't seem concerned. His focus remained on the Black Hawk that had just landed, its rotor blades slowing down.

Watching all this, Eddie, true to form, felt the urge to lighten the moment. With the key fob in hand, he slowly lifted his arm over his left shoulder and activated the security system. *Chirp! Chirp!* It rang out.

The men looked at one another and then back at Eddie, seemingly amused by this action. That made Eddie smile. He took his cigar out, looking at the tactical-clad group and commenting in a deadpan fashion. "Can't be too careful nowadays, what with bandits and such all about. Never know who you're gonna run into in the middle of nowhere."

For now, Eddie figured if they had intended to shoot him, they would have done it already. And yet, the uncertainty lingered—they still might.

In the distance, he watched as the door of the Black Hawk slid open and a figure jumped out and moved toward them in a crouched position. As the figure passed the rotor wash, he stood upright, walking crisply past the others until he stopped directly in front of Eddie. He was of medium build, blonde hair combed back, and for the moment, sported a casual smile that belied the tough-guy persona he had conveyed over the phone.

He smiled directly at Eddie, who smiled back at him in defiance. Radar had quietly eased closer to Eddie and was focused intently on this man standing in front of them. Eddie noted that Radar seemed to be broader now, as if he were readying for battle.

The blonde-haired figure noticed it too. He looked at Radar, then back at Eddie, still sporting his casual smile. "Nice dog," he finally said. The first words spoken between the two men in person. Eddie responded in defiance.

"At the moment. He is a nervous sort though. so I'd be careful." Although he and Radar were outnumbered, Eddie wasn't folding just yet. There were still cards to be played.

"Looks like he has your same attitude," came the reply. Now the verbal game was on.

"Yeah, well, he's not keen on machine-gun-wielding Black Hawks hovering outside his window in the middle of the night, either." Eddie upped the ante.

In the back of his head, he could hear his father's words of long ago encouraging him to stand his ground firmly in an uneven situation. *"Never let your opponent see fear, son. Always let them think you have more than they can see. You have to show them that you are willing to take whatever they give and come back for more and say, 'Is that all you got?'"*

Although he doubted his father ever had this scenario in mind, Eddie gave his best *I don't give a damn* pose and looked at the man in front of him right in the eyes and began.

"Okay, sport. Let's chat."

The blonde-haired fellow grinned. "Well, Mr. McVane, I'll give you this. You obviously are not intimidated by us and that's good. I like a man who stands his ground, even in the face of overwhelming odds. Says a lot about you."

He had a New York accent and the attitude to go with it, Eddie surmised. And so he countered.

"Yeah, well, I'm a realist. I take whatever comes my way and adjust accordingly. I figure, if I'm gonna go out, I'm gonna do my best to do it on my terms. Besides, I don't like being caught off guard by strangers who come at me out of the dark and want to 'friend me' in the middle of the desert. Doesn't set well with me in today's environment. A lot of hijackers and con artists out there. I usually don't tolerate such tactics but, at the moment, yours is bigger than mine. So, how 'bout let's get to it?"

That brought a chuckle Eddie's way. "Sorry about that, but we have important matters at hand and time is of the essence."

He stepped forward and extended his hand. "My name is Colonel Nathan Travis. I run a special operations unit that oversees matters of international and homeland security where it pertains to transportation-type terrorist threats."

Eddie made no move to accept his hand but instead asked to see his ID. The blonde-haired man retracted his hand and complied.

"Okay, Fair enough request."

The Colonel produced his credentials.

After looking them over, Eddie again met Travis' eyes and then offered his hand. Travis responded in kind and as the men shook, Eddie went right to it.

"Okay, Colonel. Homeland Security, eh? So, are you thinking I'm a threat?"

The Colonel gave a cocky smirk.

"If I thought you were, 'Sport', I would have blown your ass to bits first and then sifted through the pieces for answers afterward. I don't tolerate nonsense much myself."

"Good to know. I feel much better now" Eddie quipped. Radar was still staring at Colonel Travis even though it was less tense between the men; the dog wasn't yet ready to relax.

The Colonel made a motion with his hand toward Morgana, which now appeared as a tall, imposing figure with piercing eyes and an intimidating presence, seemingly reading to attack if given the command.

"Nice hot rod you got there. Fast, too. I believe you were testing some new upgrades?"

Eddie offered no response or expression but kept his eyes locked on Travis. He didn't know how much he knew or didn't know— but he wasn't giving it out for free. He let the silence build.

After a few seconds of Eddie not answering and looking at him expressionless, the Colonel nodded and continued. "Okay, I get it. So anyway, it has come to my attention that you and your eccentric friend back home in the 'Bat Cave' have managed to build a very fast rig— one that has a lot of interesting gadgetry. And it's rumored to reach 200 mph or more, given the chance. That alone, my friend, makes you very interesting to us."

Listening, Eddie wasn't liking where this was going, but admittedly, he was a captive audience. So, he puffed and listened as the Colonel continued.

"You guys have created quite a buzz on the Internet as well. You're actually considered a legend, of sorts." Pointing and looking at the truck, Travis continued, "This thing has a huge following and a lot of theories as to what makes it tick." The Colonel looked back at Eddie and grinned. "That is, if it really existed." He paused for a moment before continuing. "So far, it's just rumors of a so-called 'ghost truck' that shoots flames and roars like a lion."

At this point, Eddie had no idea what the Colonel was talking about with the Internet, and honestly, he didn't care. He had just had himself pulled over by an attack helicopter, its imposing presence a sharp reminder of the dangerous situation he was in. The helicopter was commanded by a man capable of getting in the middle of his communications with Jimmy, who, by the way, was last heard to say he was facing a tactical team as well. It didn't seem likely that Travis went through all this trouble just to discuss how Jimmy and Eddie were trending on social media. Feeling the pressure and wanting to keep things moving, Eddie leaned back slightly, bracing himself as he pushed to accelerate the pace of the conversation.

"Colonel, I don't mean to be rude, but can we cut to the chase? I got a 7 a.m. delivery of fish to make the day after tomorrow, and so far, all I can gather is you know a little bit about me, Jimmy, and this truck, and that, apparently, you have a man crush on us. Now, like you've already said, if you thought I was a threat, you would have blown my ass to bits. I know you hacked into our system and probably know a good bit about us. You sent a tactical team to what you call our Bat Cave, and you have your men there, heavily armed, of course, and again, your also heavily armed Black Hawk is parked right over there. But somehow, you went through all this just to have a chat and tell me about our Internet following? Am I missing something here?" Travis put his hand up to calm Eddie's fears.

"Regarding your friends, they're fine. My guys are just making sure Jimmy and your team don't try anything stupid while we're talking, like maybe needlessly destroying files, or some such thing."

Eddie took note that the Colonel apparently was not aware that it wasn't only Jimmy who had that capability. Travis continued.

"Yes, we did do our homework on you boys. Jimmy is somewhat of a legend, too, according to our research. It seems you two were quite the team back in the day."

Back at the compound, Jimmy, who had been listening the entire time perked up. He liked the sound of that word—*legend*. Jimmy the Hammer. Legend.

"Mostly in the old racing forums," Travis explained, "but I have to admit, it is a pretty impressive resume. And, although they don't know it's Jimmy behind the alleged *Super Truck or Ghost Truck*, the diesel geeks worship the guy who built its power plant and have given him an almost godlike status on their posts."

****

Now, Jimmy was loving every word of this. *Geek? Legend? Godlike? Cool!* He glanced at the two tactical guys who stood rigidly by him at attention. Their faces were expressionless masks, betraying nothing.

Jimmy sprang to life, addressing them directly. "Hey, are you guys okay? Need a drink? Have to pee? Anything you need, you just tell me." He waited for a response. There was none.

"Nothing? Okay, then, carry on." He leaned back slightly in his chair, crossing his arms while settling into a watchful position, then back to listening to the exchange between Eddie and the Colonel.

****

Eddie, feigning disinterest in the history lesson of him and Jimmy, pushed the Colonel to pick up the pace.

"Yeah, yeah, yeah, I know, good ole' days, blah, blah, blah. Got it. Back to the point of all this, please."

Travis's smile went to a smirk as he stuck his hand up to his shoulder and barked an order, "Taggart!"

Just then, one of the shadows came jogging up and placed a pad in the Colonel's hand. Travis opened it and began reading off what seemed like Eddie's entire life story.

"Edward Francis McVane, born 14 June 1954. Parents, John Edward and Edith Marion McVane. Graduated from Parkland High School in 1972. Joined the Army and served as a transport driver hauling fuel and supplies toward the end of the Vietnam War. Expert marksman during boot camp. Achieved the rank of Sergeant, honorably discharged. Married Katherine Lillian Morgan, one son, Edward McVane, Jr. Raced cars professionally until your father's death in 1988. Took over and ran the family business until your mother's death in 1999. Sold said business two years later in 2001. Started McVane Trucking in 2002. Wife was killed in a car accident in 2014. Six months later you sold the business, bought a new rig and leased on to Consolidated Fish Co. During your time with Consolidated, you also hauled heavy equipment, prefabbed buildings, and various other types of van and reefer loads before leasing onto Parkland Institute for Advanced Green Diesel Research and Technology, Inc., in 2017. Eight months ago, as you were traveling on I-20 westbound just outside of Shreveport, Louisiana, you were in a fatal crash that involved a drunk driver heading eastbound, sending you off the road, totaling both your truck and trailer. The drunk driver died on impact while you sustained minor injuries in the accident."

Travis handed the pad back to the one called Taggart.

Now Eddie was visibly uncomfortable and did not like being at anybody's mercy, especially someone who seemed to have his whole life wrapped up in a folder. He responded bluntly, voice low and controlled,

"Point." he growled.

"Getting there, Mr. McVane. Please have patience. Now, up until the accident, you had managed to live a pretty mundane, solitary life. In fact, as far as anybody was concerned, you didn't even exist. Then three months ago happened. That's when a trucker in Virginia who had lost his brakes and was coming down a mountain out of control, posted an amazing story about a ghost trucker who came out of nowhere in thick fog at an even more amazing speed to get in front of him and slow him down so he could get on a runaway ramp to safety. After that, there's the Highway Patrol Officer out in Weatherford, Texas, who called in a report that he was in pursuit of an 18-wheeler traveling at speeds in excess of 150 mph! Of course, nobody took him seriously at the time, because, well, 18-wheelers just don't travel that fast. Right? Plus, he couldn't produce any evidence to the contrary. So, yeah, *you* didn't exist, but you can't say the same for your exploits.

"Problem is, those kinds of stories tend to get around, hence the Internet theories and rumors. By the way, that Officer is still pissed. From what I understand, he apparently blew up his patrol car trying to catch said 18-wheeler."

Eddie was unaware of that information. He continued leaning back against the grill of his truck, puffing on his cigar, the desert wind rustling loose gravel around his boots. His eyes stayed narrowed, expressionless.

Travis paused for a few seconds, noticing that Eddie was still defiant and unmoved, cigar smoke curling into the air so he continued.

"Anyway, like I said, the story went viral on the Internet about a super ghost truck that goes over 150 mph. Now, as you can imagine, somebody is going to want to find out if it's, shall we say, a real UFO sighting or just another hoax. In your case, UFO means an *Unidentified Fast Object*."

Eddie rolled his eyes. "Cute," he snorted.

"Unfortunately for you, Mr. McVane, one of my guys loves these kinds of stories. Follows them religiously on the Internet. Just can't get enough. He is always on blogs searching for the latest updates and the story of a ghost truck is a particular favorite of his. Equally unfortunate for you is that he is also a drone operator and analyst for us who was given an assignment to do a search around a rural area off Interstate I-20, just outside a certain town in Texas.

"Now, while he didn't see anything related to what we were looking for, he did notice a very unusual anomaly. When he went back and reviewed the tape of this anomaly, he couldn't believe what he was seeing. Yes, sir, my man was so excited he couldn't wait to show me the video footage. I must admit, I was pretty impressed myself, Mr. McVane. The first time I watched it, there was nothing. Literally, nothing. Then *poof*! Two bright flashes of fire light up the night sky from a truck on the highway below, and then, *zoom*! Gone! Like nothing I've ever seen before. Would you like to take a guess as to what town that was, Mr. McVane?"

Eddie removed his cigar and replied in a deadpan fashion, "I heard it was Abilene."

The Colonel smiled.

"Nice try."

Figuring he would fight to the end, Eddie spat out, "Again, your point?"

"Well, you know, I…" Then Colonel Travis gestured at his men before continuing. "We just had to meet you, Mr. McVane. After all, who doesn't want to meet a legend?"

Eddie, looking somewhat bewildered, replied "Seriously?"

Now he'd heard enough. He wasn't sure where all this was going but his patience was gone. Eddie pushed himself forward off the grill of the truck and planted both feet on the ground, dust kicking up around his boots. He looked at the Colonel, pursing his lips in one final act of defiance.

"So. This is how it ends for me, eh, Colonel? And all this time, I was kinda hoping for going out in a blaze of glory, like driving off a cliff in a ball of fire and exploding into a confetti rainbow or something cool like that. Instead, I get busted by a bunch of thrill-seeking government employees out in the middle of nowhere, Oklahoma. Bummer. You guys are totally harshing my mellow right about now."

Eddie was annoyed for sure, but decided to go the distance, bracing himself for whatever came next…after he lit up Travis just a little bit more.

"So, let me get this straight. You guys came all the way out here in a Black Hawk helicopter with other assorted tactical hardware, just to bust my balls and to say what? You got me? You know things about me? You could have sent any local cop to scoop me up at any truck stop in the country, but no, you wanted to do it in person. Sounds kinda creepy if you ask me, but I won't judge. Tell you what, how about an autograph? A t-shirt? No, wait, a selfie of us by the truck, maybe. Oh, wait, I know! You wanna ride in the big truck and honk the horn. Yeah, everybody wants to do that."

Eddie had tired of the game and was done, but also figured by now they weren't there to kill him. He folded his arms and leaned back against the grill of his truck, the desert night wind tugging at his jacket, waiting for a comeback that he made sure he'd get by finishing his retort with a final challenge.

"Alright, let's get on with it. Fish or cut bait. What is the damn point of all this?"

The Colonel chuckled, as did the shadows in the background, their silhouettes flickering in the dim light from the truck's headlights. "Thanks, but I have something better in mind."

"And that would be?"

"I want to hire you."

Eddie froze for a moment, staring blankly at Travis, the desert around them eerily quiet except for the faint hum of the helicopter behind the Colonel and his team. He tried to process what he had just heard. Of all the crazy things that had happened to him in the past several months, this was off the charts.

Slowly, Eddie leaned forward and stood up, glaring at the Colonel and the others, looking back and forth to each. Finally, words started to form and he went off.

"Whoa, wait just a minute. What? You want to what? Are you freakin' kidding me? This...this is a job interview?" He stammered out, "Seriously? Are you freakin' kidding me?" Eddie started pacing and spewing expletives.

The Colonel tried to calm him down. "Now, Mr. McVane…"

Eddie held his hand up, trying to stop what he was hearing.

"No! No! No! This is not happening! This is bullshit! No, this is total insanity! Really? Hire? You want to..." He never finished his thought, pacing back and forth, running a hand through his hair, trying to get his head around what he just heard.

At this point, Eddie was talking out loud to no one in particular.

"Ya know, all I wanted to do was just come out here, drive my truck, mind my own business, and live out the rest of my frustrated, miserable life in peace! But *no*! I had to let Jimmy talk me into driving this crazy ass truck and test new technology for the future. *It'll be fun,* he said, *it'll be like the old days*, he said. *You would be doing a good thing*, he said."

Travis tried to interject. "Mr. McVane," but Eddie wasn't listening.

"Damn you, Jimmy Wagner! Now look what you've gotten us into! What the hell was I thinking?"

Jimmy shrank into his chair a little, eyes darting nervously between Steve, Bobby, and Danny, then to the tactical guys standing silently behind him. He half-smirked saying, "Eddie's just an excitable boy. He'll be okay once he calms down," and returned to looking at his monitor.

The Colonel started toward Eddie, trying to get his attention. "Mr. McVane! Eddie"—more sputtering—finally, the Colonel shouted him back to reality, "***Eddie!***"

Eddie spun around and started walking back toward him, still spewing.

"What? I'm supposed to be okay with this? You bunch of government yahoos come out here in the middle of nowhere in the middle of the night on a taxpayer-funded joyride to harass me and my friend, and then, after all this drama, you say you want to hire us? And that's supposed to sound reasonable to me? That's a double-barreled shot of bullshit, bubba! This is blackmail! Pure and simple blackmail! I'm a civilian, for crying out loud! I have rights, you know! Besides, what the hell do you guys need with us anyway? Me, I'm just a truck driver. You can get them anywhere. Jimmy, I could maybe understand. And besides that, you're the government. You got all our money to begin with. Go build your own damn truck! *Jeeze!* What a bunch of weasels."

He continued his rant a little more before starting to slow down. His chest heaved from the exertion, his hands gesturing wildly, and his face flushed with a mix of anger and disbelief. Finally, with his back to Travis and the world, Eddie lamented, "I don't need or want any of this in my life right now. I just got a girlfriend."

Jimmy perked up at that news, leaning forward in his chair, eyes widening, "Say what?"

The Colonel, feeling somewhat bad and trying to smooth Eddie over, offered, "Look, relax and let me explain."

Eddie spun around to face him.

"Relax! Seriously?"

"It's not what you think," said the Colonel.

"Not what I think? Not what I think? Okay, Colonel, how about telling me what I should think?"

"First of all, please calm down before you have a stroke or something." Eddie threw his head back and just laughed.

"God, I should be so lucky! At least I wouldn't have to deal with any more of this insanity."

Eddie threw his hand up in frustration as he walked away down the side of the truck again. Travis started to follow him, but stopped as Radar moved between them, tail low, chest forward, still holding his gaze on Travis and emitting a low, warning growl.

Travis stopped in his tracks and decided to wait. "Okay, okay, nice doggy," he said, smiling.

Eddie, trying to form a response, was muttering under his breath. "What the hell am I supposed to do with this can of worms?"

Jimmy was feeling guilty now. He spoke into Eddie's earpiece, hoping to calm him down. "Eddie, I..."

Eddie stopped dead, waving his hand in the air and growled firmly, "NO! Not a word! Not...one...word, Jimmy! I will deal with you later."

"Sorry, man."

"Yeah, well, sorry, ain't gonna feed the bulldog this time, bubba!"

Eddie was starting to calm down some when the Colonel tried to explain again.

"Look, the reason we contacted you..."

Eddie spun around and rebutted, "Contacted? You mean abducted! Hijacked! Truck-napped…and with a loaded Black Hawk no less!"

"In all fairness, it wasn't really loaded," replied Travis, trying to lighten the mood. "Just had to let you know we were serious."

"Well, it worked! Scared the life outta me! Jeeze!" Eddie shot back. He stood with his hands on his hips, still stewing, but listening.

"Look, the reason we *detained* you is that we needed to talk to you. We need you guys and your truck to help us with something. While I can't give you all the details, for obvious reasons, we have a situation brewing that is potentially a matter of national security—maybe a possible terrorist attack on American soil. I can't let that happen on my watch. We were trying to find a way to fly under the radar and move around undetected in order to try and catch whoever is trying to do this. And yes, we do have access to a lot of technology, hardware, and resources, but we are still governed somewhat by certain officials. The other problem we have is that we've discovered that some of these officials have been compromised, not to mention everything we have is bugged with a tracking device. We're not sure who they all are yet. That's why when we stumbled across you on a drone video out in Texas, we had to check you out. Upon further investigation, we discovered that the technology you guys have come up with would help us move around wherever we need to go without being tracked. And, because nobody really knows you even exist except us, I'd like to keep it that way. The fact of the matter is, you guys are way ahead of us with this technology, and we need that technology to help us. You have the speed and stealth technology to move faster than anything we have on the ground at the moment. Listen, we really don't want to rain on your parade, or bust up your little high-tech freak show here, although we have every right to. We just need your help."

Eddie, though calmer, was still breathing heavy as he thought through the implications while listening to Travis.

"That's why when my people verified you were real, it was imperative we find you and try to convince you to work with us."

That brought a sharp comeback from Eddie.

"Yeah? Well, your interview process sucks! Just sayin. Hey, here's a thought. How about next time, *try a phone call!*" he said emphatically.

"Well, perhaps another approach could have been used, but like I said, there are bigger things at stake here and time is of the essence. Maybe we were just a bit overzealous."

Eddie looked at the Colonel and cocked his head.

"Overzealous? Gee, ya think?"

"Maybe, just a bit. Look, you would be serving your country and you'd be helping us keep some very bad people from potentially taking a lot of innocent lives. All you have to do is move us from Point A to Point B fast and under the radar, when we need you. You'd be doing a good thing, Mr. McVane. And, if it helps any, we really are fans as well. So whaddaya say?"

The Colonel smiled, arms relaxed, waiting for a reply.

Eddie looked at all of them with a dumbfounded look.

"Fans? Seriously? Good grief! Have you people lost your damn minds?" Exasperated, he shook his head and started pacing slowly back and forth to his truck.

Despite his agitated state of mind, Eddie was thinking about what the Colonel was saying. He really didn't need or want any more drama in his life right now especially with a new woman and looking forward to building on that. On the other hand, the Colonel was right that he and Jimmy both could get into a lot of trouble and possibly go to jail. For a long time.

But Eddie needed time to think. Despite the fact that the Colonel and his sales pitch seemed legit, he needed time to think and talk it over with Jimmy. That is, if Eddie didn't kill him first. His head was spinning. Here he thought he was on the downside of life, just living out his last days on the road he loved, minding his own business, and actually beginning to have some fun and living life again instead of living under a cloud and now this.

Shaking his head, Eddie walked around the truck, lamenting about the good ole' days, the wind brushing against his face, headlights casting long shadows behind him. Again, he started talking to no one in particular.

"Man, I wish I was on the backside of the Rocky Mountains, checking out the scenery, cruising along to some old tunes, listening to Fat Betty's nice rumble as we rolled along...God, I miss that truck."

Finally, Colonel Travis's voice broke his rant, pulling him back into the present.

"Mr. McVane?"

Eddie's head dropped for a moment and then he turned and walked back to stand firmly in front of Travis with his hands on his hips and gave him his answer.

"Listen, Colonel. Tell ya what. As much as I've enjoyed your little Black Ops version of *Let's Make A Deal*, I need some time to think. I mean, this is nuts! Do you realize what you're asking of me? Of us? And I'm guessing we don't really have a choice in the matter. After all, you tell me what you could do to us and then ask us to help? Kind of a crappy proposal if you ask me."

"I do, believe me. I do, Mr. McVane. But understand this. Desperate times call for desperate measures. There are some very bad people planning to do some very bad things, and I intend to stop them any way I can. That said, I will use every resource available, including recruiting civilians, to keep that from happening. So, understand this: For the moment, you can take some time and think it over. But like I said, time is critical. That being said, keep in mind that I can reach out and touch you whenever I want to now. So, no funny business. Got it?" Eddie stood there frowning as he stared Travis eye to eye. The mood between them now was more serious and somewhat tense. He resisted the urge to say anything else for the moment.

"Got it," Eddie answered with a tightness in his jaw.

"Alright, I'll be in touch." The Colonel waved his arm in a circle over his head signaling the others to wrap it up while the chopper started picking up rotor speed. As the rest of the team were scrambling to exit, Travis turned to Eddie.

"Just so you know, you came highly recommended as a man of integrity and someone who could be trusted. I hope you'll do the right thing, Mr. McVane." Then he turned and hustled back to the chopper. Stunned at that new information, Eddie bordered on anger and surprise.

"What?" he shouted at Travis and the retreating horde. "Who the hell would that be?" But no reply came as the others got in their vehicle and the Colonel jogged back to the Black Hawk. Standing there, Eddie just muttered to himself.

"Man, I'd love to know who hates me enough to refer me for this...this...whatever this is. A recommendation? What the hell?"

Then it hit him.

"Who else knows about us and this truck? And because of that, we've been recruited by Homeland Security?" Eddie looked down at Radar.

"Can they do that?" The dog had no reply, his ears twitching slightly in the wind.

The SUV sped off while he watched the Black Hawk take to the air, disappearing into the night, leaving Eddie in the swirling dust cloud that came after with just his frustration, the truck, and the dog.

****

Back at the compound, the two tactical guys also retreated after hearing the stand down order in their ear com, slipping away silently into the shadows. Jimmy watched them go and waved goodbye to their backs, saying, "Party on, guys! It's been a hoot. Don't come back soon."

He spun around in his chair, the glow of multiple monitors reflecting off his glasses, looking at the others who were still shaken by the events of the evening.

"The feds want to use our technology. This is gonna be awesome! Wait till the rest of the kids hear this!"

Although Jimmy was excited about the prospect, he was still annoyed at being hacked and infiltrated so easily. "That won't happen again," he said under his breath.

"Okay, guys, time to check in on Eddie."

Jimmy tapped his earpiece

"Um, Eddie?"

Eddie snapped out of his trance when he heard Jimmy's voice and barked into his earpiece.

"*No!*" He shouted. "Not talking to you right now, Geek, Legend, God Boy! I will call you when I no longer feel the urge to choke the life out of you for getting me into another of your harebrained schemes! I've had enough nonsense for one night." Taking out his earpiece, he threw it into the darkness. "*Enough*!" he yelled into the darkness.

Exasperated and exhausted, Eddie fell back against the grille of Morgana, arms hanging at his sides, staring up at the starry night sky in defeat.

"I just want some damn peace and quiet and to be left alone for a while. I need to think. And I need some Jack Daniel's. No... I need a lot of Jack Daniel's."

****

Jimmy cut off the com and glanced around at his team. Their faces were showing a mix of exhaustion and confusion as they tried to process what had just happened and more importantly, what might come next. Despite the tension lingering in the air, Jimmy spoke calmly, as if nothing unusual had occurred, his steady voice drawing the team's attention.

"I think we should leave him be for a while," Jimmy said, rubbing the back of his neck thoughtfully.

"Eddie's had a rough day. He'll be okay once he calms down. But we do need to find out more about this girlfriend. I knew something was different with him. When did that happen? That's why all the trips to Oregon and always the same street. Anyway, the government boys want to use our rig to help them. That's awesome. Opens up a whole new bunch of possibilities. Although we definitely need to beef up our security and firewalls. They were able to hack our cameras and satellite feed as well. They must have some seriously good hackers on their team. For now, though, let's keep this quiet from the others until we get some more info on what the gig is. Okay, guys, that's a wrap. Go home and get some rest. We'll have to schedule the long-run test for another day. She was starting to sail pretty good, though. A buck seventy ain't too shabby and steady as a rock, and everything was working as it should. Perfect!"

Steve, Bobby, and Danny exchanged bewildered looks, their eyes wide and brows furrowed, clearly struggling to digest the rapid-fire update. After a brief pause, Steve cleared his throat, breaking the silence. "Boss?"

Jimmy turned his head with a raised eyebrow. "Yeah, Steve."

"Can we get a raise?"

CHAPTER TWENTY
FEELS LIKE CRAZY

It was now 4:30 in the morning in Oklahoma and a very exasperated Eddie McVane was still trying to get a handle on the events of the past hour.

Standing there leaning against the grille of his truck, he lamented about the events of the evening.

"Man. My life is just getting stranger and stranger by the day. What am I supposed to do with all of this now? I didn't ask for any of it."

He was frustrated to say the least and just wanted it all to go away. As he started to walk away to clear his head, Radar began to follow suit beside him like he always had. Looking down at the dog, Eddie snapped at him.

"Oh no! No! No! No! You! You stay away from me! I've had enough of all this." The dog stopped as Eddie walked a short distance away. Looking back at him, he started voicing his frustration, "Okay, enough. I wanna know what's really going on. Why is all this happening to me? I know you have something to do with all this and I'm not crazy either!" Radar grunted and cocked his head.

"And don't give me that, 'I have no idea what you're talking about' look either. "Ever since you came into my life, it's just been one weird encounter after another. I've had enough, you hear me? Enough!" He glared at the dog and Radar started grunting and barking at him in short bursts and then stopped.

"Really?" replied Eddie. "That's all you have to say?" He spun around and paced back and forth some more, still ranting and talking to no one in particular. "Of all the crazy things I have been involved with in my life, this takes the cake. What the hell am I doing here? Traipsing all over the country driving this stupid freak show of a truck, hanging out with a spooky hair bag of a dog who is clearly from a bad *Twilight Zone* episode and acting like this is okay. What was I thinking? Now I'm being blackmailed into doing, God only knows what, for Homeland Security? Seriously?" He stopped in front of Radar again. "Did I leave anything out? You! All this stuff started with you!"

Radar started barking as if arguing with him, only this time making more grunting and whining noises.

Eddie started to respond but caught himself. "Oh, yeah! Well…" but he didn't finish his thought. He just stopped and stared at the dog for a moment before replying,

"Ya know, I really have no idea what the hell you're saying." Exasperated, he turned away from the dog and began pacing and talking to himself some more.

"Now I know I'm losing my mind. I'm not only talking to myself; I'm arguing with a damn dog. Yes. I am totally losing my mind. Is this what it feels like to go crazy?... And how would I know? It sure feels like crazy." Throwing up his hands, he walked off again complaining. "Good grief!"

He started thinking of all that had happened from the time he picked the dog up. The accident, first of all. Would he have gotten into that wreck anyway? Would he have missed it completely if he hadn't taken the time to mess with him in the first place? He did warn him. But how, and why? Was it fate? Was it a God thing? And what about the Old Indian? What did all that mean? He did meet Debbie and that was a good thing. But all the rest? Jimmy and this crazy truck, Homeland Security, government conspiracies? As he paced back by Radar, the dog grunted at him again but Eddie was having none of it.

"Nope! Still not talking to you." At the moment he was not in the mood for hearing from anyone, especially a dog.

He glanced up at the stars, studying them for a moment, trying to imagine what advice Kate would give him right about now. But as he stood there hoping for answers, all he heard was silence. Finally, sighing, he looked back down at the ground in defeat wondering what to do next. Just then his phone started ringing.

"Now what?" Looking at the screen, he saw that it was Debbie. He almost didn't answer but slowly softened his demeanor to answer her call.

"Hello."

"Hey," came the cheerful greeting. "Couldn't sleep so I thought I would check in on you. How's it going? I'm not interrupting anything, am I?"

Eddie looked around him at the truck, the dog, and the empty area behind the barn in the middle of the night, somewhere in Oklahoma, and thought how ironic the question was.

"Um, no. Not at all. I was just taking a break, actually. Have to, now and then, you know."

"Oh, I'm sure. Don't push yourself. Make sure you get plenty of rest. The load will wait. Besides, you usually make pretty good time. Right?"

More irony, Eddie thought. "Yes, ma'am. I do alright."

"Do you know what day you will be here yet? I have a nice dinner planned for you and Radar. By the way, how's my buddy doing?"

Just then Radar barked. Eddie glanced over at him with a scowl, pointing his finger at him to stop.

"Oh, you know. Doing what dogs do. Being a dog. He says hi, by the way." As upset as he was, Eddie couldn't deny the calming effect she had on him. Her cheerful and pleasant tone was reassuring and comforting right now. He wished he could tell her what had just taken place, but how do you bring that kind of news to a new relationship?

Debbie was pleased with that report. "I heard him. That is so cute."

Still frowning in the dog's direction, Eddie tried to respond in a lighthearted fashion. "Yeah, he's cute alright. Just one big ball of furry cuteness." Radar just cocked his head and grunted in reply. Eddie finalized his response. "Yeah, hon, it's looking like Wednesday. We should be there around 3:00 or so, I think. I'll text you when we hit town."

"Great. Can't wait."

Debbie sensed there was a little tenseness in Eddie's tone. "Everything okay?" she asked. "You sound a little stressed."

Eddie again changed his tone hoping she wouldn't pick up on his frustrated state of mind. "Nope. All good. Just a little road weary is all. I'm fine."

"Alright, sweetie, well, you drive safe and don't take any chances. I'll see you guys' Wednesday."

"Sure thing. See you soon. Bye."

Standing there looking at his phone, Eddie was still upset but her call calmed him down. Putting the phone back in his pocket, he walked around some more with his hands in his pockets and his head down, mulling things over. He began to realize he was okay with everything up till now, even though it was all a bit weird. Now it was more than just weird. It was full-on bizarre and going to a whole other level. Pacing in the darkness in the middle of the Oklahoma desert, with only the moonlight and the headlights from the truck to see by, Eddie was beginning to realize that what was going on was bigger than anything he could have imagined.

In his world, everything in life had a price. Up until a few months ago, he really had no life at all and had managed to shut most of the world and his past out and live in relative obscurity. When he let his guard down and allowed people, and this dog, to come into his life, things began to change. Despite the odd beginnings, he had become comfortable with the new arrangements and even welcomed the challenges with an air of anticipation. The renewed relationship with his son, his new young team that reminded him of his racing days, the truck, and most importantly, his budding romance with Debbie. All this was good. And all since acquiring this dog.

He glanced over at Radar who was patiently waiting. As he replayed the Indian prophecy in head, he heard the words again, *"His spirit will guide your spirit,"* in a different way now. Slowly he began to come to terms with the facts at hand. The animal was here for him and this time in his life. Clearly, he was chosen for a specific purpose—some of it yet to be determined. The bill for all the good things that have been happening to him has come due. An old scripture from a sermon he heard years ago echoed in the back of his mind. *"To whom much is given, much will be required."* He thought about that for a while longer. Finally, he concluded that, indeed, he was just handed the bill for said, *good things*.

Pondering this revelation for a few more minutes, he decided that if he was chosen for this task at this point in time, he couldn't shrink away from it despite his misgivings. All the evidence now pointed to this truth. Seemed simple enough. But now, how was he going to go about explaining this to the new woman in his life? How do you explain such a thing? He had no clue. Especially since he had a hard time understanding it himself. Finally, looking back up at the stars a few more minutes, he looked over at Radar. They stared at each other for a time.

Then Eddie finally broke the silence. "So, you are my so-called '*guide*' in all this?"

The dog responded with a grunt and a low bark.

"Okay, well, assuming that was a yes, I don't know why me, but I suppose it is what it is. Whatever this is." He sighed and then lamented. "Okay. Let's get on with it. I ain't getting any younger." As he started walking back to him, Radar started coming toward Eddie but then just kept walking past him a short distance before stopping and looking back. Eddie watching him as he went by, just stared at him for a moment.

Finally, he asked, "Okay, now what?"

Radar barked and put his nose to the ground where he had stopped. Eddie walked over and knelt down where he was looking. Squinting and barely able to notice the small spec in the sand, with the moonlight he saw it was the earpiece he had thrown away earlier. Picking it up, he blew the sand off of it and stuck it in his pocket. As he and the dog exchanged glances, he remarked, "Seriously? Now you're just showing off. Come on. We got a load of fish to deliver."

The dog grunted and assuming his original routine, he heeled at his right side while they both began walking back to the truck. Just before they got there, Eddie looked down at the dog and asked, "I don't suppose you have an instruction booklet stuffed somewhere in that mass of fur somewhere, do ya?" Radar just grunted without looking up and waited at the door.

"No, huh? Well, I got questions. We'll work on that later."

Eddie opened the door and let him in. As he was walking around the front of the truck, he mumbled to himself, "Okay then. I guess we will see what happens next. Besides, what could possibly go wrong?" Again, more irony.

After firing Morgana back up, Eddie and Radar returned to the deserted Oklahoma highway, which now seemed to be even longer and more mysterious. The only thing he was certain of now was that his life was never going to be the same and that the final prophecies of the Old Indian had not yet been completed. This meant that the struggles with his past and his hopes for the future were both on hold until then.

For Eddie McVane, a new journey, without a road map nor a specific destination, was about to begin. And even as fast as he was, the one thing that even Eddie couldn't outrun, was his own destiny.

EPILOGUE

It had been almost three hours since Eddie's encounter with Homeland Security and Travis' ultimatum to Eddie to help them with whatever dilemma they were dealing with. Now, a quiet ride for Eddie and Radar with just the dull tones of the highway and the steady rumble of Morgana's engine. Absent was his usual music and occasional chatter towards Radar about whatever was on his mind at the moment. As Eddie checked their current location, he realized that the restaurant he usually stopped at wouldn't be open for a few hours so he found the next rest area to head to and maybe try to catch a nap. While he was pondering some more, Radar started making grunting sounds as if he was trying to break the silence out of boredom.

Without looking at him, Eddie just mumbled a somewhat terse, "What?" After a moment, the dog began a short series of low whining noises and Eddie noticed that he was looking at him with his head cocked. Glancing towards Radar and looking into those big dark eyes, he couldn't help but get the feeling that the dog was trying to apologize or something. Eddie admitted to himself that he felt a little bad for yelling at him back there in the heat of the moment and now, it seemed like Radar wanted things to be normal between them again. Finally, Eddie gave in.

"Okay, okay, I'm sorry I yelled at you. I'm not really mad, I guess. I'm just, well, to be honest, I don't really know what I am right now. Truth is, I've never been here before. I mean, I've dealt with some pretty crazy stuff in my day, but this? This is a bit over the top." Radar patiently listened as Eddie continued.

"I mean, it wasn't that many months ago that I was perfectly content to be happily miserable. Just trucking around the country, doing what I do, brooding on the past and not bothering anybody. And now…"

Eddie didn't finish his thought but instead, shaking his head, he went silent again. Radar, seeming to understand his frustration, just laid down on his seat, head on his paws, and joined Eddie in going back to being quiet.

After their stop at the rest area, they finally arrived at the restaurant they were headed to just outside Sharon Springs, Kansas to take a break and grab some breakfast. On the way, Eddie realized that he wasn't so much mad at Jimmy *or* Radar for what happened. He knew none of this was either of their faults. Not really.

Truth was, Eddie was more upset at being interrupted by Travis and his demands *right after* he finally got up the courage to tell Debbie how he felt. Although he had calmed down some, he still wasn't happy about any of it. Especially when they were pretty much being forced to volunteer. Right now, though, Eddie just wanted some quiet time to work on what to do next.

After parking his truck, the two of them walked over to the entrance of the restaurant where Radar stopped to take up his sentry position like always only this time Eddie stopped as well. Without saying a word, he reached over and gave the dog a reassuring pat on the head and a rub on the side before continuing inside. It was Eddie's way of letting the dog know it was okay. They would figure it out, together.